"If you don't want me to worry about you, fine. I won't."

Her eyes narrowed. "But Seth is part of *both* our lives, and if you think that child isn't picking up on how overworked and exhausted and stressed you are, you'd better think again."

"Okay, I'll admit I'm going through a rough patch right now, but it's nothing I can't handle."

"Then you'd better tell that to Seth."

She laid her hand on his arm. Joe frowned down at her fingers and told himself it was just a trick of his imagination that a single light touch could make him that hot, that fast.

Dear Reader,

Winter may be cold, but the reading's hot here at Silhouette Intimate Moments, starting with the latest CAVANAUGH JUSTICE tale from award winner Marie Ferrarella, *Alone in the Dark.* Take one tough cop on a mission of protection, add one warmhearted veterinarian, shake, stir, and…voilà! The perfect romance to curl up with as the snow falls.

Karen Templeton introduces the first of THE MEN OF MAYES COUNTY in *Everybody's Hero*—and trust me, you really will fall for Joe Salazar and envy heroine Taylor McIntyre for getting to go home with him at the end of the day. FAMILY SECRETS: THE NEXT GENERATION concludes with *In Destiny's Shadow,* by Ingrid Weaver, and you'll definitely want to be there for the slam-bang finish of the continuity, not to mention the romance with a twist. Those SPECIAL OPS are back in Lyn Stone's *Under the Gun*, an on-the-run story guaranteed to set your heart racing. Linda O. Johnston shows up *Not a Moment Too Soon* to tell the story of a desperate father turning to the psychic he once loved to search for his kidnapped daughter. Finally, welcome new author Rosemary Heim, whose debut novel, *Virgin in Disguise*, has a bounty hunter falling for her quarry—with passionate consequences.

Enjoy all six of these terrific books, then come back next month for more of the best and most exciting romance reading around—only from Silhouette Intimate Moments.

Enjoy!

Leslie J. Wainger
Excecutive Editor

Everybody's Hero

KAREN TEMPLETON

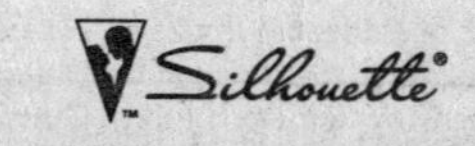

INTIMATE MOMENTS™

Published by Silhouette Books

America's Publisher of Contemporary Romance

ISBN 0-373-27398-3

EVERYBODY'S HERO

This edition published by arrangement with Harlequin Books S.A.

Visit Silhouette Books at www.eHarlequin.com

Printed in U.S.A.

Books by Karen Templeton

Silhouette Intimate Moments

Anything for His Children #978
Anything for Her Marriage #1006
Everything But a Husband #1050
Runaway Bridesmaid #1066
†*Plain-Jane Princess* #1096
†*Honky-Tonk Cinderella* #1120
What a Man's Gotta Do #1195
Saving Dr. Ryan #1207
Fathers and Other Strangers #1244
Staking His Claim #1267
****Everybody's Hero*** #1328

Silhouette Yours Truly

**Wedding Daze*
**Wedding Belle*
**Wedding? Impossible!*

†How To Marry a Monarch
*Weddings, Inc.
**The Men of Mayes County

KAREN TEMPLETON,

a Waldenbooks bestselling author and RITA® Award nominee, is the mother of five sons and living proof that romance and dirty diapers are not mutually exclusive terms. An Easterner transplanted to Albuquerque, New Mexico, she spends far too much time trying to coax her garden to yield roses and produce something resembling a lawn, all the while fantasizing about a weekend alone with her husband. Or at least an uninterrupted conversation.

She loves to hear from readers, who may reach her by writing c/o Silhouette Books, 233 Broadway, Suite 1001, New York, NY 10279, or online at www.karentempleton.com.

Author's Note

Children with Down syndrome display an enormous range of ability, interests and mental acuity; therefore, the character of Kristen Salazar is in no way meant to represent *all* children with DS, but merely *one* child; nor are her limitations meant to infer that other children and young adults with DS might face the same limitations.

I'd like to thank the many posters on the message boards at the National Down Syndrome Association for their help and guidance during the early stages of writing this book, especially those of you who took the time to write to me privately to share your stories. The children in your care are truly blessed by your love.

Karen Templeton

Chapter 1

The child's cry knifed straight to her soul.

Although how in heaven's name Taylor heard it over the din of little banshees currently running amok in the Sunday school room, she had no idea. Frowning, she scanned the swarm of Frazier and Logan kids streaking across the room, but nope—everybody certainly seemed fine in here….

Seven-year-old Noah Logan bounced off her thighs, knocking her off balance.

"Sorry, Miz Taylor," he mumbled breathlessly, taking off again as she grabbed the window sill to right herself…and saw the man standing outside by the mud-splattered SUV, the sobbing child clinging to him as though he'd fall off a cliff if he let go.

"Keep an eye on things, Blair, would you?" she said to the auburn-haired teenager a few feet away and then scooted outside, her retinas cowering in the blazing June sunlight. Barely eight in the morning and heat already oozed off the parking lot blacktop, welding her feet to her running shoes and promising to be one of those just-wanna-take-off-your-skin days. Then a dollop of shade bumped the sun from her eyes and *heat* took on a whole 'nother definition. Even without being able to fully see the man's face.

Strong, broad back underneath a khaki workshirt. Broken-in jeans smoothed over a butt that was truly the stuff of fantasies. Bourbon highlights etched in short, dark, finger-tingling wavy hair. Tall enough to definitely get a girl's attention.

And send that girl's libido streaking like an overfriendly pup through the door of her common sense.

With a sigh, Taylor grabbed her libido by the scruff of the neck and yanked it back inside, slamming shut the door, thinking, *Joe Salazar, I presume.* The man Didi had told her about yesterday, who was here for the summer—and *only* the summer—to oversee the remodel of the Double Arrow, Hank Logan's guest lodge. Only, judging from the obviously unhappy child currently sobbing his heart out in Joe's arms, right now the dude had more on his plate than the renovation of an old motel.

Maybe around eight or so and the picture of misery, the little boy noticed her still standing several feet away. Pure terror widened deep brown eyes, which vanished into the man's neck as he wailed, "Don't l-leave me, Joe, please don't leave me!"

"Hey, buddy…we went all over this, remember?" Tanned—and no doubt competent—fingers rubbed the space between the boy's shoulder blades, belying the frustration lurking at the edges of the low, country drawl not uncommon to Latinos born and bred in this part of the world. "There's lots of other kids here—"

"But I d-don't know any of them! What if they're m-mean? Or they don't like m-me?"

"I know, I know, this is all real scary. And believe me, I don't want to leave you, either—"

"Then why are you?"

Taylor saw Joe gently set the boy on his feet, then stoop to look him in the eye. "I don't have any choice, Seth," he said softly, massaging one frail-looking shoulder. "You know that. I've got work I can't put off anymore. Lots of people are depending on me to do my job, which I can't do if I'm worried you might get hurt. It's not safe, letting you hang around a construction site, you know? Besides, you'll be bored out of your mind—"

"I don't care! And I won't get hurt, I promise! I'm big enough to take care of myself! I used to stay home alone all the time!"

Taylor's stomach clenched at the child's admission as Joe stood, his body language reeking of displeasure. "Maybe so. But things are different now. And I could get in a lot of trouble if I didn't make sure you were looked after properly while I was at work. So let's go—"

But the boy saw Taylor again and backed away, shaking his head and whimpering. Joe turned and saw her, too, the *help me* expression on his face undeniable.

And undeniably dangerous for someone whose sorry libido piddled on the carpet at the mere sight of wide shoulders and a nice butt. However, the guy was obviously in a bind, and Taylor was obviously going to help him because that's what she did. Either that, or the heat was already getting to her.

"Let me guess," she said with a smile, slipping her hands into the back pockets of her white denim shorts. "Somebody's not exactly hot on the idea of day camp."

She caught a flash of annoyance in eyes even darker than the boy's; the tensing of a jaw already hard enough to break something over, both of which seemed at odds with the tenderness he'd shown the child just seconds before. And an immediate, second flash of what she guessed was guilt. "We came by yesterday, talked to the pastor's wife," he said. "I'm Joe Salazar. And this—" he touched the boy's curly hair "—is Seth."

"Yes, I know," Taylor said softly, tearing her gaze from those treacherous, conflicted eyes and back to the child's wary, wet ones. Lord, it was killing her not to gather the little guy into her arms and hug him to pieces. But even if doing so wouldn't spook the poor kid, she had a real strong feeling it would take a lot more than a hug or two to ease the deep, deep sadness weighing down his small shoulders. She glanced back at Joe long enough to catch his puzzled expression. "Didi told me about you, said you'd probably be bringing Seth this morning."

The child shifted closer to Joe, his long, spiked eyelashes canopying blatant distrust before he scrubbed away his tears with the hem of his T-shirt. That got another borderline anxious glance from his father, although Taylor gave him megapoints for not fussing at the boy or telling him to stop being a sissy, that big boys weren't supposed to cry, like a lot of the men around here were inclined to do with their sons. And maybe because of that, or the humidity, or because her libido had nosed open the door and slipped out again, she picked up a whiff of aftershave-soaked male pheromones that damn near shorted out her brain.

Joe looked back at her, sunlight slashing across prominent cheekbones to create some very interesting shadows on his face, sharply defining a mouth straight out of an Eddie Bauer catalog. "We might have a problem here," he said.

You have no idea, Taylor thought, only she said, "I can see that," because she imagined the man had more pressing things on his mind than her wayward hormones. And God knows, she did. So she thrust out her hand, hoping like heck the man's would be clammy and limp when she shook it.

As if. Still, she smiled and said, "I'm Taylor McIntyre. I run the day camp with Didi." Then she let go of the not-clammy, not-limp, extremely male hand and smiled down at the little boy, who wore the cautious expression of someone on the lookout for fangs. "How old are you, Seth?"

Long pause. Then: "Eight."

She squatted in front of him, trying to look as unthreatening as possible. A gust of hot, humid wind yanked a strand of curly hair out of her ponytail, tangling it in her eyelashes. "I know how scary new situations are," she said gently, "but it sounds to me like your daddy's got a lot of work to do—"

"Joe's my brother," the boy said. "Not my dad."

Taylor's eyes shot to Joe's, only to meet with a guarded expression. Seth's brother? He looked to be around Taylor's age—in his early thirties at least—which would make the child more than twenty years younger. However, she could tell from the look on Joe's face that whatever questions she might have would have to wait. If he would ever be inclined to answer them at all. Not that Taylor was any expert on the male thought process, God knew, but in her experience, men with stony expressions like Joe Salazar's didn't tend to be the most forthcoming souls in the world.

Then again, the frustrated-hand-through-the-hair gesture said plenty. "I'm sorry," he said with what Taylor was going to accept as genuine regret, "but I've got a crew waiting for me, I really need—"

"Got it." She smiled at Seth, steeling herself against the wobbly lower lip. "Okay, sweetie, let's go inside—"

"No!"

But Joe swung the kid up into his arms and started for the building, his cowboy boots pounding the sun-baked earth. Over the standard "It's gonna be okay, buddy" noises, a veritable swarm of pheromones drifted back to Taylor on the warm, muggy breeze.

She mentally stood aside and let them play on through, then followed Joe and Seth inside.

The place was crawling with kids.

No, *seething,* Joe silently amended. Like ants on a melting Popsicle. Sweat trickling down his back, he watched, vaguely horrified, as many, many short people pinballed around the dozen or so tables dotting the large, bright room's flecked industrial carpeting. They were laughing and shrieking their heads off, acting like normal kids, making him uncomfortably aware of just how unused he was to being around kids anymore.

Just as he was uncomfortably aware of the fresh-faced, soap-scented, round-hipped redhead beside him.

"Is it always like this?" he asked.

"Actually, no," she said, although she had to raise her voice to be heard. And step closer. Closer was not good. A paper airplane soared over their heads; a half dozen little boys swerved around them to retrieve it. Seth huddled closer to Joe's hip, vibrating like a plucked guitar string. "Once we officially start at nine," she said, "things calm down quite a bit."

Joe could feel a scowl burrow into his forehead. "I don't see a lot of adults."

Taylor turned, her entire face lighting up into a smile that easily made it into Joe's top ten female smiles. Maybe even the top five. "That's probably because the kids've tied them up outside."

The scowl burrowed deeper. Because it was killing him to leave Seth when he knew the kid wasn't ready to be left yet, because the trio of lazy overhead fans weren't doing squat to stir the hot, sullen air, because this woman and her damned top-five smile reminded him how long it had been since there'd been a woman in his life for more than ten minutes and because his body apparently had no qualms about bringing that lamentable fact to his attention.

"Just kidding," she murmured. Dammit, she wasn't even all that pretty, really, with her spice-colored hair yanked back into that ponytail and her pointy little nose and wide mouth and not a speck of makeup that Joe could see. But the way she looked at Seth, like it was everything she could do not to wrap her arms around him, was seriously messing with his head. And if all that wasn't bad enough, then she glanced up at Joe, and he saw something in copper-fringed eyes that couldn't decide if they were green or gold or gray that made him suspect she might be thinking about wanting to hug him, too. And, well—he looked away—it made him mad. At life in general and his life in particular. But most of all at himself, for half thinking he wouldn't mind being hugged right now. Especially by a pretty—okay, fine, he'd been kidding himself about that part—lady who looked soft and smelled sweet and whose smile, it pained him to notice, edged damn close to number one every time she looked at his baby brother, as if she could see straight through to his battered soul.

"Didi—that's the woman you talked to yesterday, the pastor's wife?—is always here, plus me, plus at least one parent volunteer for every ten kids, and several teenagers as junior counselors. Didi and I are CPR-trained, and three of the teens have their Red Cross lifesaving certificates. For the aboveground pool outside. Building's up to code, you don't want to light a match for fear of setting off the sprinklers, and no chips, candy or soda allowed. How's that?"

An exasperated breath left his lungs. "That's fine," he said, because it wasn't as if he hadn't given Mrs. Meyerhauser the third degree yesterday when he'd called, for one thing. And for another, it seemed everyone he talked to either had their own kids in the camp or knew somebody who did. Hank Logan's own daughter was even one of the counselors. So he had no doubt Seth would be safe and well cared for here. It was just—

A whistle blast nearly stopped his heart as every kid in the room froze. "Okay, y'all," Taylor's surprisingly strong voice rang out as the whistle bounced back between her breasts. "Seems to me you should've burned off most of the excess energy by now. So Blair, Libby, April…why don't you guys take your groups outside for a bit? And Blair, take mine, too, would you?"

The noise level sank considerably as the kids all scrambled over each other like puppies and out the two open doors at the back of the room.

"Impressive," Joe said.

"Thanks," she said, and she turned that smile on him, just for an instant. Just long enough to singe him right down to his…toes.

Seth tugged on his arm. His lashes were all stuck together in little spikes, and he still didn't exactly look thrilled about being here, but at least there seemed to be a lull in the hysterics, for which Joe was extremely grateful.

"I gotta go."

This much Joe had learned in the three weeks since Seth had come into his life. He looked over at Taylor. "Rest rooms?"

"Right over there. Follow me."

After a mild tussle over whether Seth could go in by himself—which Joe won by reassuring the boy he'd never be more than a few feet away—his brother pushed through the door, while Taylor swung around the reception desk to extract a blank file card and fee schedule from a drawer.

"This'll only take a sec," she said, rummaging through a second drawer for a pen, which she handed to Joe with the card. "I just need his name and age, your name and where we can contact you while he's here. Oh, and any allergies you might know about. Day camp hours are nine to three, generally, but we always have a few kids who need to stay until six or so—"

"I'd like to pick him up around four, if that's okay," Joe said as he filled out the card, tamping down the spurt of panic that he had no idea what the boy might be allergic to. "I promised Seth I'd be done work by then."

"Four will be fine."

Joe frowned at the fee schedule. "'All fees are *suggestions only?*'" he read aloud, then lifted his eyes to hers. "What does that mean?"

"It means this is a small town and money is sometimes pretty tight. And Didi swore when she and Chuck came to Haven nearly thirty years ago and started up the camp, that she'd never turn anyone away who couldn't pay." She smiled again. Full out. Laugh lines around the eyes and everything. "And before you ask how she manages, let's just say Didi has, um, connections."

"One of those 'the Lord will provide' types?"

Taylor laughed. "No, one of those 'the Lord helps those who help themselves' types. Rummage sales, car washes, carnivals—you name it, Didi does it. And if that doesn't bring in the funds, she has no qualms about shaming people into coughing up a donation."

There went that damn smile again, more of a grin this time, actually, partnered by an open, direct gaze as ingenuous as a child's. Only far more potent. At least, to a man who hadn't spent a whole lot of time gazing into women's eyes in the last little while. To his surprise, that grin and those eyes reached way deep inside him, way past the heaviness he'd begun to think would be a constant companion for the rest of his life, and tugged loose a chuckle.

"Sounds like a Hallmark TV movie, doesn't it?" Taylor said, and Joe's chuckle gave way to, "Just what I was thinking," which was about the time some outlandish idea bubbled up out of his brain about how he wouldn't mind standing here the rest of the day shooting the breeze with this woman. The bubble popped, though, as bubbles always do, and he returned his attention to filling out the card.

His mouth, however, had apparently missed the bulletin about the bubble-popping.

"I'm pretty much a city boy myself. Never spent any time to speak of in a small town."

"Me, either, before I moved here a couple years ago."

"Oh, yeah? Where from?"

Small talk, is all this was. Just something to fill the silence while he finished filling out this card, the kind of stuff you asked to be polite, not because you were really interested. As long as he didn't look at her, he was safe.

"Houston," she said, which immediately got Joe to wondering how on earth she ended up in tiny Haven, Oklahoma. *Why* she'd ended up here. But asking her would indicate he was really interested, which he wasn't, so he didn't.

Sure made him curious, though.

The card finally finished, he handed it back, running smack into the woman's sympathetic gaze.

"And if there's anything, um, out of the ordinary about his situation we should know about?" she said softly, and he realized he wasn't the only curious one here. As he would be, too, in her place. Wasn't every day a grown man came along with an eight-year-old brother in tow, he imagined. With Seth standing right beside him yesterday, Joe hadn't felt comfortable discussing many of the particulars with the pastor's wife. But there was nothing stopping him now.

Just as there was nothing stopping him from getting his own gaze tangled up with Taylor's. As a rule, Joe didn't have much use for sympathy, since sympathy had a bad habit of degenerating into pity, which he had no use for at all. But this wasn't about Joe—it was about a little kid who right now needed all the comfort he could get. The kind of comfort Joe wasn't sure he knew how to give.

"Seth and I didn't even know about each other until three weeks ago," he said quietly, seeing in her concerned expression the comfort he sought. For Seth, that is. "We met for the first time about a week after my father and Seth's mother were killed in a car crash."

"Ohmigod," Taylor said on a soft exhale, her eyes darting to the men's room door. "I figured it was something serious, but..." Her lower lip caught in her teeth; she shook her head and then looked back at Joe, her expression one big question mark.

"There was a will." Joe's mouth flattened. "After a fashion. For reasons known only to my father, he'd appointed me guardian in case anything happened to both him and Andrea."

"Even though you and Seth didn't know each other?"

Joe crossed his arms over his chest, as if that might somehow armor him against her incredulity. "Apparently, there's nobody else," he said, then added, "This has been real rough on the kid."

Her steady gaze momentarily threatened the composure he'd fought like hell to hang on to from the first moment he'd laid eyes on Seth, especially when she then said, "I don't imagine it's been any picnic for his brother, either."

Inside Joe's head, a warning bell sounded. He'd never allowed sentimentality to color his feelings or decisions, and damned if he was going to start now. A humorless smile pulled at his mouth. "You play the hand that's dealt you, you know?"

The dulled sound of a toilet flushing, followed seconds later by Seth's reappearance, derailed whatever she'd been about to say. Even though it nearly killed him, Joe realized he had to make a clean break. Now. Before his brother's big brown eyes sucked him back in.

Before Taylor's soft green/gray/gold ones made him forget how crowded his life already was.

"Okay, you're all set," he said, cupping Seth's head. "I'll see you at four."

Tears welled up again in the little boy's eyes, but Joe ruffled the kid's hair and strode outside, where he was free to let his emotions beat the crap out of him, even if he wasn't exactly on a first-name basis with most of them. His gut churned as he got into his middle-aged Blazer and twisted the ignition key, that he had to go to work when he knew the kid needed him right now. But if he didn't work, all the other people who needed Joe would be screwed.

And no way in hell was he going to let that happen.

As befitted anyone who'd lived through as many first days of school as she had, Taylor wasn't particularly surprised that Seth's tears dried up as soon as Joe left. That didn't mean she was particularly relieved, however. On-the-surface acceptance was not the same as being at peace with the situation.

An observation which she imagined applied equally to the child's big brother, she thought with a little pang of…something.

Except for the occasional tremor in his lower lip, the boy was doing a bang-up imitation of a statue, standing right where Joe had left him and staring blankly at the open door. His attachment to someone he hadn't even known a month wasn't all that odd, considering how desperately he probably wanted something, anything—any*one*—solid and real and alive to hang on to. Not that losing a parent was easy at any age, but eight was particularly difficult: old enough to fully understand the extent of the loss, but not old enough to understand, let alone believe, that things would ever feel "right" again.

"Seth?" Taylor said gently. After a long moment, the child turned, but his gaze was shuttered, provoking a twinge in the center of her chest. Although his hair was so clean it shimmered, tears had ploughed crooked tracks down dust-filmed cheeks. He looked so vulnerable and frightened Taylor briefly entertained the idea of throttling his big brother. "I know you're probably pretty unhappy right now, but I promise I won't say a word about how everything's going to be fine, because you wouldn't believe me, anyway. Would you?"

A burst of laughter from outside bounced in through the open window; Seth's eyes veered toward the sound for an instant, then back to Taylor. Wordlessly, he shook his head.

Her heart knocked against her ribs. At times like this, all those child psychology courses seemed about as practical as mittens in July. What on earth do you say to a child whose world had just been ripped apart? God knows, nothing anyone said to her after how own father died had made a lick of sense.

"Okay, let's try this," she said, squatting in front of him. "We usually do all sorts of stuff—play games, arts and crafts, go for walks, swimming..." She smiled. "Do you like to swim?"

A shrug.

"How about Slip 'N Slide?"

Another shrug.

"Well, why don't you just hang out today and get a feel for the place? If you want to participate in anything, fine. Go ahead and jump right in. But you don't have to do anything you don't feel like doing. No pressure. How's that?"

That got a little nod, but nothing else. Not even a glimmer of relief.

"Okay, then." Taylor stood. "You'll be with the other seven- and eight-year-olds, which means Blair's your counselor. I'll introduce you when she comes back in with the other kids—"

"I can't stay with you?"

How could one little face be so sad? "Oh, sweetie...I'd love to have you with me, but I've got the fives and sixes." She made a face. "You really want to be with—" she lowered her voice "—the babies?"

Taylor could see the struggle going on underneath all those curls, but eventually, he shook his head. Amazing how early the old male pride kicked in.

"I didn't think so," she said as the kids began trooping back inside. "Besides, Blair's totally cool."

She led Seth over to Blair's group and introduced them, whispering just enough in the teenager's ear to clue her in, even as she caught Wade Frazier's and Noah Logan's intrigued perusal of their new campmate. But as she returned to her own group of eager, rambunctious little ones, the conflicting feelings slamming around inside her head stunned her silly.

Not once that she could remember had she ever felt reluctant about falling in love with a child. For good or ill, that's just what she did, who she was. And already, little Seth Salazar was worming his way into her heart, big time. The problem was, though... this kid, she didn't want to fall in love with. Because falling in love with the kid would mean dealing with the kid's big, handsome, hormone-agitating brother on a regular basis.

And if that didn't have Bad Idea written all over it, she didn't know what did.

Chapter 2

Despite his personal worries heckling Joe from the edge of his thought like those two old Muppet dudes, he could always count on the adrenaline rush from starting a new job to make him feel in control again. This one was a walk in the park in comparison with most of the projects he oversaw, but that also meant he'd only be spending the summer in this two-bit town. A fact for which he was even more grateful after his encounter with Taylor McIntyre, Joe thought grumpily as he steered down the road leading to the Double Arrow office. Not that Haven didn't have its charms. Everyone he'd met so far certainly seemed friendly enough—although that, Joe thought with a tight grin, might have something to do with the dearth of strangers passing through—but there was that whole everybody-knowing-your business thing that rankled the living daylights out of him.

Joe never had been much on sharing his personal life with all and sundry. Not that he had anything to hide, he just didn't think it was anybody's business but his own, for one thing. And for another, he figured most folks only showed an interest out of politeness. Either that, or they got that oh-you-poor-thing look in their eyes that Joe detested. Especially since those eyes so often belonged to the kind of woman who was easily hurt. So the way he saw it, keeping to himself just saved everybody a lot of trouble.

And saving people trouble was what Joe did best, he mused as he pulled up alongside one of a series of dusty pickups in the small parking lot. He supposed he had a bit of a rep as somebody you could count on to follow through on his promises, which didn't bother him one bit. Not considering how hard he'd worked to earn that rep.

His cell rang, rousing him out of his ponderings.

"Joe?" said a gruff voice. Wes Hinton, his boss. "Got a minute?"

"Sure. What's up?"

"You know that lot on the north side of town we bid on last month?"

"You mean the one we didn't get?"

"Yep. Sale fell through, agent called today, asking if I wanted another shot at it. I said, hell, yes—you know I thought a strip mall would be perfect in that part of Tulsa. So I made another offer right on the phone, agent said it was as good as done."

Joe frowned. "Thought you were up to your butt with that new condo development in Albuquerque. You think you can swing this?"

"No guts, no glory, son. I've always landed on my feet, don't plan on changing my stripes anytime soon. But why I called is… I want you on the job."

"Well, yeah, I suppose, after I get this one squared away—"

"No, I mean while you're overseeing the Double Arrow. I've already got tenants lined up, but we'll lose 'em if this isn't ready to roll as soon as possible."

"I don't know, Wes…with the commute between here and Tulsa, that might be tricky."

"Oh, the Double Arrow project is small potatoes and you know it. You could oversee that one blindfolded and with both hands tied behind your back."

"Yes, I know, but—"

"And there's a real nice bonus in it for you, too. And with you now having more family responsibilities and all, I figured some extra cash probably wouldn't hurt. I know only too well how expensive kids can be."

Joe's mouth stretched into a wry smile. With three teenagers, two of them in college, Wes knew all about hemorrhaging bank accounts.

"Of course," Wes was saying, "if you don't think you could handle it, I suppose I could always hand it to Madison."

A robin landed in a birdbath a few feet away; Joe distractedly watched it splash around as his boss's veiled threat reverberated inside his skull. For the past several months, Wes had been making noises about taking semiretirement at the end of the year. And about appointing Joe as his successor—a position which would not only mean a damn good income for somebody who'd been doing well to graduate from high school, but also a chance to stop bouncing from job site to job site all over the Southwest. But there was a fly in the ointment: Riley Madison, a hotshot business school grad who'd come to work for Wes a couple years ago. That Riley was also jockeying for the position was no secret, especially to Wes, who wasn't above playing the two men against each other every chance he got.

"That wouldn't be you blackmailing me, would it?" Joe said quietly.

"I prefer to think of it as…laying out the options. Joe," Wes said before he could respond, "you're my first choice. Not just for this job, but future opportunities, shall we say. But I gotta have someone I can count on, someone able to juggle several projects at one time. Riley might not know construction as well as you, but he sure as hell is eager and available. And that counts for a lot." A pause. Then, kindly, "Don't let me down, son. Be who I need you to be. You hear what I'm saying?"

Yeah, Joe heard, all right. When Wes was still in construction, he'd taken Joe on as a seventeen-year-old high school senior suddenly saddled with the responsibilities of a man. A kid who knew squat about building, but figured it was something he'd be good at. As Wes's business evolved and grew, so had Joe. He'd learned from Wes's mistakes, but he'd learned.

And he owed the man an immeasurable debt.

Joe shut his eyes and massaged his forehead for a moment, then let out a sharp breath. "Fine, I'll do it. Somehow."

"Glad to hear it. Knew I could count on you."

Joe snapped shut his phone and blew out another breath. Well, hell—he'd spent most of the past fifteen years making sure everyone could count on him. Guess he had nobody to blame but himself for accomplishing his goal.

He got out of the car and walked over to the office, where Hank Logan stood outside with a mug of coffee in one huge hand and a grin spread across a face nobody in their right mind would call handsome. Joe guessed the lodge's owner to be around forty, although you sure couldn't tell it from the flat stomach and impressive biceps evident through the plain white T-shirt. Taller than Joe by a good two or three inches, the intimidation factor was nicely rounded out by nearly black, straight hair and a nose that looked like it was no stranger to a barroom brawl.

Joe had liked, and trusted, the ex-cop practically on sight, which was anything but his usual reaction to people. By nature, he preferred to take things slow when it came to getting to know a person. Not that fostering friendships was something he'd had much time for in the past several years, in any case. But now, seeing that grin, he let himself entertain an idea he rarely did, which was that it might be nice to put down roots someday. Have a friend or two to shoot the bull with now and then.

To have something resembling a normal life.

"Just made a pot of coffee," Hank said. "Want some?"

"Hell, yes."

The two men walked into the lodge's office, which, with its tired fake wood paneling and cast-off furniture, had seen better days twenty years ago. Soon it—along with the rest of the original utilitarian motel—would be transformed into a "rustic" counterpart to the individual cabins farther up the road, nestled here and there in the woods blanketing most of the property. Hank had bought the place cheap a few years back, apparently figuring he'd fix it up and sell it. Enter Wes, who'd run across the motel and wanted to buy it. But from what Joe had been able to glean through the grapevine—one rooted firmly in Ruby's Diner in town—the addition of a wife and daughter to the former recluse's life had changed his mind about selling outright. Since Wes had still believed the property had a lot of potential as a small resort, he suggested he and Hank become partners in the venture.

Which is where Joe came in.

"So who all's here?" he asked, taking a swallow of coffee strong enough to wake the dead.

"Plumbers, mostly, deciding how to get water up to the lots where the new cabins are going. And the grader got here right after you left, started leveling the lot closest to the lake." Another grin etched deep creases in the weathered face. "Told the guy he took out so much as a sapling, there'd be hell to pay."

Joe chuckled. He was usually wary of hands-on property owners, since more often than not they either got in the way or botched things up—if not both—which ended up costing everybody time and money. But not only were the renovations that Hank had done himself on the original cabins top-notch, Joe got the definite feeling Hank Logan was not a man who tolerated stupidity. In himself or anybody else.

Not only that, but he made coffee with serious *cojones.*

"The electrical contractor should be here, soon, too," Joe said.

"He already was," Hank said. "Since you weren't back yet, I suggested he go on to Ruby's for breakfast."

Joe grimaced. "Sorry."

"Don't worry about it," Hank said, frowning into his empty mug, then going back for a refill. "Breakfast at Ruby's has a way of mellowing a man." He poured his coffee, then glanced over at Joe. "How's the boy doing?"

Other than thinking I'm slime? Joe thought, then said, "He wasn't too sure about things. But they seem like nice people over there at the camp."

"They are that. Seth's in good hands, believe me. Hey," he said, apparently changing the subject. "You see my kid? Blair? Kinda tall, long red hair?"

"Maybe. For a moment. Until the other one shooed everybody outside."

"The other one?"

"Taylor? Another redhead. Said she ran the place with Didi."

"Yeah, that's Taylor." Hank took another swallow of coffee. "She teaches kindergarten up at the elementary school, went in with Didi when Bess Cassidy moved to Kansas to be with her kids two summers ago." Nearly black eyes seemed to assess him. "From what I hear, Taylor's got a magic touch with kids. They're crazy about her, and she's crazy about them. One of those women you figure would like nothing more than to have a batch of her own."

Joe found himself staring hard at his coffee. "I suppose that's an admirable trait in a teacher."

"True. I don't know her too well, myself, but Blair thinks the world of her."

Now it was Joe's turn for a second cup. "You have to wonder, though, how she ended up here." At the silence following his comment, he turned to see Hank's slightly puzzled expression. "Coming from someplace like Houston, I mean. Must be a big adjustment, living in a small town."

"No argument there." Hank knocked back the rest of his coffee, then twisted around to set the empty mug back beside the coffeemaker. "Guess it just depends on what you're looking for at the time…. Well, hey, gorgeous."

The last was directed, with a big smile, for a slender blonde dressed in shorts and a tucked-in sleeveless blouse who'd just come into the office. The woman was attractive in that way of women over forty who are unconscious of their beauty, her straight hair held back from her finely featured face with a couple of clips. Slipping a decidedly proprietary hand around her waist, Hank introduced her to Joe as his wife, Jenna, with a pride in his voice that Joe decided was due not to Jenna's being his as much as that she'd chosen *him.*

He told himself the burning sensation in his gut was due to Hank's coffee.

She welcomed him to Haven, a generous helping of crow's feet splaying out from the corners of her eyes as a warm smile stretched across her face. While Joe was pondering her lack of Oklahoman twang, Hank asked Joe if he'd read any of his wife's books—in her other life, she was the mystery writer Jennifer Phillips.

"For heaven's sake, Hank," Jenna said, swatting him lightly in the chest. "Quit putting people on the spot like that! You're embarrassing both of us!"

Joe smiled. "I've heard the name, but I'm afraid I'm not much of a reader. Not anymore, at least. Not since…" He pushed aside the cloud of memory to think back. "Not really since high school." The realization surprised him—had it really been that long since he'd indulged in the simple pleasure of reading a novel?

Fortunately, before these people managed to find out what size drawers he wore, the electrical contractor returned, giving Joe an excuse to sidestep any further discussion about his personal life and retreat once again into the safe, generally orderly world of bids, supplies and schedules, a world over which he had a fair amount of control.

As opposed to the world where he had virtually none.

On brutally hot days like this, by midafternoon not even the littlest ones were much interested in moving. So Taylor usually settled them in the grass under one of the big old cottonwoods out behind the church, reading aloud until their parents came to get them or they nodded off. She loved changing her voice to match each character, seriously getting off on the glow of delight when she'd glance up and see a batch of wide eyes and, sometimes, open mouths. And the giggles. She lived for the giggles.

And at the moment, she'd give her right arm to hear Seth Salazar giggle.

When he wasn't checking the huge watch smothering his narrow wrist, the boy was attentive enough, sitting cross-legged a little apart from the rest of the children. Although his slender fingers absently plucked at the blades of grass in front of his ankles, his solemn gaze stayed on her the entire time she read. But when the other kids howled at Junie B. Jones's antics, Seth would barely crack a smile. His body was there, but clearly his mind was elsewhere.

"Joe!" he cried, leaping to his feet.

Like wondering when his brother would come rescue him, Taylor guessed, as the boy tore across the yard.

While the younger counselors herded the remaining kids inside for the last snack of the day, Taylor got to her feet, her knees protesting at sitting on the hard ground for so long, her brain giving her what-for for putting off the inevitable. Which would be—she turned—seeing Joe Salazar scoop his little brother up into his arms.

Strong, solid arms.

Against a strong, solid chest.

All barely hidden underneath the soft folds of a dusty blue workshirt.

Yep, it was just as bad as she thought it would be.

Taylor plastered a smile to her face and trooped over to the pair, just in time to hear Seth give Joe grief about being late.

"It was only a couple minutes, buddy," Joe said, lowering his brother to the ground. "Besides, I didn't want to interrupt the reading."

"You were listening?" Taylor said, thinking, hmm…when was the last time some guy had made her stomach flutter? No, wait, she remembered: Mason. Her ex.

The fluttering might have degenerated into a vague nausea had Joe not smiled for her. Not exactly a laid-back, no-holds-barred smile, but a smile nonetheless. A smile sparkling in a face darkened by a suggestion of late-day beard shadow.

As Blair and company would say, this was *so* not fair.

"I was listening," Joe said, and something in his voice or eyes or somewhere in there made Taylor suspect she wasn't the only one here dodging a few red flags. A revelation which, aggravatingly enough, managed to flatter and annoy her at the same time. "Although I'm not sure who was having more fun—you or the kids."

He wasn't flirting, she was sure of it. Well, as sure as someone who hadn't been flirted with in about a million years—except for Hootch Atkins, and he definitely did not count—could be. Then she noticed Seth's head bopping back and forth between them, and Didi's cocked eyebrow when she came outside and saw them standing there, and then fourteen-year-old April Gundersen tripped over a tree root because she was gawking at them instead of watching where she was going. Taylor realized she wasn't sure of anything anymore, except that she didn't feel much older than April, which probably wasn't a good thing.

Then, to her horror, she heard herself going on about how she'd always been a big ham ever since she was little, how she'd set up her stuffed animals in rows—and her little sister, if she could get her to sit still long enough—and perform, making up stories as she went along and how she'd even thought about becoming an actor at one point, but had given it up when she realized all she really wanted to do was…teach…kids.

Whoa. Hot flash sneak preview. Not fun.

"Well," Joe said, not looking a whole lot more comfortable than Taylor felt. "You're very good." Then he turned to Seth. "So how was your first day?" When all he got was a noncommittal shrug in reply, he added, "That good, huh?"

Another shrug.

"Guess he forgot about the worms we had for lunch," Taylor said, which earned her startled looks from both brothers.

One day, maybe she'd start acting like a normal person. But the world probably shouldn't hold its breath for that one. Joe muttered something about their needing to head to the store to find something for dinner, then left, Seth's hand securely in his.

"Don't look now," Didi said behind Taylor, scaring her half to death, "but you look like you just saw the mother ship land in Cal Logan's pasture."

Taylor grunted and headed back to the Sunday school building, thinking she'd take a close encounter with a horde of little green men over one with Joe Salazar any day.

And if that didn't make her certifiably insane, she didn't know what did.

What the hell had just happened?

Joe yanked a grocery cart loose from the nested mass at the front of the Homeland, making Seth jerk beside him. Blessedly frigid air-conditioning soothed his heated skin, but not the dumb, pointless, totally off-the-wall fire raging inside him.

Five minutes. Five lousy minutes, he'd spent with Taylor. Five minutes of inane, completely innocent conversation. No sexual overtones whatsoever. Yet here he was, fighting to walk straight. What kind of man gets turned on by a woman reading a children's story, for crying out loud?

The kind of man who was currently standing in a crowded supermarket with an eight-year-old beside him and thinking about breasts.

What the hell? Joe never thought about breasts, for God's sake. At least not as often as he did when he was seventeen. Or twelve. But now, suddenly, mammary images crowded his thoughts like steak a starving man's on a desert island. He shut his eyes to get his bearings, and saw nipples. Pink ones, on pale, translucent skin.

Like redheads had.

"So…you like spaghetti?" he barked to the child depending on him not to get distracted by things like sex and breasts—

No less than five women scowled at him.

—and a silky voice that changed like mercury as she read, making children laugh.

"Not really," Seth said.

Joe let out a long, ragged breath and the breasts went away. Thank God. Strangling the grocery cart handle, he glowered at his little brother. "Whoever heard of a little kid who didn't like spaghetti?"

The poor kid flinched, his brows practically meeting in the middle. "It makes me gag."

Terrific. The one thing Joe knew how to cook with any reasonable success, and the kid didn't like it. They'd eaten out most of the past three weeks, but that was in Oklahoma City where there were a few more restaurant choices than Ruby's Diner or the Dairy Queen halfway between here and Claremore. Not that Ruby's didn't seem like a great place, but he'd lay odds Ruby Kennedy was the kind of women who had pity running in her veins. For hurting kids, for lost souls, for lonely men who couldn't cook and who hallucinated about breasts in supermarkets because they couldn't remember the last time they had sex worth remembering.

And anyway, if he was going to have this kid living with him for the next ten or so years—a thought which damn near stopped his breath—they couldn't eat out every night. Which meant one of them was going to have to learn to cook.

"So what do you like?"

"Tacos?"

Okay, he could probably swing that. Joe steered the cart toward the meat section, Seth not exactly trotting along behind him. Every few feet or so, somebody would smile and nod, or say, "Hey." Joe nodded and smiled and heyed back, but all this friendliness was beginning to get on his nerves.

If he didn't know better, he'd say he felt trapped. In this town, in this life, by circumstances. By phantom, probably pink-tipped breasts he was pretty sure he'd never get to see.

A smile he'd never get to kiss.

"What else besides tacos?" he said, tossing a package of ground beef into the cart.

"Hamburgers. And fries."

Yeah, the kid had put a few dozen of those away. Once he started eating again, that is. The first week had been sort of dicey, with Joe beginning to worry he'd be jailed for letting the kid starve to death. Not that Seth ate much even now, but Joe's mother had reminded him that he'd never eaten much as a kid, either, not until he hit his late teens, at least.

Thinking about his mother brought him up short, making him realize it'd been nearly a week since he'd talked to his mom and Kristen, his sister. A dull pain tried to assert itself at the base of his skull.

"I like fried chicken, too." Just as Joe was about to say he wasn't sure he could handle fried chicken that didn't come out of a box, the boy added, "But only Mama's."

Joe muttered a bad word under his breath, only to realize this was the first time Seth had mentioned his mother since the boy had come to live with him. The lady from social services in Oklahoma City had said Seth's talking about his parents would help him to accept their deaths and eventually heal some of his pain, but that Joe shouldn't worry if it took a while for that to happen. Joe knew nothing about his father's second wife—she could have been a saint, for all he knew, even though he did know the couple hadn't been living together at the time of their deaths—but he sure as hell knew his father. And a not-so-small, unhealed part of himself was hard put to wonder how, or why, the child would grieve Jose Salazar at all.

Except Joe certainly had, hadn't he, all those years ago?

"Joe?"

He looked down at Seth. The boy's forehead was a mass of wrinkles.

"You mad at me?"

"No," Joe said on a rush of guilt. None of this was Seth's fault. And there was no way he would've refused to take his brother on. Still, that didn't mean he was a hundred percent okay with the situation, either. Full-time responsibility for an eight-year-old boy you'd never met before wasn't something easily slotted into your life, especially one already crammed to the gills. But more than that, Seth's sudden appearance had stirred up a whole mess of issues Joe'd thought he'd dealt with years ago and was not at all amused to discover he hadn't. Not as much as he'd thought, at least. The social worker had suggested counseling to help Seth through this, but Joe was beginning to think maybe he was the one who needed help getting his head screwed on straight. "Just got a lot on my mind, that's all. And it's been a long day."

Seth nodded, but didn't say anything, leaving Joe wrestling with another brand of guilt—that he didn't feel more for the kid than he did. Sure, he cared about what happened to him, and he hated seeing the boy so unhappy, but if he thought he'd feel a strong attachment right off just because they were brothers, he'd been dead wrong.

"Hey. You want some ice cream?"

After a moment of apparent contemplation, Seth said, "C'n we get chocolate chip?"

"That your favorite?"

Seth nodded.

"Huh. Mine, too. Let's go see if they've got some."

As they walked up and down the aisles until they found the frozen-food section—not only did they have chocolate-chip ice cream, they had five different kinds—it struck Joe that he'd better damn well work on forming that attachment, because right now the only thing that mattered was making this kid feel secure again. And the only way that was going to happen was by Joe's devoting as much time and attention to him as he possibly could. No distractions allowed.

Especially distractions with red hair, a generous smile and green-gold eyes that saw deeper inside a man than this man wanted them to see.

Chapter 3

Taylor was officially in a cruddy mood. And it had nothing to do with the heat, or her hormones, or even that Oakley, her four-legged roommate, had devoured the salad she'd made for lunch today, leaving her with nothing but tuna fish. She only kept tuna fish in the house because it was easy to fix and lasted forever in the can, but truthfully, she wasn't all that fond of it. No, her cruddy mood had something to do with Joe Salazar. She just wasn't sure what, exactly.

From her perch on the edge of the Sunday school room's low stage, Taylor took a bite of her tuna sandwich, but it tasted like dust. Fishy dust, at that. For heaven's sake, she'd barely even seen the man this past week. He dropped Seth off every morning and picked him up every evening—although Taylor did notice he got later and later every day—but mostly he talked to Blair, since she was Seth's counselor. Which was just how Taylor wanted it.

But even totally non-Joe-related events or situations would set her off. Like last night, when she got home and her house was empty. Well, duh, she lived alone; of course her house was empty. But usually she walked in and felt "Ahhh." Last night, she walked in and felt…actually, she wasn't sure what she felt, but it wasn't pleasant. And why she should connect this unpleasant, undefined feeling to a man she didn't even know made no sense whatsoever. But there it was. And there she was, in a cruddy mood.

"How's he doing?"

A cruddy mood clearly destined to get worse.

Taylor didn't have to ask to know who the pastor's wife was talking about. She glanced across the room at Seth, listlessly picking at his sandwich and still doing his best to ignore the other children. Since Didi could obviously see for herself how he was doing, Taylor guessed the older woman wanted her take on things. Which unfortunately smelled to high heaven of ulterior motives.

"Maintaining. Barely." Compunction about not letting herself get too close to the boy had been increasingly gnawing at her for several days. "Mostly he's just hung back and watched."

She most definitely did not like the silence that greeted her comment. "I don't mean to butt in," Didi said at last, almost provoking a laugh, "but don't you think you should, um, get a little more involved?"

"Blair's doing fine."

"Yes, she is. But Seth isn't. Honey, this is a special case—"

"I know that."

"Then why in tarnation are you sitting back and doing nothing?"

"I'm not sitting back and doing nothing. I'm here if Blair needs me. And it's not as if I'm ignoring the child."

"Taylor." Didi hauled her petite, but ample, form up onto the stage beside her, setting short, fading blond curls all aquiver. "The poor kid follows every move you make. If anyone could help him over this, it would be you."

"And there's also a real danger of his becoming too attached—" she bit off another corner of her sandwich "—and then what happens when the summer is over and he has to leave?"

"You'll heal."

"I'm not talking about me—"

"Aren't you?"

Oh, yeah, her mood was definitely worsening. Especially when Didi added, "And I don't think it's just the boy you're afraid to get close to, either."

With friends like this…

"No comment?" Didi said.

"Not in a million years."

That got a chuckle. Then Didi crossed her arms and said, "Still, sometimes you gotta worry about the present and trust the future to take care of itself." A pause. "And hiding out from life isn't exactly trusting, now, is it?"

This was hardly the first time the pastor's wife had hinted that she had problems with some of Taylor's choices, most notably her moving to an itty-bitty town where there *weren't* a whole lot of choices. In jobs, in housing, in prospective relationships of the man-woman variety. But it wasn't as if Taylor hadn't known from the start what she'd be getting into when she accepted the teaching job here. Still, after her marriage's collapse, there was a lot to be said for being able to go to sleep every night grateful for her relatively complication-free life.

A cop-out? Maybe. But ask her if she cared. She loved her job, and her little house nestled in the woods, and she was perfectly content with her safe, calm, orderly life, one where she could face the world each morning with a smile that she didn't have to pull out of a drawer and paste on. So how come Didi's words weren't rolling off her back the way they usually did?

As Taylor watched Seth's large eyes alternate between cautiously surveying his surroundings and withdrawing into his grief, old wounds began to seep open. Wounds she'd thought had long since healed. Memory yanked her back to just past her eleventh birthday, right after her father died, when she'd been convinced she'd never be happy again.

Seth was only a little kid. All he knew was *now.* And somehow, she had the feeling his big brother, although he meant well, was as clueless as the kid. Conflicting instincts clashed inside her—compassion versus self-preservation, the need to help duking it out with the realization that wanting to help didn't necessarily mean she could.

But could she live with herself if she didn't at least try?

Taylor slurped up the rest of her bottled juice as she watched Blair sink into a small chair beside Seth, trying to engage him in conversation, as she'd been doing without much success the whole week. If anyone could get through, it was Blair. Not only did the teen adore little kids—she'd already talked to Taylor about majoring in early childhood education in college—but she, too, knew what it was to lose someone she loved. In her case, it was the uncle who, with Jenna, had adopted and raised her before anybody knew Hank was her father and who had died of cancer a few years back. But after a minute or two, the little boy shook his head and Blair got up, shooting Taylor a helpless glance before sitting down at another table where a group of little girls were having giggle fits over heaven knew what.

Never in her life had Taylor been able to see a hurting child and not try to comfort him or her. And she had about as much chance of success at trying to resist comforting this one as she did of staying away from chocolate.

"Maddie Logan's coming in this afternoon to help. She could take over your group," Didi said, as if reading her mind. And with that, Taylor sighed, heaved her duff off the edge of the stage and gave in to the inevitable.

Even if the distrust in Seth's eyes as he watched her approach wasn't exactly inspiring her with confidence. She shooed the rest of the kids outside and then sat at the table beside him. He'd brought his lunch today, a banana and cookies along with the sandwich, Taylor saw. She imagined Joe packing it for him, unable to squelch the warm feeling attendant thereto.

"Hey, honey." She angled her head to peer into the glowering face. "That looks like a good lunch you've got there."

He poked at his peanut butter sandwich and then shrugged. "I'm not hungry."

"Well, that's okay. It happens sometimes. So…you and

your brother are staying in one of the cabins up at the Double Arrow, huh?"

A nod.

"I hear they're very nice—"

"She made you come over here and talk to me, didn't she?"

"Who?"

He nodded toward Didi. "Her."

"Oh. No. She didn't. Totally my idea."

After a long pause, Seth said, "You wanna see a picture of my mom?"

"Sure."

The boy reached around and yanked out a slim cloth wallet from his back pocket, opening it to a photo of a smiling young woman with dark hair and eyes.

"Oh, Seth…she was very pretty."

"I know." He contemplated the photo for a couple of seconds, then said, "Do you think I'll see her again? In heaven?"

Oh, boy. "Maybe," Taylor said. At his distressed look, she smiled. "I don't actually know how all that works. But I've always thought I'd like to see my father again."

His eyes met hers, interested. "He's dead, too?"

"Yeah. For a long time, now."

"You still miss him?"

"Sometimes. But I can think about him now without it hurting so much."

Seth broke the eye contact, slapping shut the wallet and shoving it back in his pocket. "I don't want to talk about this anymore."

"Okay."

"What time is it?"

"About twelve-thirty."

"How long till Joe comes to get me?"

"He said he'd be here at four."

"He didn't get here until five yesterday."

"Guess he got tied up—"

"Can I go outside now?"

Taylor said, "Sure." But she caught the boy's sticky, warm hand as he rose. He didn't try to get free, but he kept his gaze fixed firmly on the tabletop. "It's all really awful, isn't it?" she said.

For a long moment, he just stood there, his breath spurting from his nose in ragged little pants. Then, finally, his eyes shot to hers, all his sorrow and confusion upending on her like a bucket of cold, grimy water before he yanked his hand from her grasp and strode wordlessly away.

So help her, if Joe didn't show up on time today, she was going to string him up by his…toes.

At four-fifteen, Didi informed Taylor she had a call, she could take it on the phone in the church office. Taylor locked eyes with the older woman for a moment, just long enough to get that sick feeling in the pit of her stomach that always accompanied bad news. Her imagination was all set to take flight when Didi rudely yanked it back to earth with, "It's Seth's brother."

Taylor frowned, not processing either the information itself or all the wherewithals behind it. "Why's he calling me?"

"That, I couldn't tell you. But he didn't sound so good."

Taylor tromped off to the office and picked up the phone, plucking at her T-shirt's neckline. There was actually an air conditioner in here, but the secretary—who only worked three mornings a week—always turned it off when she went home, leaving the small room feeling like a recently vacated shower stall.

"This is Taylor—"

"Taylor, Joe Salazar. I'm really sorry, but I'm running behind and it looks like I'm going to be late picking up Seth tonight."

"Again?"

A pause. "Again."

She shut her eyes. "How late?"

"I'm not sure. I've got people here, we've got a lot of ground to cover… If I leave here by five-thirty, I'll be back in Haven by half past six or thereabouts. I know you all don't stay open that late—"

"Whoa, hold on—it doesn't take an hour to get here from the Double Arrow. Where *are* you?"

Another pause. "Tulsa."

"*Tulsa?* Why the heck are you in Tulsa?"

"For work. It's a long story. Which I doubt you want to hear."

"You'd be surprised."

"Then I'll tell you sometime. Right now, though, I've got a whole bunch of people giving me dirty looks because I'm over here talking to you and not over there talking to them, so the upshot is…" Big sigh. "Look, I know this stinks, but is there any way somebody could watch Seth until I get back?"

Taylor shut her eyes again, praying for patience. Her prayer was not answered. "Oh, I suppose…"

"Could you do it? I mean, I know that's asking a lot. And you probably have plans…"

"No, I don't have plans" flew right out of her mouth before she could catch it, only then she lost her breath. "But I'm not real sure that's such a good idea—"

"I agree. But you're the only one he talks about. I think he likes you."

Setting aside his "I agree" comment to examine at a later date, she said, "He sure has a funny way of showing it."

"Taylor, please. I'm desperate. And I'll make it up to you, I swear."

His words set off a series of echoes in her head, reaching way back, words that had taught her the meaning of disappointment and distrust.

"Seems to me I'm not the one you need to be making anything up to."

Silence. Then a soft, "I agree. And God knows I'll probably get an earful from my brother when I get back. If he even talks to me at all. I know this makes me dirt in everybody's book, but I'm really stuck."

More echoes, this time of genuine regret.

Taylor sighed, inwardly muttered something that was anything but a prayer, and said, "You know the first road you get to after you turn off from the highway, going up to the Double Arrow?"

"Yeah?"

"Make a left, then go all the way to the end. That's my house. I'll take Seth there after camp closes."

"Thank you so much—"

"And don't mind the dog. He's loud but harmless."

"Got it." Joe paused. "Can I bring dinner to pay you back?"

"No," she said, and hung up.

"Well, this is it," Taylor said to the stone-faced child buckled up next to her in the Chevy pickup she'd bought off Darryl Andrews last year, after the dirt road leading to her place finally did-in her old Saturn. She was about to add something about the dog, except she noticed Oakley hadn't budged from his spot on the porch, guarding the front door. Blocking it, anyway. Oakley's method of watch-dogging ran more along the lines of "Look who's here, let's party!" than "Get your good-for-nothin' butt off my property before I rip you to shreds." Also, nobody'd clued Oakley in to the fact that the image of the lazy bloodhound was an inaccurate stereotype. Taylor often wondered what, if anything, the dog did during the day while she was gone, since he never seemed to change position between when she left and when she returned. If it weren't for the piles of poop that magically appeared in her absence, she'd have no proof that he actually moved.

"You got a dog?"

Taylor couldn't quite tell if that was interest or trepidation in Seth's voice, but at least it was a response. "After a fashion," she said, unlatching her seat belt and opening the truck door. A breeze would be nice right about now to wick the moisture off her back and bottom from sitting on the truck's vinyl seat. But no such luck. Even the wind chime on the end of her porch was dead silent.

"Does he bite?" Seth asked, making no move to open his own door.

Trepidation, definitely. "Honey, half the time I'm not even sure he breathes. Come on, it's okay."

Seth had taken the news about Joe's lateness more calmly than Taylor might have expected, but she knew he was ticked. When she'd said they were ready to go, the boy had collected his things and walked out to the truck like a prisoner resigned to his fate. Just warmed the cockles of her heart, is what.

"Seth?" she now said. When he finally looked at her, she smiled like a goon and said, "Really, this is going to be fun."

Somehow, she got the feeling he didn't believe her.

Tempted to mutter things she shouldn't, Taylor got out of the truck. Seth, however, didn't. Not until she went around to the passenger side and opened the door for him, anyway. Then, with excruciating slowness, the child slithered down from the seat, his eyes glued to the comatose dog the entire time. When she started toward the porch, however, the kid grabbed her hand.

"Seth, honey? I promise you, I've yet to hear of a bloodhound eating a child. He might slobber you to death—" she twisted her mouth at the prone mass on her porch "—if he ever wakes up, but Oakley's as gentle as a lamb, I swear."

Perhaps her voice finally pervaded the beast's consciousness, because at that moment the big red dog hauled himself to his feet, his skin taking a few extra seconds to catch up, and let out a bay of joy before bounding over to them. Seth let out a scream and hid behind Taylor, shaking so hard she thought he'd break.

"Oakley! Doghouse!" she said, and the dog gave her a wounded "What did I do?" look before morosely lumbering off to his garage-sized doghouse at the side of the house. But he'd no sooner gone in than he turned right back around, sitting hunched inside the opening with a baleful expression. Taylor glanced down to see Seth staring at the dog as hard as the dog was staring at him.

"He looks like his feelings got hurt," he said.

"Oakley loves kids," Taylor said, continuing toward the house. "And they love him. He's never run into one who was afraid of him before, so I guess he's kind of confused."

"But he's so big."

So's your brother, but I'm not afraid of him, Taylor wanted to say, except then it occurred to her maybe she was a little more afraid of Joe than she wanted to admit. Or at least, afraid of her reaction to him. The man was like chocolate—even though it always gave her a headache, she couldn't completely shake her affinity for it.

Would someone please explain to her why she was so attracted to driven, focused men, when she knew damn well that driven, focused men made lousy mates?

"Come on, let's go inside," she said, leading Seth into her house, a little two-bedroom bungalow with a sunroom off the living room and an eat-in kitchen. But it had been a steal, and it was all hers—or would be in twenty-nine years—and the lot was plenty big enough to justify having a bloodhound, even if she'd spent a small fortune on an invisible fence to keep the beast from following the scent of every rabbit or possum that wandered across the property.

"I'm hungry," Seth announced from the middle of the living room, even as she noticed those big eyes taking it all in—the one whole wall filled with books, the mismatched, garage-sale furniture, the old Turkish rug from her father's office that she'd discovered wasn't colorfast when Oakley peed on it as a puppy.

"Yeah, me, too." He trailed her into the kitchen—she'd replaced the ugly black-flecked floor tiles with a pretty white-and-gold linoleum, but she'd have to live with the harvest gold appliances and burnt-orange cabinets for a while yet, she imagined—where she opened the freezer. "You like Healthy Choice?"

"What's that?"

"Frozen dinners. There's…let's see…lemon pepper fish, Salisbury steak and some Mexican chicken thing."

"C'n I have the Mexican chicken?"

"Sure can."

Outside, Oakley started baying at something. Seth wandered over to the kitchen window, which looked out over the front yard. "I think he's lonely," he said as Taylor put his dinner in the microwave.

"Could be. He's used to coming inside with me when I get home."

"Oh." The boy turned to her. "Guess it's not fair, huh? That he has to stay outside?"

"He'll live. Right now, your feelings are more important than his. Okay, I'm out of milk, but I can make iced tea."

Seth gave her a long, considering look before saying, "With lots of sugar?"

Taylor smiled. "How else?"

Oakley bayed again—*Owrooowroooowrooooooo.*

"Will he come if I call?" Seth asked.

"In a New York minute," Taylor said, and the boy went to the front door and did just that, then hid behind the door when a hundred pounds of dog galumphed into the house, looking pleased as all get-out.

It was closing in on seven o'clock by the time Joe got to Taylor's. Translation: His butt was in a major sling. As he pulled the Blazer up in front of the little white house with the gold shutters, he wondered who would be more ticked off with him—Seth or Taylor. His money was on the redhead. Shoot, the chill in her voice when he'd called had damn near given him frostbite. Then again, maybe it was nothing more than paranoia and a squirrelly connection. A guy could hope, right?

Candy and flowers in tow, he got out of the SUV, strangely disappointed at the lack of a welcoming committee. No glowering redhead with evisceration on her mind, no little boy tearing down the steps and up into his arms, not even the promised dog he shouldn't pay any mind to. For a moment, he wondered if maybe he had the wrong house, until he heard it, just faintly—Taylor's laughter drifting out the open window next to the front door, as soft and rich as the notes sporadically floating out from the wind chime hanging from the porch eaves.

Joe simply stood there, absorbing it, much the same way he was absorbing the almost-cool breeze sucking at his damp back. It was still hot, too hot, but the whispering of thousands of still-tender leaves, the calm *whoooo...whoooo...whoooo...*of a mourning dove soothed his frayed nerves, just a little. It would be another hour or more before the sun set, but the late daylight gilded the roof of the tiny house and set the masses of flowers ablaze in more containers than he could count scattered across the front of the porch and alongside the steps. There wasn't much grass in the yard to speak of, but a great big old mulberry tree kept it shaded. Off to the side, the heady, peachy fragrance from a mimosa in full bloom mingled with the sweetness given off by the honeysuckle vine smothering the post-and-rail fence along one side of the house, arousing him in some way he couldn't even define.

Just then, the largest dog he'd ever encountered nosed open the screen door, got Joe in his sights, and bounded down the steps, barking his head off. Before Joe could brace himself, ham-sized paws collided with Joe's shoulders, sending him sprawling in the dirt with a loud "*Oof!*" And if having the wind knocked out of him wasn't enough of an indignity, a gallon or so of dog spit now washed over his face. Then he heard Taylor yell, "Oakley! Drop it!" and he could breathe again. Move, no, but definitely breathe.

"Ohmigod, I'm so sorry..." Taylor grabbed his hand and, grunting, hauled him to a sitting position. "Are you okay?"

"Yeah, yeah, I'm fine," Joe said, cautiously testing assorted limbs to make sure he was. On her knees in the dirt beside him, Taylor was close enough for him to catch a whiff of her scent. Yes, even over the mimosa and the over achieving honeysuckle. He'd almost forgotten how good women smelled. And to make matters worse, her hair had come loose, swirling around her face and shoulders in a mass of glittery, untidy waves that looked hot to the touch.

"Gross," Seth said, over what sure sounded like choked laughter. "You've got dog slime all over you!"

Joe's gaze shot to his brother. Hearing him laugh was almost worth the sore butt and dog spit. Then his eyes swerved to Taylor's, who sure as hell looked like she wanted to laugh, too, and for a split second, he felt the dumbest spurt of connection or something. Almost angrily, he yanked his shirttail out of his waistband and started mopping his face, only to then remember what Taylor'd said to get the dog off him. He dropped his now soggy shirttail and looked at her again. "'Drop it'?"

"It's one of the few commands he'll obey," she said, her forehead crinkled for a moment before she pulled a tissue out of her pocket, grabbed Joe's chin and daubed at his still-wet face like he was one of her kindergartners, for Pete's sake. The sensation of soft fingers against his skin sent awareness jolting through him, settling nicely in his groin. Terrific.

"He loves to play fetch," Taylor went on, totally unaware of her torture. "But he has a problem with the part where he has to let…go…"

She went stock-still, her gaze fixed on his mouth. Then her hands yanked away and a little hiss of air escaped her lips, her cheeks turning practically the same color as the bright pink petunias spilling out of the whiskey barrel planter a few feet away.

Now it was Joe's turn to barricade the laughter threatening to erupt from his gut, even as he had to tamp down the urge to plow his fingers through all that bright, glittery hair and plant a hard, fast kiss on that funny mouth of hers just because, well, he felt like it.

"Sorry," she mumbled as Seth, bless him, got everybody back on track.

"You said six-thirty, Joe," he said, indignant as hell. "It's after seven."

"I know, I know," Joe said, collecting the slightly battered flowers and candy—which the dog had slobbered all over—and getting to his feet. "Traffic out of Tulsa was a bi…bear. Then the skies ripped open right outside Claremore and I had to pull off the road until it let up some." He shifted everything to one hand and hugged the kid to him, his physical instincts fully operational even if the jury was still out on his emotions. "I'm really sorry. But I got you something, it's in the car. And these—" Joe wiped the candy box on his jeans as the kid took off, and then shoved both candy and flowers at Taylor "—are for you."

She stared at them like she wasn't sure what to think.

Well, hell, Joe never had been much good at the keeping-women-happy stuff. He didn't suppose it helped matters any that by now the flowers looked like something he'd filched from a neglected grave and the candy box was still slightly damp.

He blew out a breath. "It's lame, I know, but I thought, hell, I should do something. But I didn't have any idea what you might like. Since I don't really know you, I mean. And the Homeland was the only thing open by the time I got here. But I figured I was probably safe with candy and flowers. I mean, don't all women have a thing for chocolate?"

Why wouldn't she say anything? She just stood there, staring at the flowers with a peculiar expression on her face. After what seemed like forever, she finally brought the daisies and carnations up to her nose and inhaled deeply. Daisy petals fluttered off in all directions; one carnation head plummeted to the dirt. She bent to pick it up, then lifted her eyes to his. "They're lovely, thank you. But unfortunately chocolate gives me a headache."

Behind him, the Blazer door slammed shut; small feet pummeled the earth as Seth returned, holding aloft his prize, a toy police car Joe'd gotten when he'd picked up the flowers and—he now realized, pointless—candy.

"This is so cool! Thanks, Joe!"

Joe's heart turned over in his chest. It was a stupid two-buck toy, for crying out loud. But like the dumb TV commercial, the look on his brother's face was priceless. Seth looked like a normal little boy. A *happy* little boy. Joe knew better than to think the worst was behind them, that this was anything more than the sun's piercing the clouds for a moment. But it was a start.

And he'd made it happen. Okay, the toy had made it happen, but Joe had made the toy happen, right?

"You're welcome, bro," he said, and the boy beamed even more brightly, and Joe noticed Taylor watching him like maybe she expected him to sprout wings or something.

"I guess we'll be getting out of your hair now," he said, just as she said, "Have you had dinner?"

"No, ma'am," he said after a long moment. "But I don't want to put you out."

She smiled. That full-out, first-place smile. "Don't worry," she said. "You won't."

Chapter 4

Flowers, for God's sake.

The goofball had brought her *flowers.*

And candy she couldn't eat.

Taylor eyed the Russell Stover box, sitting there so innocently on the kitchen counter.

Shouldn't eat, anyway.

With a sigh, she climbed up on a kitchen chair to get down a cut-glass vase she'd gotten as a wedding present and couldn't remember ever using before this. Partly because nobody—including her ex—had given her flowers since her marriage, and partly because, even though she was perfectly capable of giving herself flowers, glass anythings and bloodhounds were not a good mix. But then, she mused as she located the vase in amongst the million and one other wedding presents she had no use for but couldn't bring herself to pitch, one could always stick flowers in a milk jug if one really wanted flowers in the house.

She thought there might be something profound in there, somewhere, but she was too tired to figure it out. Just as she was too tired to figure out what the heck had been going on outside when she'd for some reason thought wiping the dog spit off the man's face would be a good idea and he'd gotten this look in his eyes that had clearly told her it had been anything but.

"Need any help?" she heard behind her, and the vase nearly fell out of her hands. Joe reached up and relieved her of it, setting it carefully on the counter and sending yet another life-is-so-unfair rush through Taylor.

Things were much easier when she was mad at him. Only then he had to go and do stuff like bring her battered flowers and chocolates and get that confused, helpless, I'm-really-trying-here expression on his face when he looked at Seth. Dammit, not only could she not stay mad, she invites the man to dinner.

But then, she wasn't having visions of abandoned, uneaten chocolates in the trash, either.

However, she noticed Joe glowering at her as she got off the chair, and a small, hopeful flame of annoyance tried to rekindle itself.

"Standing on chairs isn't safe," he said.

The flame grew a tiny bit brighter, even though his voice was all growly soft and he was standing there with his arms crossed over his chest. By seven o'clock, his five o'clock shadow had reached the should-be-outlawed stage. So she puffed on the flame a little to make sure it didn't go out.

"Yeah, well, I've been standing on chairs since I was two, haven't broken my neck yet, so I'll continue to live dangerously, thank you. Where's Seth?"

"Out front, playing with the car."

She actually considered keeping her big mouth shut, she really did. But since that was like trying to keep rain from hitting the ground, she said, "You know, distracting him with gifts will only work for so long."

Joe's eyes darkened, but he leaned one hand against the counter and slipped his other into his jeans pocket, as if nothing or nobody was going to ruffle his feathers, by golly. "And it might not hurt for you to cut me some slack here, Miss McIntyre. I'm doing the best I can."

His reproof was gentle, but dead-on. Her cheeks burning, Taylor turned her back on Joe to run water into the vase, after which she grabbed the flowers from beside the sink and plopped them into the vessel. Oakley trotted into the kitchen, his nails clattering against the tiles. From outside, she heard Seth making assorted, if subdued, high-speed chase noises with the little car. She glanced up to make sure he was okay, just in time to see a robin the size of Texas scamper across the yard, tweetering his little robin heart out.

And Joe's pheromones flooded her kitchen, flooded *her,* settling into every nook and cranny of her person and making her puff so hard on that damn flame she was about to hyperventilate.

"So," she said. "Dinner. Frozen or canned?"

After a slight pause, she heard, "You don't cook?"

"I cook. When the mood strikes. It didn't tonight." Or most nights, actually. Which was a shame, in a way, because she wasn't a half-bad cook. But it was like the giving herself flowers thing—basically, she couldn't be bothered. "Anyway," she went on, twisting to set the flowers in the center of the table, where they actually looked very pretty, if still a bit shell-shocked, "I've got canned chili, some of that Chunky soup stuff, and a freezer full of frozen dinners."

"I think I'll take my chances with the chili."

"Good choice."

That got a half laugh. Then he plunked himself down at her table, looking as though he belonged there. How bizarre. "So how come you invited me to dinner if you're still pissed at me?"

Her gaze shot to his. "I'm not—"

He chuckled. She huffed.

"Damned if I know."

The corners of his mouth curved up. "Don't take this the wrong way, but you are one strange woman."

"So I've been told."

The grin stretched out a little more. "You're also very pretty."

She barked out a laugh, which somewhat blotted out the *uh-oh.* What little makeup she'd put on this morning had long since melted off, her shirt was stained with everything imaginable (and a few things that weren't), and her hair had that fresh-from-the-wind-tunnel look.

"Oh, man—we'd better get some food in you, quick. Hunger must be making you delusional." She tromped over to the cupboard. "And even if it were true, that's not going to stop me from being pissed."

"I didn't think it would. And I'm not delusional. Or a suck-up."

She arched one brow at him, which tugged a sheepish grin from his mouth.

"Okay, the flowers and the candy were a suck-up." Then his smile…changed, somehow. Seemed to be coming more from his eyes or something. "Stating a simple fact isn't."

Unlike Abby, her younger sister, Taylor had never been good at accepting compliments. And she wasn't all that sure what to do with this one now. So she decided to set it aside, like a sweet, but totally impractical, present, and said instead, "Would you like crackers with your chili?"

She could feel his gaze, warm and intense on her back, making her shiver slightly. "Sounds good. And I didn't really mean that about you being strange."

"Yes, you did." The can of chili duly retrieved, she yanked open the utensil drawer and found the can opener, then handed both to Joe. "I'm a firm believer in audience participation," she said when his brows lifted. Shaking his head, he set about removing the lid; at the sound of the can opener, Oakley planted himself next to Joe, his entire face undulating as it swiveled from Joe to can to Joe.

"I don't suppose chili's part of the dog's diet," Joe said.

"Not unless you want to wear a gas mask for the rest of the night."

"Got it. You know," he said, frowning at the dog as he cranked the opener, "his face kinda reminds me of an unmade bed."

"Hey. Don't talk smack about my dog."

"Oh, I don't know. Unmade beds are kinda nice, if you think about it." His mouth twitching, he handed the open can to her. "Cozy. Inviting."

Taylor rolled her eyes—mostly to keep from staring at him bug-eyed—and he laughed. After she dumped the chili into a bowl and put it in the microwave, Joe asked, "How'd you come to have a bloodhound anyway?"

"A question I've asked myself many times," she said with a sigh. "Only thing I can figure is that since I couldn't have a pet when I was a kid—not even a hamster—when I finally got this place, I sorta went overboard." Oakley angled his head backward to give her a reproving look. "Not that I don't adore the big lug," she added, "but a bloodhound isn't exactly the most practical choice in the world. Oh, Lord..." She grabbed an old towel off a cabinet knob and beckoned to the dog. "Come here, Niagara mouth."

"And let me guess," Joe said as she sopped up a small lake's worth of drool from the dog's jowls. "You're by nature a very practical person."

"Let's see," she said, dumping the towel in the sink and washing her hands. "I teach kindergarten in a flyspeck of a town, I bought an eighty-year-old house that I swear was made by the first little pig, and last month I picked up a sequined evening dress at a garage sale just because it was pretty."

"What's wrong with that?"

"Hello? Where would I wear a sequined dress around here? To one of Didi's potlucks?"

Joe angled his head. "Don't tell me you never leave Haven. Not even for a night out now and again?"

She flushed. "Well...no. I mean, sure, I suppose I could. It's just been a while since I have. God. That really sounds pathetic, doesn't it?"

They stared at each other so long and so hard a blind person—in China—could have seen the sexual sparks leaping between them.

Joe sighed. Then chuckled, a low, warm, rough sound that did a real number on her nerve endings.

"Um…we've got a problem, don't we?" she said.

"Only if we act on it."

"Are we thinking about acting on it?"

"Don't know about you, but I am. A helluva lot more than I've got any right to." He leaned back in the chair, one wrist propped on the table. "I don't suppose…"

"No," she said, waving her hands in front of her. "I was just…curious. If I was imagining things."

"You're not. But I'm not looking for…entanglements."

That was relief she felt, right? Sitting like a lump in the pit of her stomach? "No, of course you aren't. Because you're only here for the summer."

"Right. And I'm not much for starting things I can't finish."

"Not to mention that you've got enough on your plate already. With Seth."

A fraction of a second shuddered between them before he said, "Exactly."

"Well," she said. "That's good then. That we got this out in the open." *Oh, yeah, let's hear it for responsible adulthood.*

"Just what I was thinking." His gaze nestled up to hers and settled right in. "So nobody has to wonder. About what might happen."

"Right."

"Sure can't help wondering what it would feel like to kiss you, though."

A short laugh burst from her throat even as her eyes—the traitors—zinged right to his mouth. "Did you really mean to say that out loud?" she said, looking at his mouth.

"Just figured you for the type of woman who likes to know where things stand."

Heaven knew how long she stood there, staring at his mouth and thinking wayward thoughts, before she finally said, "This is true." Then she added, because it seemed like another one of those good ideas, "But it wouldn't be a good idea."

"No. It wouldn't." His brow creased. "Why wouldn't it?"

"Because if the kiss was good, I'm not sure I'd want to stop."

His eyebrows practically shot straight up off his face.

"Did I shock you?" Taylor said.

"No. Of course not. After all, why shouldn't a woman—"

"—be just as sexually up-front as a man? I agree." Then she leaned forward. "My divorce was nearly four years ago. I've been celibate since. You do the math."

His stare was hard and long and impossible to misread. "You're not making this any easier."

"Just letting you know I'm probably not the safest bet to fool around with if you're not looking for entanglements."

"Real dry kindling, I take it."

"Oh, buddy, you have no idea."

Praise the Lord, Seth chose that moment to wander into the kitchen, because if they continued this conversation any longer, she was going to pull a Meg Ryan-in-the-deli right there and then. And she *wouldn't* be faking it.

"C'n Oakley come outside with me?" he asked.

Taylor smiled. "If he wants to, sure."

Apparently the dog did, since he actually roused himself with something resembling enthusiasm and followed the boy outside. Joe got up from the table to watch them through the kitchen window. "I know this was all unplanned," he said quietly, and the atmosphere calmed down enough for them to function like rational adults instead of bonkers bunnies, "but I think being here is doing him some good. Having something else to focus on besides his pain."

Taylor came up beside him—but not too close—just in time to see Oakley bring the boy a stick to throw. Seth took hold of it willingly enough, but when the dog wouldn't let go, he gave up, plopping himself back onto the ground to mess with the car.

"How can you tell?" she asked.

"He's actually playing with the car. He wanted the dog to come out with him. Believe me, that's an improvement. And I have to think part of it's because he's in a real home, even if only for a little while." He glanced at her and then back out the window. "We can't let that happen again."

Confused, she looked up at the side of his face. "What?"

A muscle flinched in his jaw. "Flirt like that. Because right now, I can't let myself get sidetracked from getting that little kid healed up." He rubbed his chin and then slipped his hand back in his pocket, still not looking at her. "Because it's been a long time for me, too."

The longing in his voice wrapped itself right around her heart, a longing she suspected went way beyond sex. "Ah. Got it. Um, should I step away?"

"Wouldn't hurt."

So she did. Then she said, "You don't have a real home?"

"Oh, I've got a place in Tulsa." Joe walked away from the window and sank back down at the table, his legs stretched out in front of him. "An apartment I'm rarely in. So I've never really bothered to fix it up much. Besides, since it took me the better part of two weeks to sort out the mess my father left behind, we came straight from Oklahoma City—where I picked Seth up—to here. Kid's been living in a motel of one kind or another for nearly a month. That can't be helping him any."

Taylor unhooked her gaze from Joe's and again looked out the window, at the sad little boy now sitting under a tree, absently watching one of the robins. And once again, she felt herself being sucked in by the vulnerability edging Joe's words, by her own inability to resist wanting to help. But she didn't want to get sucked in, dammit, by either the kid or his big brother, didn't want to give in to impulses she knew would bring nothing but aggravation and heartache. Because there'd been a time when she *had* wanted entanglements, the kind of entanglements that led to waking up beside the same man for the rest of her life and potty training and training wheels and soccer games and crazed, noisy Christmas mornings. All the things she'd thought she'd have with her ex but realized weren't going to happen. All the things that had never really happened with her own family.

All the things she could tell would never happen with the man sitting at her kitchen table.

The microwave dinged, shaking her awake enough to edge back from that emotional vortex. She got out the bowl and set it in front of Joe, handed him the box of crackers, poured him a glass of tea, sat down at the table and said, "So what *were* you doing in Tulsa earlier today?"

Huh. So she'd decided to go on the attack. Interesting, if a mite disconcerting, since he'd apparently hit a nerve he hadn't meant to hit. Not this time. Yeah, when he'd told her she was pretty, he'd definitely been trying to get a rise out of her. He'd had a long day, he was stressed to the gills and for a single, stupid moment, he thought it would be amusing to rattle her chain. But this…this was different. This reaction, he couldn't quite figure out. Except that something must be threatening her sense of control—an illusion, if ever there was one, but it wasn't as if Joe couldn't relate—so she became the aggressor.

What she didn't know, however, was that if she wanted the upper hand, she'd have to fight him for it. So he scarfed down several spoonsful of chili before answering. "My boss asked me to take on another project at the last minute. I couldn't turn it down."

"Why?"

What she also didn't know was that Joe'd always had a thing for women who didn't make a man turn cartwheels trying to figure out what was going on in their heads. For some weird reason, the more direct the woman, the more turned on he got. Which, in this case, was one of those good-news, bad-news things.

"Because I need the extra cash, for one thing," he said. "And because I need to prove to Wes—my boss—that I'm the right person to take over for him when he takes semiretirement next year."

Taylor turned her glower on his empty tea glass, like she was trying to figure out how to be a good hostess without giving him any ideas about women serving men. Then she got up, apparently deciding the solution was to plop the pitcher in front of him so he could refill his glass any time he wanted.

"But how on earth are you going to handle two projects in two different places?"

"I have no idea. But I'll manage." He picked up a cracker and dunked it in his chili. "I have to."

"You don't sound all that happy about it."

Happy? When had he last thought of his life in those terms? The muscles in his upper back mildly protested when he shrugged. "Just being realistic, is all."

She snorted. "Honestly—what is it with men and their need to prove themselves? No matter what the cost?"

His gaze fixed on his food, Joe stilled and then lifted his eyes to hers. "I'm not sure how being responsible is the same as *proving* myself. Besides, seems to me men don't exactly have the market cornered on ambition."

A second passed before she pushed out a breath. "You're right," she said, and he thought, *point to him.* "It's just that…I don't know. Men get this whole protective thing going and…"

"And what?"

"And they can't see that they're accomplishing exactly the opposite of what they think they are."

Joe leaned back in his chair, brows drawn, arms folded across his chest. "You think there's something wrong with a man wanting to provide for his family?"

"No, of course not. Except…" He was startled to see her eyes soften with tears. "Except when he neglects his family in the process."

He thought of all the things he could ask, wanted to ask. Wouldn't ask. Not now, at any rate. Probably not ever, if he were smart. Because asking questions might get him answers, but it could also get him involved. And getting involved, now, with her—with anyone—wasn't in the cards.

So he did what any sane man who didn't want involvement

would do—he turned the tables on her. Not rudely, or meanly, but with the conviction of somebody who didn't need some female making him question his own motives, for crying out loud.

"You know," he said quietly, "you're cute and all, but you've got a real problem with judging folks when you don't know them worth squat."

She flinched a little, then recouped. "I'm not judging you. I'm just familiar with the signs."

"Of what?"

Another breath. "My father was a workaholic, Joe. So was my ex-husband. And it sucks."

The words were brittle, as if years of acid had eaten away at them. And they arrowed straight from her heart to his.

"Your father…"

"…Literally worked himself to death. When I was eleven."

"I'm sorry," Joe said softly. "But I'm not a workaholic, Taylor."

For several seconds, their gazes tangled like a pair of kids scrapping over a toy, until Taylor got up from the table and walked over to the kitchen window, her hands stuffed in her back pockets. "How many hours a week do you work? And that includes work you bring home."

His eyes narrowed. "It's the sex thing, isn't it?"

She whirled around. "What?"

"You don't know what to do about this attraction between us, so you're picking a fight with me."

"I'm not picking a fight with you. And this has nothing to do with…that. I just asked you a simple question. How many hours a week do you work?"

"And how is this any of your business—?"

"Sixty? Seventy?"

Joe's jaw tightened. "Somewhere in there, yeah."

She turned, brows arched. "And you don't think you're a workaholic?"

"No, I think I'm somebody who can't stand the thought of letting people down who depend on me."

"And what the *hell* do you think you did when you didn't pick Seth up on time tonight?"

Though spoken barely above a whisper, her words exploded around him like buckshot. And Joe wasn't real partial to picking buckshot out of his butt. Man, if this was what she was like when she wasn't picking a fight, he'd sure hate to be around her when she was.

"I didn't have a choice, Taylor. You know that."

"There's always a choice! And right now, that kid needs *you!* Not what your paycheck can buy him!"

And what he didn't need was this woman in his face about this, a fact the chili was only too vigorously corroborating. Direct was one thing; deranged was something else entirely. Except Joe was as ornery as she was. He'd never in his life walked away from a challenge, and he wasn't about to start now. Even if he didn't have a clue in hell what this one was even about. His manhood, maybe. His honor, definitely. But there was more going on here than a simple disagreement about lifestyle choice.

"Maybe I do have a choice. In theory. Doesn't always pan out that way in practice, though."

"You're saying it's not about the money?"

"Hell, yes, it's about the money. You think I'd put Seth through this if it wasn't about the money?"

That seemed to take the wind out of her sails for a moment. But only for a moment.

"Then *what?*"

Joe silently uttered a word he didn't think Taylor would appreciate. What the hell had he gotten himself into? Baby-sitting and chili, that's all this was supposed to be about, not a hot-and-heavy game of sexual dodgeball followed by his having to defend himself about stuff that had nothing to do with her. The last thing he wanted was to talk about his personal life, but God only knew what conclusions she'd come to on her own if he didn't. Why he should care one way or the other what she thought about him, he had no idea. That he did was no small source of worry, but it was a worry he'd have to deal with later. Because right now, his choice was to bare his own soul, at least to a certain extent, or pry hers open. That, however, was an even less palatable option than door number one, since the tiny glimpse he'd already gotten into that soul had nearly undone him. A longer, deeper look could be disastrous. And Joe had all the disasters he could handle right now, thank you very much.

"Seth's not my only responsibility," he said with as little expression as he could manage. "Because, when my father walked out of my life and my mother's, fifteen years ago, he also left behind a three-week-old baby girl with Down syndrome. My sister Kristen."

Chapter 5

Instantly, Taylor's high horse not only threw her, but took off for parts unknown. "Oh, Joe—"

He put up a hand to stop her. "Kristen's only moderately retarded, but my mother realized she couldn't go back to work and still give my sister the kind of attention she needed, so she had to take an unpaid leave of absence from her teaching job. My going to work was the only way we'd've made it."

Taylor frowned. "But you couldn't have been more than, what, eighteen?"

"Seventeen. My last year of high school."

"Don't tell me you quit?"

The horror in her voice coaxed a smile from his lips. "Mom would've had five fits if I'd tried. But I had to work. We got some help from the state for Kristen's care, but it wasn't enough. So, since construction paid a helluva lot better than fast food, I worked as a framer during the day and finished up high school at night. Oh, for God's sake…don't look at me like that."

"Like what?"

"I don't want your sympathy, Taylor. I did what I had to do, that's all."

Lord, how many times had she heard those words, or variations on that theme? "And you still are, I take it?"

"Yeah. I am. Kristen's had the best care and training available, Mom made sure of that, but she's never going to be able to live completely on her own or earn a living wage. And she's got a heart condition that needs constant monitoring. Even though Mom was able to go back to teaching once Kristen started school, you know what teachers' salaries are like. And anyway, she's not going to be able to work forever. A good chunk of my earnings goes into a trust fund for Kristen. For later."

When their gazes locked this time, it wasn't about sex. Taylor carted his empty bowl to the sink, wondering how admiration and aggravation could be so closely linked. But the question was, what was she aggravated about? Joe's dadblasted insistence on shouldering so much responsibility, or her own dadblasted weakness for men with such broad shoulders?

"What are you thinking?" he asked as she smacked up the faucet to wash the bowl.

"Why does it matter what I think?" she said over the running water.

"I don't know. It just does. So humor me."

The water groaned off, then she twisted around, her arms linked over her middle. "I think…" She blew out a sigh. "I think I owe you an apology, for one thing. For giving you grief when I didn't have all the facts." She hesitated, then said, "But when I taught in Houston, I'd see kids who'd have every gadget on the market, the best clothes, every privilege imaginable, but there'd be something in their eyes, this…enormous, gaping void, that just ripped me to pieces. Nine times out of ten, I'd eventually find out their parents weren't in the picture as much as the kids needed them to be. It kills me to see a kid being neglected. Especially when the parent has no idea that's what he's doing."

"Like…your father?" he said softly.

She smiled. "I guess I'm a little hypersensitive about the issue."

Was it her imagination, or did his eyes narrow? "S'okay," he said. "I understand."

"I imagine you do," she said, and their gazes brushed up against each other, just for a moment. Just long enough, apparently, for him to decide it was high time he got out of there.

"Well," he said, rising, "we've all got to get up pretty early, so we'd better get going."

She walked him through the living room her older sister Erika had pronounced *spartan* the one time she'd come to visit and out onto the porch, the screen door slamming behind them. Seth lay on his stomach in the grass underneath the mulberry tree, talking to Oakley, who frankly didn't appear all that captivated with the conversation.

"Time to go," Joe shouted across the yard.

The kid scrambled to his feet. "C'n I use the bathroom first?"

"We'll be back at the Double Arrow in two minutes, can't you hold it?"

"Nuh-uh."

"Go on, then." After the kid trooped back inside, Joe turned to Taylor. "Well. Thanks again. I really appreciate it."

"Any time. No, I mean that," she said when he snorted. Oakley had dragged himself up onto the porch and flopped down at her feet with a groan. One echoed silently inside her as her heart shoved her right smack in the line of fire, all the while her head was yelling, *Have you lost your mind?* But apparently there were certain aspects of a person's makeup that could not be altered, no matter how desperately you might want to. No matter how fervently Taylor might have wanted to be a practical person, in the end her heart always made her decisions for her. "I'm happy to take Seth after day camp, if you need an emergency baby-sitter."

Joe had the most honest, direct gaze of any man she'd ever known, which wasn't helping matters any. Especially when a bemused smile touched his lips. "Even though…" He pointed between the two of them.

She laughed, even as she felt herself coloring again. "Like you said, this is about Seth. And I think we're both adult enough to control ourselves."

Only he gave her this look that said, *Speak for yourself,* and she thought, *Oh, boy.* What he said, however, was, "Fine, I might just take you up on that. But only if I can pay you for your time—"

"Don't be ridiculous, that's not why I offered—"

"I know it's not. But I insist."

She let out a little huff and started down the porch steps. "Make a contribution to the church maintenance fund, then. We desperately need a new heating and cooling system."

"Okay, I'll do that."

When they got to the Blazer, she asked if he got to see his mom and sister very often. The question seemed to surprise him, making her wonder if he wasn't used to being asked. And his reply seemed hesitant, at first—no, not as much as he'd like, since his work kept him away so much. Then he went on to say that was one of the reasons he wanted his promotion, so he'd be able to stick around Tulsa more, and her common sense tapped her on the shoulder and said, *Remember this for future reference, sweetheart.*

Except then it was as if her question had let light into a room where the curtains were usually kept drawn, because he started talking about his family. "They're tough as nails, both of them," he said, then laughed. "There was one time, when Kristen was maybe three, we were in the grocery store. Mom had placed an apple in my sister's hand, saying the word, 'Apple, apple' over and over. Some idiot woman stands there, staring at them for I don't know how long, then finally says, 'You do know you're wasting your time, don't you?'"

"Ouch," Taylor said, even as she wondered, as she often did, why some people seemed to think they were exempt from exercising common courtesy.

"Ouch is right. Especially after Mom singed her ears about how at least Kristen had an excuse for her condition...what was hers?"

Taylor laughed, her smile reflecting his as something told her he probably didn't share his personal life with many people, a realization that left her feeling both profoundly flattered and more than a little nervous. "Sounds like a woman after my own heart." She paused, then gently asked, "Has Seth met them yet?"

He shook his head. "Mom took Kristen away for several weeks to visit our grandparents in Kansas. They'll be back in August. Hopefully by then...Seth will be ready. To meet his sister, I mean."

She thought perhaps there might be one or two other worries surrounding his siblings' meeting each other he wasn't addressing. But the screen door slammed again as Seth came back outside, so that was that.

Joe prodded the little boy to say "Thank you," although he apparently didn't need prodding to swiftly hug Taylor around the waist, a gesture which took her breath, emotionally and physically. The brothers got into the car; Joe argued with Seth about getting his seat belt on, then leaned out the open window and said, "By the way...what color's that dress?"

She frowned, clueless. "What dress?"

"The one you bought you said you had no place to wear."

"Oh." The breeze picked up, sending the ends of her hair into her eyes. "Royal blue," she said, brushing them away. "Like the sky, right before the sun sets—"

"I know what color royal blue is."

A smile twitched around her mouth. "Why'd you want to know?"

"No special reason," he said, gunning the Blazer's engine to life. "Just wondered." Then he drove off, and Taylor and Oakley stood there, watching the dust cloud kicked up by the tires until it blended into the early evening haze hugging the road. The sun was beginning to think seriously about setting, that robin was up in the trees somewhere, singing his lullaby, and Taylor went back inside and straight to the kitchen, where she scarfed down three pieces of chocolate before she could talk herself out of it.

Then, thoroughly annoyed with herself, she walked back out into the living room.

To see Seth's lunch box sitting right smack in the middle of the coffee table.

Seth leaned as far over in Joe's car as the seat belt would let him, his head half hanging out of the open window. He liked the way the wind tickled his face as they drove, the whooshing sound it made in his ears….

He thought maybe Joe was saying something, so he pulled his head back inside. "What?"

"I asked if you liked staying with Taylor."

"Oh." He shrugged. "It was okay, I guess."

"Well, I suppose that's something. So you'd be okay with going home with her from time to time when I'm late?"

Seth felt like somebody was squeezing his insides, but he didn't let on. Instead, he just nodded.

"How're you doing otherwise? You settling in a little bit better at camp?"

"Yeah, maybe. Um, I don't much feel like talking right now, okay?"

Joe glanced over, then looked back out the windshield. "Sure, I understand," he said, but he had that look on his face that said he didn't understand at all. His I-wish-I-knew-how-to-make-it-better face.

But he couldn't. Nobody could. Seth knew Joe wanted him to talk about how he felt, but the feelings hadn't turned themselves into words yet.

Seth stuck his head back out the window, letting his eyes go unfocused, the landscape blur into a big streak as they sped along. It was funny, the way grown-ups would ask if you were okay when what they really meant was, were you mad at them? And heck, yeah, Seth had been mad, when Taylor first said Joe wouldn't be able to pick him up on time, because Joe'd *promised* he wouldn't be late. It wasn't fair, how a grown-up could tell a kid it was wrong to make a promise you couldn't keep, then go and break their own all the time.

Except Joe was actually pretty cool, for one thing. And Seth had liked staying with Taylor, for a lot of reasons. Her house wasn't full of all kinds of stuff you couldn't touch, the way his grandmother's had been, and it smelled nice, not like those stinky sprays his mother used to use to cover up his father's cigarettes and beer and stuff before Dad moved out. And Taylor was funny, and she smiled like she was really happy to have him around, not like she felt sorry for him. Or like his mother did, a weird, kinda flat smile that always made Seth hurt inside.

Just like thinking about her did. But if he thought about Mom hard enough, he could almost pretend she was still alive. Except then he'd remember she wasn't, and he'd feel all cold and empty again. He hadn't expected things to be better at Taylor's, but for some reason they were. A little, anyway. But then he got all confused because, on the one hand, he didn't want the better feelings to go away, but, on the other hand, maybe it wasn't right. As if it meant he didn't love his mother enough or something.

His brain kinda changed channels then, and suddenly he was thinking about how Oakley'd let him lie against him, like a big old pillow, his fur soft against Seth's cheek. Like that big stuffed bear he used to have that Mom had given him for Christmas when he was real little. Joe had told Seth he could bring anything he wanted with him, when Joe came to take him after…after the accident. But Seth didn't want Joe to think he was some stupid baby who still played with stuffed animals, so he'd left the bear behind.

He pulled his head back inside and wriggled around so he could pull the police car out of his pants pocket. The car was awesome, its doors really worked and everything. It'd been nice, lying against the dog, playing with his car, listening to Joe's and Taylor's voices coming through the kitchen window. He couldn't tell what they were saying, but that was okay. At least they weren't yelling at each other, the way Mom and Dad used to.

Seth scrunched up his face, trying to remember what it was like when Dad still lived with them and Mom and Dad still liked each other. Not like at the end, when Dad would sometimes come and take Seth away for the weekend, but he never really looked happy about it.

They pulled up in front of the cabin where he and Joe were staying then both got out. It was okay, he guessed, even if the mosquitoes were about to drive him crazy. But he'd seen a deer in the woods behind the cabin, once, and the other day a raccoon had come up onto the porch, and that had been pretty cool.

"You hungry?" Joe asked when they went inside. It was real hot in here, even after Joe opened up all the windows and turned on the ceiling fans.

"I dunno. Maybe."

"How about some ice cream?"

Joe said all the cabins were going to get air-conditioning in the next couple of weeks. But it didn't really matter, since Seth didn't really mind the heat all that much, anyway.

"Sure, I guess."

He followed his brother into the kitchen, climbing up onto a stool in front of the counter while he watched Joe scoop ice cream into two bowls. Joe gave him a lot more ice cream than Mom ever did, but Seth didn't want to hurt Joe's feelings by telling him that. He figured his brother was having a hard enough time trying to figure out what to do with a little kid.

Like the way he kept asking Seth questions, about what he liked and stuff. And the way he'd catch Joe looking at him, with his forehead all creased, like he couldn't quite figure out why Seth was still there.

Oh, Joe was nice—nicer than Dad had been, at least at the end—but Seth knew he was only with Joe because neither of them had a choice in the matter. And Taylor had taken him home with her because there hadn't been anybody else, either. Maybe grown-ups didn't think kids knew the difference, between when somebody did something because they wanted to and when they had to. Well, Seth could tell, and all he had to say was, it sucked.

Joe put a dish of plain ice cream in front of him. Seth would've liked chocolate sauce on it, the way Mom used to fix it, but he didn't want to complain. Nobody liked a kid who whined about stuff. Joe brought his own dish to the counter and got up on the stool beside Seth, but he didn't look all that interested in eating it. Seth understood—there were lots of times he didn't much feel like eating, either. These days, especially.

They ate without anybody saying much. Then Joe asked Seth if he was ready for bed.

"I don't know," he said.

"You don't know?"

"Well, I always had to go to bed at nine, but Mom had said maybe I could start staying up until ten in the summer, or when I didn't have school."

Joe got this funny look on his face, as if this were something he didn't want to hear. "Well…then I guess you can stay up until ten. As long as you don't give me a hard time about getting up in the morning."

"I won't, I promise."

Then Joe kinda looked around the room, like he was hoping to find something, until his eyes came back to Seth's. "I guess you could play video games until then."

"Oh." Seth tried not to feel disappointed, but he couldn't help it. He knew he was weird, not liking video games all that much when his friends would play them until their hands dropped off if they could get away with it. But he wasn't real good at them, so if he played too long he usually ended up in a stinky mood. "Mom used to read to me, or listen to me read. Or play games and stuff. So we could spend time with each other, you know? I brought books with me, remember?" he added, just in case Joe was going to say they didn't have anything to read. Seth hadn't said anything about reading and all that before this because he hadn't wanted to seem pushy, figuring maybe Joe would offer when he was ready. Except it just now occurred to Seth maybe Joe didn't know that's what he was supposed to do, so it was up to Seth to clue him in. "And games, too. Parcheesi and checkers. If you don't know, I could teach you, they're real easy..."

Now Joe's face went all panicky looking, like Seth felt when a teacher would call on him and he didn't know the answer. Then his brother's eyes slipped over to the corner of the living room where he'd set up a drafting table and files and his computer, like an office. "Shoot, buddy, that would be great, but..." Frowning, he looked back at Seth. "I've got a ton of work to do yet—"

"But you've been working all day! Aren't you tired of it?"

Joe smiled. Sorta. "It's not a matter of whether I'm tired of it or not. It's just stuff I've gotta do. I'm really sorry, squirt, but I can't just show up unprepared."

Even though Joe's voice was real quiet, Seth got that hot, stingy feeling at the back of his throat like he was gonna cry. But no way was he gonna do that, not anymore. Bad enough he'd acted like a sissy baby that first day at camp. Especially since, when Joe'd come to get him after the accident, Seth'd heard him talking to that social worker lady, who'd said if it didn't work out Joe could bring him back and they'd try to find him another home. Like Seth was something you bought at a store and changed your mind about so you returned it, like Mom did that time with a dress that didn't fit her right. Of course, nobody knew he'd heard them talking, but he was glad he had, 'cause now at least he knew what he was up against. Maybe things weren't great, but at least Joe wasn't mean or anything, Joe was his *brother,* and if he took Seth back to Oklahoma City, he'd have to go live with strangers. Strangers who weren't even related to him.

So Seth figured he'd better keep his mouth shut and not let on like he was hurt or anythin', else Joe would figure Seth was too much for him to handle, like Dad would say sometimes—*Boy, you are too much for me, with your constantly asking me questions and stuff.* Only he didn't say *stuff*, he'd say the bad *s* word.

But, boy, did he feel like crying, because nothin' felt safe anymore, and he was getting real tired of it. So all he said was, "Y'know, I think I'm tireder than I thought, so maybe I'll go to bed after all."

Joe frowned at him. "You sure?"

"Yeah. I'm sure." He slid off the stool and started for his room.

"Seth?"

He turned around, saw how sorry and confused Joe looked, and made up his mind that if it killed him, he wasn't gonna make any trouble.

"I suppose we could play a couple of games of checkers if you want."

"No, that's okay, I don't really feel like it anymore, anyway."

"Are you—"

"Yeah, I'm sure. Really."

"Well. Okay. Another time, then."

He shrugged. "Whatever."

Joe looked at him real hard for a couple seconds and then said, "Then go ahead and get your teeth brushed, and I'll be in to say goodnight."

"No! I mean, jeez, I'm too big for that."

Joe frowned some more. "Since when?"

"Since now. So, g'night, I guess."

Another moment passed before Joe said, "'Night, squirt. Sleep tight."

But instead of answering, Seth ran into his room and shut the door, because he couldn't hold in the tears anymore. He wished like heck this was a bad dream and he'd wake up and Mom would be there, holding him and telling him it was all right, there was nothing to cry about, everything was okay.

Except nothing was okay, he thought, throwing himself on the bed and burying his face in the pillow so Joe wouldn't hear him cry. Nothing would ever be okay again.

"Dammit!"

Joe charged across the kitchen, clattered the two dirty

bowls into the sink, then slammed one hand against the edge. How the hell was he supposed to help Seth if he wouldn't let him in? He knew he'd hurt the kid's feelings by saying he couldn't play with him, but then his brother wouldn't even give him a chance to make it up to him or talk about it, nothing.

He walked back out of the kitchen, glowering at Seth's closed door, mad at himself for hoping the kid's good mood might stick around a little longer, even madder for not knowing what to do to make it stick around. For a moment, he thought about knocking on the door and trying again. Except Joe remembered what it felt like, after his father left, how everybody bent over backward to try to make him feel better—his mother, his grandparents, his teachers—when all he really wanted was to be left alone.

Joe had thought he'd get over wanting to be alone. Until it dawned on him one day that counting on people was where most people made their first mistake. Maybe his determination that nobody would ever get the chance to screw him over like that, ever again, was the knee-jerk reaction of a hurting child. But as time went on, Joe began to see the wisdom of that vow, especially in the light of his ongoing responsibilities. It was all about focus, about not letting outside…stuff get in the way of his obligations.

It was just easier this way.

With a heavy sigh, he went over to the corner of the living room he'd turned into an office, sinking into the chair behind the drafting table. Maybe Seth needed to work some of this out on his own, too. Or maybe…maybe it wasn't going to work, Joe taking care of his brother.

The thought knocked the breath from his lungs. Once again, he glanced across the room at the closed door, unwilling to believe the words still reverberating in his head, equally unable to refute them. But Joe had lived by himself for so long…just because they were brothers…if Joe couldn't be what Seth needed…the only thing that mattered was what was best for the kid…

The sound of a truck pulling up in front of the cabin startled his train of thought off its tracks. Massaging the muscles at the base of his neck, he went to the front door and opened it in time to see Taylor and Oakley get out of her truck.

Oh, yeah, *just* what he needed.

Looking none too pleased herself, Taylor came up onto the cabin's porch to hand Joe Seth's lunch box.

"He left it at my house. I figured Seth would be in bed so you wouldn't be able to come get it."

"Thanks," Joe said, and that should have been that. And might have been that if Taylor hadn't looked at him like she could see straight through his skull. "What's the matter?" she said, and he said, "Nothing, everything's fine." She frowned at him in a way that suggested she was thinking a very unladylike word.

"It's nothing I can't handle," he said.

"I don't doubt that for a minute."

"And I've got a boatload of work to do."

Her mouth flattened. "I'm sure you do. Well, I just came to give you back the lunch box. So there it is."

"Yeah." He held it up. "Thanks."

"Anytime." Taylor turned to leave, calling the dog. Moonlight kissed her hair, eased over her skin; on a faint, damp breeze, her scent floated back to him, taunting.

"It's Seth," he said before she'd gotten all the way down the stairs.

She twisted back around, a flicker of triumph in her eyes. "What about Seth?"

"Never mind, forget it, I don't want to take up your time…"

"Hey. It's summer. Nothing but reruns on TV, anyway."

Then she smiled.

Joe blew out a breath. "All I've got is beer. And milk."

"Beer is good," she said, and Joe wondered if anything would ever really be good, ever again.

Chapter 6

This was one desperate hombre sitting on the porch steps beside her.

Not that he'd be any too pleased to know that's what she was thinking, Taylor imagined. But since he'd pretty much related every detail of what had transpired between Seth and him from the moment they'd left her house until roughly a few minutes before she'd arrived, there wasn't a whole lotta doubt about it. And her heart ached, it really did, for this pair of clueless males thrown together in some lifeboat of a relationship without an oar between them.

However—she took a swallow of her beer and idly wondered if she was ever going to grow up—sympathy probably wasn't what Joe needed. What Joe needed, she decided, was a swift kick in the butt. God knows she did. For eating the damn chocolate (her head was killing her), for asking the man what was wrong…take your pick.

Of course, he wasn't actually *asking* for help. Or even advice. Nowhere in the conversation had he inserted a single, "So what do you think I should do?" or "Got any ideas how I should handle this?"

Of course.

"Okay," she said at last, figuring if she didn't prod the conversation in the direction it needed to go they'd be sitting there for the rest of the night, "not that you're asking me, but…maybe you just need to be more patient, you know? There's no magic formula for this. It's going to take time. Until you two get to know each other better, and until Seth learns to trust you, you're going to hit lots of bumpy spots."

Silence from the other side of the steps. Then, out of the dark, "How's he going to learn to trust me if he won't talk to me?"

"Well…maybe he's afraid to talk because he thinks you're going to resent being interrupted."

"Ah, hell, Taylor…"

"Hey. We've already established I'm not the type to pussyfoot around an issue."

"Yeah, *your* issues."

She washed down the bitterness at the back of her throat with another slug of beer. "Maybe so," she said quietly. "But sure sounds to me like they're your issues now."

Silence. Then a swear word. She thought, anyway, since it was in Spanish.

"I don't want to know what that meant, do I?"

"Probably not."

More silence. Then, because she clearly had a death wish, she said, "I know you want to fix this. As quickly as possible, for both your sakes. But it doesn't always happen that way."

This time, the silence stretched out so long and taut, her ears rang with it.

"You saying it's hopeless?"

"No, of course not." It was a damn good thing he was sitting as far away as he was, because she wanted nothing more than to lay her hand on his arm. "What I am saying is sometimes we have to admit we don't have all the answers before we can figure out how to solve the problem."

"That doesn't make sense."

"Life rarely does."

Oakley hauled himself up the steps, flopping down between them with a loud groan. After a moment, Joe reached over to scratch the dog behind the ears. Then he said, very softly, "It's killing me, seeing Seth so unhappy."

Taylor waited, but once again, the logical follow-up to that—a request for help—didn't come. A mild spurt of annoyance winnowed through her at that damn male pride that made so many women's lives a living hell. But right on the heels of the irritation came another, far less defined emotion—that she was probably seeing Joe Salazar about as vulnerable as he got. Something she doubted he shared with many others. That he should pick her… Well. She didn't quite know what to think about that.

"So," she said, "what are you gonna do about it?"

Again, he took his sweet time answering. But when she finally heard the weary "I don't know" from a few feet away, the fear in his voice that no amount of macho I-can-handle-it posturing could cover up, she realized she had two choices—offer the help the bleepin' man was too stubborn to ask for himself, or walk away and let him muddle through on his own.

The pounding in her head got louder.

"Okay, I'll tell you what—when Seth's with me, I suppose I can read to him or play games or whatever. And maybe…I can get him to talk to me, see what's going on inside his head." She stood up, rattling her car keys to get Oakley's attention, then looked over at the man sitting with his hands clamped between his knees, the moonlight edging a rigid profile. "But I'm gonna let you in on a secret—it's not the book and games he really wants, it's you. He needs to bond to you, not me. Because at the end of the summer, I stay here and you and Seth go…where ever it is you end up going. And there's not a whole lot of sense in letting him get too attached to someone who's not going to be part of his life after a few weeks, is there?"

Almost in slow motion, Joe lifted his eyes to hers. "No. There isn't."

"So." She swallowed. "We have an understanding?"

"Yes, ma'am, I would say we do."

Then, figuring everything had been discussed that needed to be, Taylor dragged the dog off the porch and convinced him to get back in the truck. And as she drove home, she decided she needed to tack up that look in Joe's eyes someplace where she'd be sure to see it at least a hundred times a day.

Shortly after five o'clock a few days later, Taylor herded Seth into her house, fixed him a snack, then asked if he minded if she made a couple of phone calls. The boy shook his head, then politely—he was always polite—took his snack and cup of juice out back to sit on the porch swing Taylor'd finally gotten around to putting up last weekend. Oakley, who had a particular fondness for Cracker Barrel cheese, went to keep him company.

Taylor stood at the back door for a moment or two, frowning through the screen at the child as he perched on the edge of the swing, nibbling his crackers and cheese and staring off into space, his sneakers squeaking rhythmically against the porch floorboards when he pushed off.

No wonder Joe was worried about him. The kid's silence was about to drive her stark raving bonkers; she could only imagine how it was affecting Joe.

Where at first Seth had hung back at camp, not wanting to join in, now he'd participate in or do anything that anybody suggested. But more out of a sense of obligation than any enthusiasm that Taylor could see. As if he were simply going through the motions so everybody would stay off his case. The thing was, if Seth had been obviously unhappy, or even acting out, that would have given Taylor something to work with. But this chronic close-mouthedness, his almost stoic cooperation with everybody…she had no clue what to do about that. As Joe said, it was kinda hard to help someone who wouldn't let anybody in.

With a sigh, Taylor turned away from the door and picked up

her cordless phone, punching in her mother's number. She dutifully called once a week, even though—

"You've reached the McIntyre residence," came her mother's good-old-gal Texas accent. *"Please leave a message after the tone."*

—Olivia McIntyre was rarely home.

"Hi, Mom, it's Taylor. I'm fine, just calling to see how you were doing. I'll…talk to you later."

Except she probably wouldn't, since her mother rarely returned her calls.

Next on her list was Abby, her younger sister, a hotshot Realtor in Atlanta, married to an equally hotshot young corporate attorney. Abby had informed the family, shortly after her marriage three years before, not to expect any babies since neither she nor Bryce felt particularly driven to add to the world's population. Considering Abby's first word at ten months had been "Mine!", Taylor thought her sister had made the right decision.

"Abby?" she said when her sister answered her cell. "Hey, it's Taylor!"

"Taylor! Hi!" Lots of clinking china and silverware and loud conversation in the background. "Hold on a sec…" Taylor heard something mumbled about no, they'd rather sit in the window, then: "Bry and I are meeting his folks for dinner at this new place out in Buckhead, you should see it, it's unbelievable!"

"Oh, I'm sorry, if you're busy—"

"No, no, it's okay, I've got a couple seconds before they get here…what, honey? Oh, no, I don't care, that side is fine. Okay, hold on, let me just…get…seated… There, whew. Is it as hot there as it is here? I'm telling you, ten feet from car to door and I am just a *puddle*. So how *are* you? Oh, hold on, sorry… A daiquiri, please, thanks. Now. I'm all yours. Oh, wait, did I tell you? I closed on an absolutely *outrageous* deal involving an entire chain of restaurants. Fourteen of them, to be exact. The commission is *huge*. In fact, if I wanted to retire tomorrow, I could. What, honey?" Taylor heard her brother-in-law's voice, then her sister's light, ladylike laugh. "Bry said over his dead body. Oh, he says hi, by the way, wants to know how things are out in the boonies."

"Actually—"

"You know, with this commission, we're seriously thinking of looking for a farm or something out in the country, getting away from this *wretched* traffic. What was that, Bry? No, of course not that far out, silly. Bry says if there's no health club within a five-minute drive, he's not going. So did you hear Mom's on the Opera board? So that makes I think five boards, now. Maybe six. I do not know how she keeps them all straight. Oh, I see the folks now…" Her sister lowered her voice. "Phyllis is wearing this totally outrageous diamond pin. Wonder what she had to do to get that. Or, more likely—" Abby's voice dropped to a whisper "—what Lyndon did." Breathy giggle. "So look, I've got to run, but I'm so glad you called! I'll give you a ring next week, promise! Bye, honey!"

Well. At least they knew each other was still alive. Taylor supposed that counted for something.

One more call—Erika, her older sister—then her conscience would be clear.

But Erika in Denver had just gotten in from work and had, like, two seconds to get Fleur to soccer practice and Kevin to Little League—thank God they were both in the same sports complex this time!—and why on earth wouldn't Taylor use e-mail like the rest of the world?

Because, gee, maybe Taylor liked to actually *talk* to her family every once in a while? Not that she ever actually did, she thought as she hung up the phone. She supposed there was some small comfort in knowing that they weren't singling her out—nobody talked to anyone much, as far as she could see. And she couldn't even remember the last time they'd all been together. Erika hadn't even made it to Taylor's wedding—

"Who were you talkin' to?" she heard as the screen door wheezed shut.

Taylor turned to find Seth standing in front of her, cracker crumbs clinging to his T-shirt like insects, his empty plate and cup held out like a proffered gift. A mild curiosity in his eyes ratcheted his expression half a notch above indifferent. Taylor decided to take this as a positive sign.

"I'm not sure I'd exactly call it talking. But I was calling my mom and sisters. And you know where your dishes go."

"You got sisters?" the kid said, setting his plate and cup beside the sink.

"Yep. Two. Did you get enough to eat? And what's the dog doing?"

"Yeah, I guess," Seth said, sliding onto one of her kitchen chairs and hooking his feet behind the lower rung. "And I asked Oakley if he wanted to come in, but he said no." The boy's dark curls shivered from the overhead fan as he plunked his face down into his palms, scrunching up his cheeks. "How old are they? Your sisters?"

Taylor held her breath, afraid to disturb the frail thread of trust shimmering between them. She went over to the sink to rinse off his dishes. "Erika's thirty-five and Abby's twenty-eight."

"How old're you?"

Okay, so maybe this interested she didn't need him to be. One eyebrow raised, she twisted around. Grinning. Teasing. "Hey, goof. Don't you know you're not supposed to ask a lady how old she is?"

A fly landed on the table. Seth stacked his fists, then lowered his chin on top, watching it. "How come?"

"Well, because some women are sensitive about their age."

"That's dumb."

Chuckling, she turned off the water and grabbed a towel to dry her hands. "Maybe so, but that's just the way it is."

"So how old are you?"

Oh, brother. "Thirty-two."

"That's the same age as Joe," he said flatly, plugging in the fact without reacting to it. "So you're in between your sisters, huh?"

"Yep."

"That must be nice."

Hmm. Had it ever been *nice?* "We fought a lot as kids," she said. "Then we ignored each other. Now we all have our own lives, in three different places." She shrugged. "We're not exactly close."

Seth seemed to think about this for a minute. Either that, or he was fascinated by the fly, now slowly inching across the kitchen table. Taylor put her money on the fly. Who would be history the minute the kid wasn't looking. Then he said, "Joe read to me last night."

"He did?"

"Yeah. Only he fell asleep while he was doing it. So I felt bad."

Her heart stumbled: Was it her imagination, or did the thread just get a little stronger? "Bad?" She went back to the table, sinking into the chair closest to him and asking softly, "How come?"

That got a little wrinkle, right between his brows, as he stared hard at that fly, not looking at Taylor. Finally he said, "After Dad left—"

After Dad left?

"—and Mom had to work extra so we could stay in the apartment, Mom never wanted to do much of anything, anymore. She kept sayin' she was sorry and stuff, but…but she was so tired all the time."

"Oh, sweetie…that must've been really hard on you."

His chin still propped on his fists, Seth swung his eyes over to Taylor's. Then he just looked and looked at her, as if trying to decide if it was okay to say what he was thinking. Taylor stayed quiet, waiting. "There was this one time," he said at last, "when she fell asleep right in the middle of dinner. And I got real scared, 'cause I'd thought she'd, like, died or something." Then his eyes widened, as if his words has just caught up with his brain, and he sat straight up, his gaze darting to the clock over the refrigerator. "It's after five-thirty, huh?"

Taylor glanced over and nodded. "Not too much. Five thirty-five."

"Joe said he'd come pick me up by now."

It was the same thing, every day. The same longing, the same hope sagging into disappointment. And it broke her heart. Not just for Seth, but for Joe, who, she had to admit, was only trying to make the best of an impossible situation. The worst part, though, was that it was like finding yourself tricked into watching a movie you've already seen, one you know ends badly. Only with a movie, you could at least get up and walk out, or turn off the video or DVD. Because the story wasn't real, the characters on the screen were only pretend, they wouldn't know or care or be hurt if somebody walked away from them.

Dammit.

"Seth?" she said gently.

The boy looked back at her, and this time she could see past the mask, through the silence, the politeness, the I'm-okay-ness, to the wordless, howling hurt churning inside him.

She opened her arms. "Come here, baby," she whispered.

For a split second, there was hesitation. Wariness. A flicker of fear, no doubt a reflection of her own, both consumed in an instant as the child catapulted himself off his chair and into Taylor's embrace.

And even though he didn't cry, the poor little guy held on so tight Taylor could hardly breathe. Not that she cared, as she sat there rocking him, rubbing miniature vertebrae underneath slightly damp, sweet-sour smelling cotton, her cheek nestled in his thick curls. A tidal wave of tenderness plunged through flimsy barriers, flooding her parched soul...swamping her with the realization that maybe she wasn't doing this just for Seth.

Emotion clogged the back of her throat, stung her eyes. When was the last time somebody had needed her? *Really* needed her?

Really needed *her?*

Not her sisters, certainly, or even her mother. Not Mason, who'd literally shrugged when she'd said she wanted a divorce. And you know something? That *hurt.* Oh, she was useful, and appreciated, she knew that—as a teacher, as a member of her community. She'd made some good friends here, and she was grateful. But, dammit, that wasn't the same as having somebody who couldn't wait to get home to tell you about their day, who missed you if you were gone too long, whose face lit up when you came into view. Who cared if you were unhappy or lonely, who got excited for you when you had good news.

It wasn't the same as having somebody to miss, to care *about,* to get excited *for.*

Without thinking, she placed a kiss in Seth's curls, then leaned back to smooth them off his forehead. Her heart was breaking, splintering into a thousand pieces. She'd done exactly what she'd sworn not to do—fall in love with this solemn-faced little kid. But she could no more keep her love out of his reach than she could stop the sun from coming up in the morning.

And feeling sorry for herself wasn't going to do anybody a lick of good.

"Feel better?" she said, feeling a half-baked smile tug at her lips.

He nodded. "You smell nice."

She laughed. "I do?"

"Yeah. Like clothes when they first come out of the dryer—"

They were interrupted by frantic whining and snuffling at the back door, followed by a single *"Wroww!"*

Taylor gave the boy another quick hug, then said, "Might as well let him in, he'll drive us nuts until we do."

Two seconds later, the dog burst proudly into the kitchen… and both humans clamped their hands over their noses.

"Ohmigosh, Oak!" Through her hand, Taylor still caught a strong whiff of what she could only describe as a cross between a hundred ticked-off skunks and rotten broccoli. "What on earth did you get *into?*" With her free hand, she grabbed the dog's collar with the full intention of hauling his reeking hide outside, a plan with which Oakley was not entirely in agreement. Finally, with Taylor pulling and Seth shoving his full weight up against the miserable beast's butt, they got the dog back out, where he promptly trotted over to the far corner of the backyard and flung his body down onto the ground, writhing in unbridled canine bliss.

"Stay here," Taylor said to Seth, then followed, steeling herself. The bad news was, whatever it was had passed over to the big woods in the sky quite some time ago. The good news—if one could find any in the situation—was that the animal was so far past identification stage that she couldn't really drum up a whole lot of sympathy for it at this point.

It wasn't easy trying to talk without breathing, but she did manage to get out, "Oh, Oakley…" Except she decided Oakley was more the type to take advantage of a situation than initiate one. In any case, she once again grabbed hold of his collar, dug in her heels and dragged him away to shove him in his dog run while she decided what to do with…the remains.

"What is it?" Seth called from across the yard.

She turned. "Something dead. Not real sure what."

"Is it gross?"

"Oh, yeah."

"Cool. C'n I see?"

Well, shoot—if she'd known roadkill was all they needed to bring the kid out of his shell, they could've arranged for a breakthrough long before this.

"Okay, I guess—"

Kid was across the yard in three seconds flat. "Awesome," he said. "What are you going to do with it?"

Good question. Burying it was pointless, since something would undoubtedly only exhume it later. So she trekked over to the shed the previous owners had left to get some rubber gloves and several garbage bags. Five minutes later, after the carcass had been duly shrouded and dispatched into her garbage can—while Oakley barked and bounced the whole time, protesting the loss of his prize—they both turned and regarded the heartbroken, stinky dog.

"What now?" Seth asked.

Taylor looked at the kid. "You got a problem with getting soaking wet?"

The boy's great big grin said it all.

Chapter 7

"Joe! Guess what I did yes-terday?"

Joe smiled at the exuberance in his sister's voice. Kristen had caught him on his cell just as he was getting into the Blazer to go pick up Seth. She didn't call often—although she'd phone him several times a day if Mom let her—so the last thing Joe wanted was to put her off.

"What, cute stuff?"

"I went swim-ming! It was fun! The water got up my nose, but I was o-kay!"

Joe chuckled. "That's terrific! I bet you're a good swimmer."

"I am." She laughed, a loud HA! HA! HA! that came from her belly. "And guess what?"

"What?"

"I pulled weeds from the garden. Gran gave me money."

"How much?" he said, encouraging her.

"Ten dollars. How much is ten dollars, Joe?"

"You can rent three movies for ten dollars."

"Wow. That's a lot!"

Joe smiled, but it was a smile weighted down by reality. At her last evaluation, they'd been told Kristen's mental capacity was that of an average six-year-old. And like a six-year-old, Kristen tended to see things in black-and-white, tended to obsess about unimportant details like her stuffed animals being lined up on her bed the exact same way every single day. She could read very simple books and write her name and perform clearly delineated tasks, but at fifteen, it was clear there would be no miracles.

His mother had made avail of every program, every provision, every type of stimulation out there. They could at least rest easy knowing that they'd done everything for her they could—including, perhaps most importantly, fostering an expectation that Kristen learn to do as many things for herself as possible…an expectation that had brought its share of temper tantrums over the years. But there was a difference between giving Kristen the opportunity to reach her full potential and having unrealistic hopes.

Just as there was a difference between loving her for who she was and being able to accept that loving her wasn't enough to…

To fix her.

Joe shut his eyes against the guilt that had set up permanent residence in his gut from the day his mother had brought Kristen home from the hospital. If he loved her—and he did, with all his heart—why couldn't he simply accept her for who she was and be done with it?

"Guess what we're having for dinner tonight?" Kristen said, breaking into his thoughts. "Pizza! With saus-age and mushrooms! Hey, Mom wants to talk to you, okay?"

"Sure, cute stuff."

"I miss you, Joe."

His heart cramped. "I miss you, too, honey."

His mother was slightly out of breath when she came on the phone. "Sorry, I didn't know she'd called, I hope it wasn't a bad time."

"No, but I've got to go pick up Seth, and I'm already late."

"How's he doing? Better?"

Danielle Salazar had greeted the news that her rat-bastard ex-husband had fathered another child with an equanimity Joe doubted few other women could match. But then, taking out her frustrations on an innocent child wasn't his mother's style in any case. Mom loved kids—all kids—far too much for that. Like Taylor, he thought idly, then yanked his thought back to attention by reminding himself that he still had no intention of letting Seth become his mother's problem.

"Yeah, I think. We're doing okay."

"Except you sound exhausted."

"It's the end of a long day, Mom," he said, smiling slightly as he shifted to lean against the front fender. Lacy shade from a nearby cottonwood flicked over him, shielding him from the brutal heat; in the distance, the Ozark foothills stretched across the landscape like a sleeping cat, serene and unperturbed. For the briefest of moments, he felt…not bad. "I think I'm entitled."

"Still," she said on a rush of air. "It can't be easy, suddenly having a child to care for. Especially one you don't even know. It might not be so bad if you were married, but all by yourself…"

So much for the okay moment. "Mom? Don't."

She blew out another sigh, but she backed off. Sort of. "So define, 'Doing okay.'"

"Just what I said—"

"Jose Diego Salazar. Am I going to have to come over there and pop you one?"

She'd only torment him until he cracked. "It's not like Seth is giving me any trouble or anything," he finally said. "It's just…he won't talk to me. In fact, instead of opening up, it's like he's withdrawing even further. Even Taylor noticed it."

"Taylor?"

Obviously he was a lot more pooped than he thought. "I told you about her," he said levelly. "The day-camp lady who takes care of Seth in the evenings when I can't pick him up on time."

"Oh, yes, yes, I remember now. The kindergarten teacher, right?"

"Yeah, that's her." Level voice or no, there wasn't a damn

thing he could do to keep his heart rate from kicking up a notch or two, or a memory from the other day from jarring loose and floating to the surface of his brain. He'd actually picked Seth up from camp early—well, on time—to find Taylor in the grass out behind the church with at least two dozen little kids piled on top of her, laughing so hard she could barely get her breath. When she'd untangled herself from the heap and gotten to her feet, grinning and flushed with half the kids still clinging to her like seaweed, he'd wanted to kiss her so badly he thought he'd choke.

Only then she'd done…something. A small gesture, maybe, the certain way she'd looked at the kids when they'd run off. Nothing he could put into words. But suddenly, it was as if he could feel what she was feeling, her emotions spilling from her psyche to his and ricocheting through him so sharply it hurt.

A second later, if that, she returned her gaze to his. And smiled, a half tilt of her bare lips that seemed almost apologetic, though God knew for what. And the purely libido-driven drive to kiss her from only moments shattered, to be instantly supplanted by an ache infinitely more basic and a million times more complicated, to pull her into his arms and simply *hold* her, protect her, comfort her, with gentle words and heartfelt promises he'd stopped believing in himself a long time ago.

And how dumb was that? He had no power to protect her, or anyone else, from anything. Still, the moment had jolted his emotions like a slug of bad booze on an empty stomach. Why this woman, for God's sake? And why now? Because she'd been dead right the other night, that he and Seth were leaving when the project was finished, that there was no point in anybody becoming attached to anybody else.

Even if they weren't leaving, there was no point in anybody become attached to anybody else.

"What?" he said, suddenly realizing his mother had been talking.

"I said, he's probably still grieving. After all, it's only been, what? A month?"

"Something like that, yeah."

"Just give him time, *mijo*." She paused, then said, gently, "Give *yourself* time. Nobody's watching you, waiting for you to make a mistake."

"Except Seth."

"Especially not Seth. As long as he knows you care, that's all that's important. So," she said, in her now-I'm-changing-the-subject voice. "Tell me about this Taylor."

Joe actually laughed. "Nothing like being subtle."

"Subtle is for people much younger than I am. She sounds like a sharp cookie. Is she young, old, what?"

"She's about my age," he said calmly. "As are lots of people. And she's just my brother's temporary caregiver."

"Of course she is. Is she pretty?"

"Pretty is subjective."

"Then I guess I'll have to decide for myself."

Despite the temperature still hovering somewhere between sweltering and blistering, a cold chill tramped up Joe's back. "What are you talking about?"

"In the if-the-mountain-won't-go-to-Mohammed department," Danielle said, "I called that Double Arrow place you're working on, and talked to somebody named Hank—he sounds like a very nice man—and he said, sure, Kristen and I could come stay in one of the cabins for the last week in July. As long as we understood how messy it was with all the construction going on. And that it got pretty noisy sometimes during the day."

"What?"

"From everything you said, it sounds like a beautiful place, and we got a good deal since it's under construction. And since we haven't really had a chance to see you in so long, I thought this would be a great way to kill two birds with one stone. Three, actually, since Seth can meet his sister, then, too."

The phone melding into his palm, Joe said quietly, "Do you really think this is a good idea? If Kristen thinks I'm going to be able to hang out with her all the time…"

"We've talked about it, and she understands."

Does she? he wanted to ask.

But even greater than the risk of disappointing his sister—who didn't take disappointments well under the best of circumstances—was the risk of his mother's reaction to his working the extra job. Although Danielle had always been grateful for Joe's financial help, it would be a major blow to her pride to discover the extent of that help.

"What is it?" his mother said, teetering on the brink of sounding hurt. "Don't you want us to come?"

"It's not a matter of wanting you to come or not," Joe said. "It's the timing that worries me. Look, after this project is done, why don't I plan to take a couple weeks off, and come and see you then? Seth should be more prepared to meet Kristen—"

"And then something else will come up," his mother said softly, "and then something after that, and before you know it another six months will be gone."

Joe waited out the rebuke's sting, then said, "I'm sorry, Mom. You know I'm only doing this for you guys."

"I do know, *mijo.* So I'm doing this for *us.* All of us. So we'll see you on the twenty-fourth. Brace yourself."

After she hung up, Joe yanked open his car door, climbed inside and rammed the key into the ignition. Tires squealed as Joe peeled out from the Double Arrow's parking lot and away from the motel. And once he hit the road, for a second—maybe more than a second—he was tempted to keep on going, driving away from everything and everybody who had some sort of claim on him. Maybe drive straight through to Denver. Or California. Why not? Maybe not forever—although *forever* sure seemed like a good idea at the moment—but just for a while. Just long enough to find himself again underneath this mountain of responsibilities and gotta-dos.

Except when he got to the turnoff leading to Taylor's place, he turned. With a huge sigh, and a choice cuss word or two, but he turned. Because there was a kid expecting him to and a woman who would read him up one side and down the other if he didn't.

Sometimes, life was just like that.

As he approached Taylor's house, however, curiosity nudged aside his bad mood when he noticed the commotion in her front yard. What kind of commotion, he couldn't say, since a breeze kicked up a cloud of dust just then, throwing a sandy-orange film over the whole scene. Plenty of jumping around, though, it looked like. And, when he got close enough to hear, lots of laughter.

Lots of laughter. Taylor's, mostly, but Seth's, too, his sparkling giggles darting in and out of her darker, richer belly laugh like a brightly colored bird through a lush forest. They seemed to be doing something with the dog. Who didn't look all that happy, from what Joe could tell.

A bath, Joe finally realized as he parked the car. They were giving the dog a bath.

Or he was giving them one, it was hard to tell. Woman and boy were wetter than the dog, Taylor's hair half out of its ponytail, plastered to her face and pale neck like so many dark red snakes, the tops of her breasts glistening over the neckline of the most unsexy bathing suit Joe had ever seen. Some dark color, blue, he thought, with wide straps, the bottom half concealed by a pair of baggy running shorts.

But it wasn't her body that had his attention, not now. Now all he noticed was the energy pulsing around her, from her, through the laughter that surged up from someplace deep inside her.

And Seth…*look* at him, having the time of his life, wet and filthy and giggling his head off. Like a regular little kid.

"No, hang on to his collar!" Taylor said breathlessly as she vigorously scrubbed the dog's back with a wide brush, while water spurted every which way from the hose clamped in her right hand. "Oakley! Stay still! Oh, no you don't—!"

She grabbed at the slippery skin folds sagging from the dog's neck, but the beast broke loose, knocking Seth—who was limp with laughter by this point—on his butt in the grass, only to get no more than five feet away before he started to shake, a blur as shockwaves rippled from muzzle to tail. A million water droplets flashed in the late-day sun, hovering airborne for a second before drenching them both even more. Then the dog shot away, cavorting around the yard and baying to beat the band. Taylor and Seth took off after him, half laughing, half yelling.

"Come *back* here, you miserable beast! Ooooh…!" Breathing hard, the redhead stopped, bent over at the waist, her palms pressed against her thighs as she glared at her dog, who, now safely across the yard, pranced in place with his tongue lolling out of his mouth, before letting out a challenging *"Rworf!"*

Now he was having a good time, boy, Joe thought on a chuckle.

His bad mood had all but vanished. And even though he should be bone-tired—hell, he *was* bone-tired—watching those two nuts trying to wash a dog that outweighed the two of them put together… God knows, it didn't make any sense, but suddenly, he felt downright invigorated.

"Need some help?" he heard himself call over.

"Joe!" Seth yelled, running to him as Taylor's head swung around. Water from her dripping hair sliced through the air; her smile dimmed, just barely, only to rekindle with a dazzling radiance that took Joe's breath.

While Seth started in about a dead animal and Oakley stinking to high heaven and how they were trying to give him a bath before he "fixiated" somebody, Taylor straightened, her chest rapidly rising, falling. Rising. On second thought, maybe that swimsuit wasn't as ugly as he'd first thought, especially when she brought one hand up to swipe a hank of wet hair off her forehead, parking the other on her hip. "You know anything about herding dogs?"

"Not a whole lot, no."

"Then you'll fit right in." Something like concern flitted across her features. Or maybe that was amusement. "This is gonna get messy, though."

"I imagine I'll live," he said, stepping closer. To Taylor, not the dog. "Can't do much to jeans and a T-shirt."

"You don't know Oakley."

"You can get him, Joe, right?" Seth said, hanging on to his hand.

The dumb dog had backed himself up against the white picket fence that ran along one side of the yard. "Piece of cake." He ignored Taylor's snort beside him. "So he smells really bad?"

"We're talking eau du rotting flesh."

"Charming."

"You said it."

He chuckled. When the wind blew from the east, he smelled wet, soapy woman, which was both very good and very bad. When it shifted, however, he smelled wet dog overlaid with dead animal. *Bad* didn't even begin to cover it.

"I'm getting a poodle next time," Taylor said in a low voice as they both maneuvered closer. "Something prissy with bows in its hair that sits in my lap and doesn't go rolling around in dead stuff."

He glanced over at the soggy, mud-streaked woman next to him. "Somehow, I can't see you with *prissy*."

"People change," she said, only to then let out a bellowed *"Get him!"*—good God, the woman had a set of lungs!—as she lunged for the dog. Who slipped right out of her grasp to mow Joe down like an army tank.

"You okay?" Taylor tossed out, sprinting past as Joe once again found himself communing with the sky.

This was getting real old.

"Never better," he muttered. He sprang to his feet and went after the dog again, thinking it was probably a good thing he hadn't decided on a rodeo career. Several minutes later, however, through a combination of dumb luck and macho determination—and spurred on by the cheers from his audience—he'd corralled the mutt and herded him back to his bath, where both adults hung on to him long enough for Seth to wash and rinse. At long last, Taylor pronounced the beast clean enough and they let him go.

The dog took off like a shot, barreled around the yard three times at about ninety miles an hour, then flung himself down to roll in the dirt.

Joe looked at Taylor, who was frowning at the dog. "And the point of that was?"

"Wow, Joe," Seth said. "You've got, like, dog tracks all over you."

He looked down. Sure enough, paw prints tracked from his thighs up to his shoulder. And everywhere there was a paw print, a muscle whimpered in pain.

Then he looked over at Taylor—wet, dirty, flushed and incredibly, unselfconsciously female as she strode over to the porch, where she'd apparently left a stack of towels—and everything else whimpered in another kind of pain.

So he broke the connection. Because he'd already used up his rebellious allotment for the day—the month, the year—and indulging in the kinds of thoughts that seemed hell-bent on taking over his brain would only lead to misery for all concerned.

"Here," she said, flinging a beach towel in his direction before wrapping Seth in another and vigorously rubbing his hair dry, chuckling low in her throat at Seth's squirming. "Lord, you're as bad as the dog—stay still, goof!"

A breeze whisked across the yard, making her shiver. And Joe's gaze wandered. He couldn't help it. It had been too long and she was too…there.

Taylor glanced up, then glanced down. And chuckled again, even as she got a third towel for herself and wrapped it around her breasts.

After Seth went inside to use the bathroom, Joe muttered, "Sorry."

"For what?" she said, her grin unaffected as she reached up to squeeze the water out of what was left of her ponytail. "Being human?"

Exactly.

"I'd—we'd—better go. It's getting late."

"Oh." She shook the excess water from her hands, her smile

fading slightly. "I could probably scrounge something up for dinner if you want to stay—"

"No, that's okay, I don't want to put you out."

"You wouldn't be, believe me—"

"Aw, c'mon, Joe," Seth said, the screen door slamming shut behind him as he came back outside. "Please? I was having so much fun!"

Yeah. So was I. Joe's gaze shifted to his brother's, and he saw in the boy's hopeful expression exactly what Taylor had feared would happen—that he was becoming too attached.

Just as he imagined anyone who was really looking would see the same thing in his.

"Not this time, squirt," he said, the damp towel hanging limply from his hand, the bruises on his body not nearly as tender as the ones being inflicted by the kid's big brown eyes. "I've got a lot of work to do tonight—"

"Just for a little while? Please?"

"I'm sorry, Seth."

His brother's eyes darted to Taylor—whose silence Joe didn't find the least bit reassuring—then back to Joe, before he tromped back inside to gather his things. Two seconds later he was back, stomping down the stairs and over to the car, his brows practically meeting in the middle.

Joe finally looked at Taylor, whose attention was fixed on Seth's rapid retreat. Her arms were crossed, her mouth set, but when he started to say something, she simply shook her head.

"Don't make it worse," she said, reknotting the towel under her arms before stomping over to the porch to snatch up Seth's abandoned towel.

"You don't understand—"

"It was just *dinner*," she said, whirling around, her eyes blazing. "A friendly gesture, that's all. Because you helped me with the dog and you look like you could use a couple hours off. And besides, the kid was having a good time, for crying out loud! I thought that's what you wanted, to see him feeling better!"

"I do! And I'm grateful to you! But—"

"Never mind," she said on a sigh, then held out her hand. "Give me the towel. And now you'd better go, Seth's waiting."

"I can take it back and wash it—"

"Oh, for God's sake, just give me the damn towel! It's no big deal!"

He shoved the towel at her, opened his mouth, realized he didn't have a damn thing to say that would make a lick of sense, then turned and strode off to the car, refusing to believe that had been hurt he'd seen in her eyes.

The minute Joe's car was out of sight, Taylor dropped to the porch step and gave in to a good old-fashioned sobfest. One of the perks of living out in the middle of nowhere was that she could bawl her eyes out and nobody would hear her. Whimpering in concern, Oakley hauled his much nicer smelling self up beside her and nosed aside her arm to lay his head in her lap.

"It's so s-stupid, Oak," she said, stroking him. "Like I said, it's only d-dinner. So why am I acting like an id—" her breath caught "—diot?"

She grabbed her towel to wipe her eyes, only to realize she'd grabbed Joe's instead because suddenly his scent was everywhere, pungent and arousing and comforting and frustrating. She threw down the towel with a groan, only to snatch it up again and bury her face in it because she was obviously pathetic. No, beyond pathetic—*hopeless.* Not to mention hornier than any living creature should ever have to be. All of this combined to set her off again, so she sat and blubbered until she was all blubbered out, then sat and sighed deeply until she got so light-headed she thought she might faint.

Then she sat a little longer, hugging her dog and listening to the breeze whispering in the trees, until the woman who was perfectly fine with her dog and her house and her kids, even if they weren't *her* kids, moved back inside her head. Because that other one—the whiny, weepy, pathetic one who seemed to have forgotten that she'd *chosen* this life—was a real pain in the butt.

Then Taylor hauled that butt off the porch steps, gathered up the soggy towels and carted them inside to throw them in the wash.

From the other side of the booth at Ruby's, Seth watched his big brother mess around with his French fries, like he was eating them only 'cause they were there, not because he really wanted them. Seth didn't feel a whole lot like eating, either, but his stomach kept growling so he figured maybe he'd better. Besides, he liked Ruby's a whole lot—how it always smelled like coffee and fried onions and hamburgers, the way Ruby and her husband Jordy acted like everybody was their best friend, not just a customer. Even Joe and Seth, when they'd come in the first time. Seth'd eat here every day, if he could.

Other than asking him if he wanted to come here for dinner, he and Joe hadn't talked hardly at all since they left Taylor's. Seth got the feeling Joe and Taylor were mad at each other, but he couldn't figure out why. Especially since they'd been laughing so much and stuff when they'd all been chasing the dog. Then Seth had gone inside to pee, and when he'd come out it was like a big cloud or something had come over everybody. It didn't make sense. And he didn't like it, not one bit. In fact, the more he thought about it, the madder he got. Mad enough to get up the nerve to ask his brother how come he had time for them to come here for dinner when he'd said he was too busy to stay at Taylor's?

"'Cause when you stay at somebody's house for dinner," Joe said, not really looking at Seth, "they expect you to stick around and talk and be social. This way, we can leave whenever we're finished." His lips twitched, sorta like he wanted to smile but couldn't quite work up to it. "And I don't have to cook."

"You wouldn't've had to cook if we'd stayed at Taylor's," Seth pointed out.

Joe stabbed a fry at the dish of vegetables beside the plate with Seth's cheeseburger on it. "Eat your broccoli."

"Broccoli's gross."

"Eat it anyway. It's good for you. And Ruby steamed it specially for you." Joe leaned toward him. "And if you don't eat it, no dessert."

"You heard what your brother said, baby," Ruby said from two booths over. "You wanna grow up to be big and strong like him, you gotta eat your vegetables."

Seth sighed, but one, he didn't want Joe to be mad at him, and two, he really wanted one of Ruby's ice cream sundaes. The big-and-strong stuff was just something grown-ups said when they wanted you to eat something disgusting. So he stuffed a bite of broccoli into his mouth and chewed, holding his breath so he wouldn't taste it. Then he washed it down with half a glass of milk and said, "I really like Taylor."

Joe's eyes kind of bounced off his, then he said, "Well. That's good."

"Don't you?"

"She's a real nice lady. Why wouldn't I like her?"

"I don't know. But you sure don't act like it sometimes, like the way you're always in such a hurry to leave when you pick me up and stuff."

Joe's mouth twitched again, but he didn't say anything right away. Instead, he took a bite of his burger, chewed for a good long time, and drank some tea before he finally said, "I know this might not make any sense to you, but I just don't have time to go getting cozy with some gal. Got too much on my plate as it is, what with work and taking care of you. And what's with the third degree all of a sudden?"

But Seth didn't hear the question right away, because his mind was back there on Joe saying that about taking care of him, and how that was part of what made him so busy. Then his brain caught up, and Seth realized Joe probably didn't like having Seth ask him so many questions. So he just shrugged again and said, "I didn't mean nothin' by it."

"Hey," Joe said in a real soft voice, and Seth looked up into his brother's eyes. "You can tell me, or ask me, anything. And if I get grumpy, ignore me. I just have a lot on my mind sometimes, that's all. Okay?"

"Okay," Seth said, but he noticed Joe still hadn't answered the question about Taylor, and Seth didn't think it was a good idea to ask it again, no matter what Joe said.

But then his brother said, "This is all real new for me, taking care of a kid full-time. And I'm not all that sure I'm much good at it, if you wanna know the truth."

"Don't you like having me around?" popped out of Seth's mouth before he could catch it, and he felt his face get all hot.

"Of course I do," his brother said, real fast, his eyes only touching Seth's for a second before he reached over for the sugar jar to dump some more into his tea. "It's just a lot harder than I thought it would be."

Seth felt a cold, hard lump form in the center of his chest, but he made himself say, "You don't hear me complaining, do you?"

Joe smiled. "No, I don't. But that doesn't necessarily mean everything's okay, does it?"

The lump got harder. "No, I guess not."

They didn't talk much for the rest of their meal. Then Charmaine, their waitress—she had three boys, Seth knew, 'cause one of them sat at his table in camp and was all the time talking about how he wished he was an only kid so he wouldn't have to share everything with his brothers—came over with a piece of peach pie for Joe and a hot fudge sundae for Seth. Charmaine was pretty, and kinda nice, always asking him how he was getting on and stuff, but she always stuck around longer than she needed to. Sure enough, she stood there, talking about nothing, really, acting all smiley with Joe before finally leaving to check on the people in the next booth. Joe let out a sigh, like he was glad she'd gone, but even so, Seth noticed Joe never said anything to her that might make her feel bad.

So how come he made *Taylor* feel bad, Seth wondered, scooping up his hot fudge then dribbling it back over his ice cream, when she didn't even act all dopey like Charmaine? Taylor was cool. Even if she was nothing like Mom. When she'd hugged him this afternoon, he'd felt good. And safe.

For some reason, he decided not to tell Joe about Taylor hugging him. He didn't know why, he just had a feeling Joe wouldn't like it.

Then he realized Joe was looking at him funny. Not like he was mad or anything, but like he wanted to say something but couldn't figure out how. So Seth took a bite of his sundae and said, "What is it?"

Joe tapped the end of his fork on his plate a couple of times, then said, "I need to talk to you about something. I was going to tell you later, but now seems as good a time as any, I guess." He took a breath and said, "You've got a sister. Her name's Kristen, and she's fifteen."

Well, that was about the last thing Seth expected to hear. He didn't know right off how he felt about that, except maybe a little surprised. Joe said she lived with Joe's and her mother in Tulsa, except they were away at the moment, visiting Joe's and Kristen's grandparents in Kansas.

"Will I get to see her?"

"Yep," Joe said, looking like he was trying to be happier about this than he actually was. "At the end of the month, when they come here to visit."

Suddenly, Seth wanted to know everything about her. "She's like Blair's age, huh?"

"I guess she is. A little older, though."

"Is she cool? What does she like to do? What's her favorite TV show? Does she like school?"

Joe looked like he wasn't sure where to start, but then he said, "Yeah. Kristen's cool. She likes to dance and sing, sometimes she is okay with school and sometimes she isn't, and I'm not real sure what her favorite TV show is right now, but I know she loves to watch ice skating." Then he took another deep breath and said, "Kristen has Down syndrome. Do you know what that is?"

Seth shook his head. So Joe explained that something had happened while Kristen was inside Joe's mom that gave her an extra…cromazone, or something, which made Kristen look the way she did, and made her a little slower at learning things than most people. That it wasn't something you could catch, and it wasn't like a sickness that would go away or they had medicine or anything to cure it. But that Seth had to remember she was more like everybody else than she was different, that lots of stuff made her happy, but she could get her feelings hurt, just the same as anybody else, too.

"See, there are some things she'll never be able to do well, no matter how much we try to help her learn how to do them. And sometimes she gets frustrated because she can't do some things she sees everyone else do."

"Like me and video games?"

Joe smiled. "Yes, I guess it's something like that. But the difference is, as you get older, you'll probably figure out how to play those games. Whereas Kristen's been trying to learn how to read since she was five or six, but she still can't read as well as you can now. Like the menu over the grill? She can only pick out a word here and there. But you can read most of it already." His brother got quiet for a moment, his eyes getting a funny, faraway look in them that made Seth feel uncomfortable.

He looked down at what was left of his ice cream. Only he didn't much want it anymore. There'd been these kids at school, in one of the special ed classes, who couldn't move or talk right, and Seth remembered the way the other kids'd make fun of them when the teachers couldn't hear them, calling them retards and stuff. And his face got all hot again, because, sometimes, he'd join in. But he never in a million, zillion years ever thought about what it might be like to have a brother or sister like that. Or that just because they had all this other stuff wrong, they wouldn't know when somebody was making fun of 'em.

"Wanna see a picture of her?" Joe said. Seth nodded, so Joe

got his wallet out of his back pocket and pulled out a picture, which he handed across the booth to Seth. A kinda chubby girl with shiny brown hair and glasses grinned at him from the photograph, her right hand lifted in a big thumbs-up. Seth looked real hard at that picture for some time, until he felt his own lips smile, too.

"She's the reason you have to work so hard, huh?"

Joe's eyebrows lifted, like he was surprised at Seth saying that, but then he said, "One of them, yes. Because she'll never be able to completely take care of herself, so I want to make sure she'll always have whatever she needs. And so my mother doesn't have to worry about what might happen after she can't take care of Kristen anymore. And now you, too, because…because I get the feeling you've had it kinda rough, and I want to make it up to you."

Seth stared at the picture for several more seconds, then handed it back to Joe to take another bite of his ice cream. "Did Dad ever see her?"

Joe looked like he didn't know how to answer that question, until finally he said, "He left us when Kristen was three weeks old. She never knew him. You ready to go?"

Seth was startled to look down and discover he'd finished his sundae after all. So he nodded, sliding out of the booth as Joe pulled a twenty-dollar bill out of his wallet, slipping it with the check underneath his tea glass where Charmaine would be sure to find it. As they walked out to the car, Seth couldn't decide which was fuller, his stomach or his head. Joe sure had a lot of people to take care of. No wonder he was so tired all the time. Jeez, Dad had gotten so tired taking care of just Mom and Seth, he'd left, saying he couldn't "hack it."

They'd no sooner gotten into the Blazer when Joe got a call on his cell phone, so they couldn't go yet because Joe didn't like driving and talking on the phone if he could help it. Since Seth didn't figure the call had anything to do with him, he didn't pay much attention at first, until he suddenly heard Joe say, "*What?* Are you serious?"

He looked across the seat. Even though it was nearly dark, he could see how mad his brother was by the way everything on his face was pointing down.

"What's wrong?" he said when Joe finished his call.

"What?" Joe said again, jumping a little like he'd forgotten Seth was there. But then he shook his head and started up the car. "Nothing that concerns you, okay?" he said. But then he didn't say much of anything the whole way back to the lodge, either, and Seth figured he was probably thinking about that phone call. And maybe Kristen, too, since they'd just been talking about her. So there probably wasn't a whole lot of room left over in Joe's brain to think about Seth.

Or Taylor, either, he thought. Except...

That cold, empty feeling settled in his stomach again.

Except Seth's father had left because he started to like some other woman more than he liked Seth's mom. Seth wasn't supposed to know that, but he did. He also knew that grown-ups didn't always say what they meant, especially if their feelings were all mixed up. But then, Joe hadn't said he didn't like Taylor, only that he didn't have time for her.

Just like he'd said he liked Seth, too.

His forehead all knotted up, Seth leaned against the car door, watching the sky begin to turn a pretty, deep blue over the mountains as the sun went down, thinking about how much easier life was when he'd been a kid.

Chapter 8

The sky had sagged with gunmetal clouds when Joe had gotten up the morning after Hank's bombshell phone call; by the time he got back from a quick run to Tulsa, rain was hammering the site, churning dirt into mud and making it virtually impossible to work outside. He hoped to God this was just a passing storm. Otherwise the schedule could be seriously screwed up.

By the time he'd sprinted from car to office, he was drenched. He straddled the threshold long enough to flick a veritable lake off his broad-brimmed hat onto what passed for a porch, then plunked it on top of a long table littered with brochures and junk just inside the door. On a moth-eaten braided rug under the table, a large black mixed-breed dog peacefully snoozed, despite it sounding in here like stampeding buffalo in a roller rink.

"Little wet out there?" said Danny Andrews, the college kid Hank had hired a year or so ago to help him manage the place. He cradled a tiny baby on his skinny shoulder, his spiked blond hair and earring, not to mention the mild case of acne, making him look far too young to be a father.

Joe managed a tired smile for the kid, even though his soaked denim shirt was making him shiver unpleasantly in the frigid air-conditioning. "SueEllen strong-arm you into baby-sitting?"

A big grin slid across Danny's narrow face. "You kiddin'? Only time I get to play with Scottie without her getting in my face is when she goes off grocery shopping or whatever—"

"That Joe?" boomed a voice from the open office door.

"Yep," Danny said, then leaned forward and said in a low voice, "He's real pissed about something, though, so I'd be careful if I were you."

"I heard that!" A second later, a glowering Hank appeared at the doorway. "And what makes you think I'm pissed?"

"Just a hunch," the kid said with a grin.

Hank grunted, took a second to peek at the sleeping baby, then motioned for Joe to follow him back into the office. Of course, Joe not only already knew that Hank was definitely pissed, but what he was definitely pissed about: Wes's check to the cement company had bounced clear to Oklahoma City and back. Now Joe squeezed his frame into a space barely large enough to fit him, let alone anybody else. Some opera or other was booming from the CD player on a shelf over Joe's head. Not that Joe had a problem with that, in theory, but he could do without the sensation of hearing the music from inside the singer's throat.

Hank aimed a remote at the CD player and sank into a rolling chair behind his desk as Joe said, "I've tried calling Wes three times, but his secretary keeps saying he isn't in yet. And he's not answering his cell."

"I know," Hank said. "I've been trying to get him all day, too."

"Swear to God, Hank, I've never known him to do this before."

Not-amused eyes lifted to Joe's. "Dougherty'd already made out his payroll based on that check."

Joe let out a choice cussword.

"My sentiments exactly," Hank said. "So I figured I better cover it, and fast, before word got out to the other subcontractors."

"Wait a minute..." Joe frowned. "*You* covered it?"

"Deposited funds directly into his account this morning."

"You shouldn't've done that, Hank. It's not your responsibility."

Hank leaned back, his arms crossed over his chest. "Technically, maybe not. And you better believe your boss will pay me back every single cent. But like I said, I don't want any problems. Hell, half the place is torn up—if it all falls through now, I'm up the creek."

"That's not gonna happen, Hank. And you've got my word on it."

Hank's eyebrows lifted. "And what would you have done? Made good on the check yourself?"

"If I'd had to, yeah."

Hank looked at him hard for a moment or two, then said, "Wes Hinton and I are partners in this deal. You're his employee. Your boss screws up, it's not up to you to fix it."

"Technically, maybe," he said, echoing Hank's words. "But if it's my project, I guess I feel I've got a personal stake in it."

"Then why the hell are you working for somebody else?"

The question broadsided him. Not because it was out of line, but because, over the past year or so, that very question had begun popping into Joe's head with unnerving regularity. He'd love nothing more than to be his own boss, have his own business. Maybe in development or construction, maybe something else. But self-employment was for people who could afford to take the kinds of risks Joe couldn't. However, he was hardly going to go into all this with Hank, so all he said was, "Maybe one day I will. When the timing's right."

Hank's gaze held his for a second or two before Hank turned his head, listening. "Sounds like the rain's let up." He pushed himself to his feet, pulling a pack of gum out of his shirt pocket and proffering it to Joe before pulling out a piece for himself and unwrapping it, the silver liner glittering as it fell into the trash can by his desk. "Let's go up to the new cabins. I want to make sure the roofs held up."

Joe stuck his own gum in his mouth. "Still not convinced the prefabs are 'real' buildings?"

"You got that right."

Hank whistled for the dog, who jumped up and shook himself awake, and they headed out to trudge up a muddy hill determined to suck their boots off. Fat, cold water droplets occasionally dive-bombed them from the trees as Hank said, "You always been the type to take everything on your own shoulders?"

Joe shrugged. "Least this way, I'm sure of things getting done."

"Yeah, I know how that goes," Hank said on a low chuckle. "But you know—and you can tell me to shut up if this is none of my business—if it's one thing I've learned, it's that the tighter we hang on to the reins when life tries to get away from us, the more we're liable to break something when we get thrown."

"You're right," Joe said quietly. "It's none of your business."

Hank's craggy features rearranged themselves into a big grin. Mutt—the dog—trotted up with a stick for Hank to throw, then went tearing through a sodden layer of forest debris to retrieve it after he did. "Figured you'd say that. But look at this…" His hands in his pockets, he stopped and looked up, taking a deep breath. Joe stopped, too, following Hank's gaze. A shaft of sunlight had knifed through a fissure in the clouds, gilding the rain-heavy branches, brilliant against the deep blue-gray of the sky. "Is that awesome or what?" Hank said.

Joe grinned in spite of himself. "Somebody's been hanging around a teenager too long."

That got a funny look, then Hank said quietly, "I see a lot of me in you, Joe. Or the me I was a few years ago. So damned determined that I was in charge of my life, that nothing or nobody could make me do or feel anything I didn't want to do or feel. No, hear me out," he said when Joe shook his head, smiling. "When I became a cop a million years ago, I sure as hell couldn't've told you it was because I had control issues, or whatever you want to call it. I just knew I liked being on the side that caught the bad guys and put them away. At least often enough to make it worthwhile." He looked away and said softly, "Until some trigger-happy idiot killed my fiancée in a robbery, and then got away with it because nobody could ever find him."

"Oh, man..." Joe let out a breath. "That must've been rough."

"Let's just say I wasn't fit for human company for a long time after that. So I quit the force, came back here, bought this sorry-assed place and spent the next three years taking out my frustrations on every two-by-four I could reach. Knowing I could lay down a shingle and hammer it into place, right where I wanted it...that was my therapy, I guess. All I wanted was to be alone, just me and my hammer and nails." A sardonic smile twisted his mouth. "Then Jenna and Blair showed up and blew that idea right out of the water."

Joe listened as Hank told him about Blair's being Jenna's niece, that her sister had never told anyone who her child's father was until Hank's name surfaced after her death and Jenna looked him up, because she figured he had a right to know his daughter.

"Except the last thing I needed, or wanted, at that point in my life was a kid. And the *very* last thing I wanted in my life was to ever feel about another woman the way I had about Michelle. Until I finally got over myself long enough to realize maybe I wasn't doing myself any favors by closing myself off from the world. Damn," he said when they reached the crest of the hill and the first of the new cabins. "*I'd* pay good money to stay here! Would you look at that view?"

Breathing a sigh of relief that the unasked-for lecture was apparently over, Joe followed Hank's gaze. Yeah, it was pretty damn spectacular up here, especially with the air all rain-washed and the sun slicing across the valley...

...perfectly spotlighting Taylor's house through the trees. And like a video playing in his head, he could see her chasing the dog around the yard, rubbing Seth dry with the towel on her porch, hear her laughing.

See the rejection in her eyes when he wouldn't stay for dinner.

He knew Seth was probably wondering why Joe had been so

quiet after they'd left last night. The truth of it was, Joe'd been too angry to talk for some time. Not with Taylor, though, not exactly. With the fact that being around Taylor made him want things he had no idea how to get.

Not the sort of stuff he could exactly discuss with an eight-year-old boy.

Loneliness threatened to take him under, combined with a *wanting* that was so intense, he could hardly breathe. And it was no use pretending that Taylor wasn't a major part of that wanting. Oh, man...looking into her eyes was like recognizing some part of himself he hadn't even realized had gone missing. As if his entire being had gone numb and then he'd met Taylor and all those little nerve endings were shrieking in agony as feeling rushed back in.

"Looking good," Hank called from the cabin's porch.

Joe turned, startled to discover he hadn't even been aware of Hank's leaving. He walked back toward the cabin, forcing a grin. "Told you."

"Okay, okay, so I needed a little extra convincing," Hank said as Joe joined him inside, his voice echoing in the empty space, rich with the scent of new wood and damp forest. Mutt rushed around the cabin, trying to smell everything at once; Hank's boots clumped against the cement slab when he walked over to one of the windows and cranked it open. In the distance they could hear the sound of hammering reverberating through the woods as the crew, now back in action, worked on one of the other cabins. "When's the flooring coming?"

"Couple of weeks," Joe said. "Once the rest of the cabins are up."

Hank turned to him. "You know, it concerned me a little, how you were going to handle two projects at once. But from this end at least, I'm impressed as hell."

Joe stuffed his hands in his pockets and nodded his thanks. "That mean you'll put in a good word with my boss?"

That got a speculative look, then a nod in return. "Sure. If that's what you want." Hank walked over to the kitchen area, currently a collection of gaping holes and marks on the walls indicating where the cabinets and appliances would go. "Think this might be finished by the time your mom and sister get here?"

"Probably. But I thought you were putting them in one of the original cabins."

"This is farther away from the main building, which should be a real mess by then."

"Yeah. I suppose you're right."

Hank hesitated, then said, "I know about your sister's…condition." At Joe's frown, he added, "Taylor mentioned it to Jenna, who probably wouldn't've said anything if I hadn't told her they were coming to visit. And don't go getting all bent out of shape because Taylor said something. She was just being sympathetic, is all."

"Sympathetic?"

"Yeah. You got a problem with that?"

Joe waited out the surge of irritation, then went back outside, only to feel it lance through him all over again at Hank's "Mind telling me what's got your boxers in a bunch?" behind him.

"Nothing. I'm fine."

"Bull."

Joe whipped around to look Hank square in the eye. "See, this is what I hate about small towns—not only does everybody know your business, but they all seem to think it's their divine right to tell you how to conduct it!"

"Yeah. It's called giving a damn."

"It's *called* sticking your nose in where it doesn't belong! Why is it so freaking hard for everybody to see I just want to be left the hell alone?" He stomped off, only to let out a "Hey!" when Hank's hand landed on his arm in a steel grip.

"I said—"

"I know what you said," Hank replied, shaking Joe's arm before letting go. "I also know a front when I see one. Because I've been there, and for damn sure I've done that."

Joe looked away for a moment, trying to regain some control. Then he met the other man's gaze again. "And like I said, it's none of your business."

"If whatever it is you're going through messes up this project, you better believe it's my business. You are right on the edge, you know that?"

"Hank?" Joe felt like his heart was about to pound right out of his chest. "I mean no disrespect, but go to hell."

"Fine. You don't want to talk to me, don't. But you need to talk to somebody, and bad. You got somebody you can go blow off some steam with? You know, go out for a beer, play some pool for a couple hours?"

"And how the hell would I do that? I've got an eight-year-old to take care of, remember?"

The instant the words were out of his mouth, Joe realized he'd walked right into Hank's trap. Especially when Hank said, "So maybe Blair wouldn't mind watching him for a couple hours some evening. Or what about Taylor, since Seth goes over there already anyway? Or better yet, leave Seth with Jen and me and take *Taylor* out."

"For a beer and some pool?"

Hank shrugged. "Why not?

Joe gawked at the man for a second, watching as a grin marched across the hard angles of his face. Then he shook his head at the absurdity of the situation, feeling the anger leak out of him like air from a tire. "That wouldn't be an attempt to hook Taylor and me up, would it?"

"Hell, no. Far as I can tell, the two of you are no more suited to each other than ice cream and ketchup. Just thought both of you could use the diversion, that's all."

Then Hank started back down the hill, the dog ambling along beside him, and Joe followed, his head about to explode from trying to puzzle out all of this. Especially the part about Taylor and him not being suited to each other. Not the truth of it—that went without saying—but why Hank would say it. Especially after suggesting Joe take her out.

"She dated my brother Ryan once, a couple years ago," Hank said, and Joe thought maybe he was about to get the answer to his question. "He's the doctor, lives in that great big corner Victorian in town. Like I was saying, he asked Taylor out before he married Maddie. You've probably seen Maddie around—about five-foot-nothing with big gray eyes? Real pregnant? She makes the pies for Ruby's."

The thought of Maddie's pies sent Joe's brain off on a little detour. "She makes good pies," he said wistfully.

"*Damn* good pies. You had her apple?"

"Oh, yeah. But the peach…"

"And don't forget the cherry."

As if he could. Both men drifted into reverential silence for several seconds to reflect on Maddie's pies, until Hank finally got to his point, which was that while Ryan and Taylor wouldn't have worked out in any case—his already being crazy for Maddie at the top of the list, with Taylor's not being interested in getting involved with another man married to his work running a close second—as far as he knew the poor gal hadn't been out on a date since then.

"And that was a good year and a half ago. Just seems to me the two of you would be doing each other a favor."

Now back in the parking lot in front of the office, Joe glared at the bigger man. "You know, I'm not sure which one of us you're making sound more sorry."

Hank laughed. "You forget you're talking to a former hermit. For more than three years. You wanna talk *sorry.* You and Taylor don't even come close. Besides…" One brow lifted. "You can't tell me you don't like the woman."

"But you just said…"

"A man and woman don't have to be suited to spend a couple hours in each other's company, right?"

Joe stared at Hank for a long moment, then shook his head and walked away, thinking there was nothing worse than a reformed loner.

Especially when that reformed loner went around planting dumb ideas in people's heads.

Chapter 9

As the days marched on and the sky took on that hazy, pallid blue of high summer and the mosquitoes threatened world domination, the only thing Taylor was sure about was that she wasn't sure about a damn thing.

Well over a week had passed since the dog-washing debacle, a week during which her hormones settled down enough for her to start acting like a rational human being again. A week during which she and Seth got closer, which probably wasn't good but there was no way she could fight it, while she and Joe acted as though one of them had a highly contagious disease, communicable merely through conversation with the other person. All in all, a good thing, since she wasn't about to kid herself that she had a will of iron where Joe Salazar was concerned. Shoot, she'd be doing well to muster up a will of straw. Because, honey, if that man were to ever even *hint* he'd like to fool around…

Oh, yeah. Definitely a good thing he was keeping his distance.

Of course, there was the possibility that he wasn't being strong at all, but that he simply no longer had the hots for her. Since this was a depressing idea, she thought as she rinsed out her coffee cup and set it in the drainer, she decided to reject it in favor of her original theory.

Through her kitchen window, Taylor heard Jenna Logan's bicycle bell chirrup.

"Be right there!" she hollered. She and Jenna often jogged together in the early mornings, but at least one Saturday a month they'd bike into town to Ruby's to pig out on waffles and bacon and omelets and yak their heads off. In the past couple of months, Jenna's two sisters-in-law had taken to joining them—Dawn Gardner Logan, freshly married to the youngest Logan brother and with a brand-new baby boy; and Maddie Logan, who was so pregnant with her and Ryan's baby that the first words out of Taylor's mouth when she set foot outside were, "You know if Maddie's gonna make it?"

"As of an hour ago, yep," Jenna said with a grin, redoing her ponytail. "Although she said if the kid gets any lower, one good sneeze and he'll *fall* out."

Taylor chuckled, feeling some of the tension melt from her shoulders at the prospect of hanging out with her friends for a couple of hours. She got her bike from the side of the house, checked her fanny pack one last time to make sure she had her wallet—lack of sleep over the past few weeks were wreaking havoc with her brain cells—told Oakley to be a good boy, and they took off.

Even though nobody would exactly call the morning cool, there was at least enough of a breeze to fake them out, and the humidity had dropped enough so a body could at least breathe without fear of drowning. The two women cruised the hilly first mile or so of the five-mile ride in silence, enjoying the sunlight sprinkling over them through the trees and the nagging of a thousand mama birds trying to teach their babies to fly. In the distance, the Ozarks smudged the horizon, and Taylor could almost believe she felt content. Maybe not as much as when she'd first moved here, when the countryside proved to be the perfect balm for her divorce-tattered nerves, but enough to remind her of why she loved this area of the world.

"God, what a gorgeous day," Jenna said, her back straight, her long, muscled legs at rest as they hit a level stretch of road. Even though Jenna had a good ten years on Taylor, there was nothing even remotely middle-aged about the blonde. She'd once said she'd taken up jogging and biking as an antidote to both her sedentary lifestyle as a writer and a propensity toward stress-eating, resulting in a trim figure that belied an addiction to potato chips and luxury ice cream. Taylor, whose hips were clearly determined to hang on no matter how much she exercised, didn't hold her friend's slimness against her, which she thought was very generous on her part.

"Thank God," Taylor said, adding when her friend glanced over, "For the gorgeous day. Otherwise I was beginning to think I might have to kill somebody."

"Ah..." A war-torn pickup trundled into view; they passed it single file. Jenna yelled from behind, "Are we talking a generic somebody, or a specific somebody?"

"Generic." They came to a hill; both bent over their handlebars, pumping their loyal steeds upward, and Taylor got out between puffs, "For now."

The hill conquered, they coasted down the other side, the wind tangling in their hair as they whizzed past sloping orchards and cornfields and pastures dotted with lazy cows and horses. "God," Jenna shouted, "this is so gorgeous I can't stand it!" Only when Taylor didn't reply, she glanced over and said, "Okay, what's up?"

Taylor's front tire wobbled when it hit a pebble in the road. "Nothing's up," she said, fighting for a second or two to steady the bike. "Why do you think something's up?"

"Because I've never known you to pass up a chance to give me grief for sounding like the deprived city slicker rhapsodizing about the countryside."

"It's too hot."

She could feel Jenna's I-don't-believe-you-for-a-minute glance on the side of her face, but then the other woman faced front again and Taylor—naively—thought she was out of the woods. Until she heard, "So how's it working out with Seth Salazar? If Joe's said it once, he's said it a dozen times, how lucky he was to have you to fill in the gaps between day camp and when he gets home."

And just like that, Taylor lost her admittedly dicey grip on her better mood. Because when it came down to it, whether she and Joe ignored each other or not, filling Seth's gaps only widened the chasms in her life she'd been doing her best to ignore for the past few years.

"He's doing much better," she said. "Seth, I mean. He's pretty excited about getting to meet his sister next week. A good distraction, I think. Something positive to look forward to."

"So Joe told Seth?"

"About Kristen's having Down syndrome? Apparently so. We've been reading up about it online, and from what I can tell, Joe's being very open with Seth about what to expect."

"Sounds good," Jenna says, only to add a second later, "He talks about you all the time."

"Seth? Yeah, I guess he would, since we spend so much time together—"

"Not Seth," Jenna said. "Joe."

Taylor pedaled a lot more vigorously than was necessary. "*All* the time?"

"Okay, maybe I'm exaggerating. A little. To make a point. But he does seem to bring up your name an awful lot."

"And how often…does he happen to bring up *my* name…because of *your* lead-in?"

"You have a very suspicious mind."

"With good reason, obviously."

They pedaled for another hundred feet or so. Then Jenna laughed.

"Okay, so maybe I did have something to do with your name coming up…"

Taylor grunted.

"...but that's not why you're blushing."

"That's exertion."

"No, that's blushing. Not that I blame you. That is one seriously hot dude."

"And you have been hanging around Blair too long."

"I won't argue with you there. If I'd known how bad fourteen was going to be, I'd have made a conscious effort to enjoy thirteen a lot more. But the sentiment's the same. The guy is gorgeous. And he's got that whole big-strong-protective-type-who's-a-little-lost thing going. Who can resist that?"

I'm doing my best, Taylor thought. Grumpily.

Fortunately, Ruby's loomed into view and talk turned to what they were going to gorge themselves on. Then they spotted Dawn, in a clingy, ankle-length skirt and Birkenstocks, getting out of the new Expedition her father had insisted on buying for her and Cal as a wedding present, struggling to haul Max, the World's Biggest Baby, in his car seat from the back. Jenna and Taylor angled their bikes in the rack in the little alley by the diner and then headed back around, where Dawn stood, the muscles in her arms straining with the weight of baby and carrier.

"Is it me, or is this bruiser twice as big as he was last month?" Then, without waiting for a reply, she shoved open the diner door with her shoulder, muttering, "My next kid's daddy's gonna be a hobbit."

The aroma of coffee and bacon and pancakes rushed out to embrace Taylor like a long-lost friend, making her stomach leap to attention. Jordy Kennedy yelled out, "Figured it was about time you gals got here," from the grill, his gold tooth flashing, the overhead light glancing off his dark, bald head. Then Ruby herself popped up from nowhere, herding them into "their" booth.

"Maddie's here already," the white-haired woman said. "She's just in the kitchen setting out her pies."

"She's still baking?" Dawn said. Already seated, she swung her long brown braid behind her back as she scooped Max out of his seat and immediately—but discreetly—put him to breast. "The woman's like fifteen months pregnant, for God's sake!"

"And don't I know it," Maddie herself said, waddling up to the table and collapsing into the remaining outside seat with a huge sigh. Only she had to sort of sit sideways because there wasn't enough room to fit in both her and the kid. "But bakin's about the only thing keeping me from goin' nuts. Figures I'd be two weeks late with this one." This morning, her Arkansas twang was as thick as the pancake syrup Ruby was setting on the table. "The other three were all puny little things when they were born, on account of their daddy bein' pretty puny himself, I suppose. But your mother says—" she looked across the booth at Dawn, whose mother Ivy was the town's midwife "—this one could be a ten-pounder!"

Dawn lifted her cup of decaffeinated coffee like a drunk would a beer. "Damn those Logan genes."

"At least you're tall!" Maddie squeaked in a voice that sounded like an abused violin. Underneath scraggly light brown bangs, her gray eyes were wide as saucers. "I'm barely five foot!"

"In shoes," Ruby put in.

Maddie tossed a friendly glower in Ruby's direction, then wailed, "How on earth am I gonna push out a ten-pound baby, is what I want to know."

"Carefully," Dawn said, adjusting the eagerly nursing baby underneath the receiving blanket flung over her shoulder.

"Maybe it's just as well I can't have kids," Jenna mused, stirring sugar into her coffee. "Hank's the biggest one of the brothers. I'd probably feel like I was carrying one of Cal's foals."

"You got it," Dawn said, holding up one of Max's chubby little feet. A blob with toes. "Hooves and all."

Everybody laughed, including Taylor, who was thinking, *Yeah, well, so they've all got hubbies and kiddies, what's the big hairy deal?* After all, there was a lot to be said for being free to come and go and do as she pleased, to not having to worry about anybody else's expectations. Okay, so maybe she wasn't all that down with the enforced celibacy bit, but she had nobody to blame for that but herself. If she wanted sex badly enough, she could go troll the bars in Tulsa, right?

Yeah, that was so something she would do.

Ruby took their orders, after which Maddie said to Dawn, "So how was the honeymoon?"

The brunette grinned, then one-handedly extracted an envelope from the baby bag which practically took up half the booth. "I've got pictures!"

"Cal Logan in New York City?" Jenna said. "This I've gotta see!"

"He loved it, by the way," Dawn said smugly. "You should've seen his face when the plane flew over Manhattan as we came into La Guardia. Now he says he can't wait to go back when Max is bigger."

Although Dawn had been raised in Haven, she'd left for New York right after high school, getting her law degree and then staying on in the city to practice after she passed the bar. Nobody ever expected her to return to Haven to live and start her own practice, let alone marry a horse breeder, let alone be sitting here in Ruby's, looking perfectly happy about having a monster-sized baby attached to her breast.

Just as nobody ever expected a reclusive, duty-obsessed country doctor to make room in his life for a widow with three young kids.

Or that a classy, shy blonde and a cranky teenager could melt the heart of a bitter, grief-stricken ex-cop.

Okay, so miracles happened. To other people. And Taylor was glad for them, she really was. But just because they happened for these women didn't mean it would happen for her.

At least, not with Joe.

They passed around the photos—Taylor had to laugh at the one of Cal, in jeans and boots and cowboy hat, posing with Max in front of Tiffany's—and stuffed their faces, and Maddie and Dawn shared leaking breasts stories. Taylor started to feel like a usually docile little stream after a big storm, the rushing water churning the stream bed into a froth of mud and rocks and lost flip-flops long buried and forgotten. Now, she knew once the storm passed the bed would settle back down and the water would once again be clear. Clearer, even. But she also knew nothing would end up where it had been before the storm.

Which was what worried her.

Especially when Joe and Seth walked through the door.

And Joe's eyes clamped on hers like a magnet.

Enter one storm, stage right.

She took a huge swallow of coffee to wash down the wedge of eggs and sausage caught in her throat. But coffee couldn't budge the sexual tension that had plopped down between them, hot and panting and immoveable (like Oakley, but not as endearing) from the moment Joe set foot—as well as the rest of his fine-looking self—inside the diner. Even after he averted his gaze, she could *feel* what he was thinking. And unless she was way off base, what he was thinking involved his hands on various parts of her body. Or maybe hers on his. That clairvoyant, she wasn't.

Well. The good news was, she could indulge in her original assessment of the situation with a clear conscience. Whether or not Joe still had the hots for her was no longer an issue. The bad news, of course, was that now she had to hope he'd continue to be the strong one. Because that's what she wanted. For him to be strong.

She stole a glance at his back, all muscled and what-all underneath his T-shirt.

Oh, yeah. He'd be strong, all right.

Then Maddie leaned over—well, she would have leaned over if her belly hadn't been in the way—and whispered, "Oh, Lord…I have got too many hormones to deal with *that,*" and Dawn said, "You and me both, sister," and Taylor realized estrogen levels in five counties had probably surged to new highs.

With a dry chuckle, Jenna surveyed the devastated remains of their breakfast. "So much for the eating-as-a-substitute-for-sex theory."

"Honey, there is not enough food in the world," Taylor said, and everybody looked at her. She blushed furiously and stuffed the last bite of sausage into her mouth. "Okay, I don't know where that came from."

As one, three heads now swiveled to Joe, then back at Taylor.

"Hey," Dawn whispered, "I just had sex this morning—"

"Oh, now that's just cruel," Maddie said, rubbing her stomach.

"—and the man's making my teeth hurt. I think we *all* know where that came from."

Taylor poured way too much sugar in her coffee. "Oh, come on…he's not *that* good-looking."

They all laughed. Like hyenas.

Taylor looked at each one of her friends in turn. "Are y'all really this obsessed about sex, or am I just imagining it?"

"Well, let's see," Jenna said. "I'm forty-two, which puts me at my sexual peak. Dawn is obviously still thinking about this morning…"

The brunette grinned.

"…and thinking about sex," Maddie put in, "is all I *can* do at the moment."

Dawn stretched across the table to pat her hand. "This, too, will pass, sweetie."

"I'm fantasizing about the missionary position, for crying out loud! I mean, jeez Louise, that's like the cheese-sandwich-on-white-bread of sex."

"*American* cheese," Dawn said, entirely sympathetic.

"Always did have a soft spot for American cheese," Taylor said wistfully as she lifted her coffee cup to her lips, only to nearly choke when Seth suddenly said, "I like American cheese, too!" right at her shoulder.

Grabbing a napkin to cough into, she glared at the two women across from her, both of whom seemed to be thoroughly enjoying her misery. But once her eyes stopped watering, she smiled for Seth and said, "Well, how about that?" Then she put her arm around his waist and hugged him to her, only to realize his big brother was standing right behind him. Which put his crotch right smack at eye level. And her own whimpered, *You know what would be nice…?*

She quickly lifted her eyes to see Joe giving her a bemused I-know-exactly-what-you're-thinking look. Damn him. Because she could tell herself from now to doomsday that this was nothing more than physical attraction, the effects of a good-looking man on a neglected everything. But every time she looked at him for longer than a nanosecond, she felt a connection that singed her to a place so deep inside her, she couldn't even name it. Whether he felt it or not, she didn't know. And why *she* felt it, she knew even less. But her helplessness at avoiding becoming bonded to Seth—who'd linked his arm around her neck and was snuggled up against her like a second skin—was nothing compared to the helplessness she felt around Seth's big, strong, nobody-should-be-this-sexy brother.

Or the annoyance when she also caught, behind the bemusement, the tell-tale signs of exhaustion. Irritation shot through her, about men who thought they were invincible, who were too dumb or too stubborn to see when they were overdoing it. Yeah, yeah, the guy was young and healthy, he could probably weather the stress okay. But for how long?

This was why she couldn't get involved, she told herself, even as she knew that's exactly what made him so dangerous.

And while she was pondering all this, Joe and the others were introducing themselves. Joe was being unbelievably charming, and Taylor could feel little pieces of her heart splintering off and floating in his direction. He complimented Maddie on her pies and asked how she was feeling and when she was due, and then he made over Max, even picked him up and made goofy noises at him for a second before giving him back to an obviously smitten Dawn.

Dark, almost haunted, eyes would meet hers and skitter away. Drift back, even when he was talking to someone else. And everybody kept giving Taylor these meaningful glances, the kind with the slightly raised eyebrows that said, "What are you waiting for?" Only Taylor's entire insides were vibrating, knowing, *feeling* the lie that Joe was feeding everyone. On the surface, he looked as relaxed as could be. But underneath was a whole other story.

His mistake for letting her see inside him like that.

Hers for not turning away.

"Dawn," he now said, smiling for the brunette. "You're...the lawyer, right? Cal's wife?"

"That's right." Dawn chuckled. "Hey, you're good."

"I have to be," he said, half smiling. "I'm afraid Ruby's gonna give me a pop quiz one of these days, and if I don't pass, she'll cut off my peach pie allotment."

Everybody at the table groaned in commiseration. Then somebody told him to pull up a couple of chairs, but Joe declined, saying he was headed over to Tulsa to check up on the crew who'd been called in.

"On Saturday?" somebody else said. Taylor didn't hear who, she was too busy seething and being horny and being mad at herself for both.

"This is kind of a rush job," he said, his gaze brushing Taylor's again. "And since it looks like the weather might be bad later in the week, we're trying to push through."

"An' I get to go, this time," Seth said, grinning up at his big brother.

Taylor stopped seething long enough to notice the adoration on the kid's face. He clearly worshipped his big, strong brother, even after such a short time. And who could blame him? This was a good man. Seth's hero. *Everybody's* hero, from what she could tell. How could you be tickled with someone who—she had no doubt—would put his own life on the line for his family?

Her sausages felt like little hot coals in her stomach. If the gods were kind, he'd go away in a second and she could get back to her denial in peace. Apparently, the gods weren't in a kindly mood today, because suddenly Dawn—who had far too much energy for a woman with a three-month old baby—was inviting everybody out to the farm for a cookout that night.

"Just burgers and stuff, nothing fancy. Oh, come on, Maddie," she said when her sister-in-law groaned, "it'll be fun."

Maddie's response—that the only thing that sounded like fun to her right then was going into labor—turned out to be the last thing Taylor clearly remembered for several seconds as excuses flew and Dawn batted them right back. Then she played dirty by telling Seth he could ride one of Cal's horses if he came, and of course nobody (meaning Joe) was going to disappoint the kid once that offer was laid on the table. And whatever lame excuse Taylor might have made about being too busy died on her lips the instant Seth looked at her with those big, brown, pleading eyes—a ploy he'd clearly picked up from Oakley—and said, "You're gonna be there, right, Taylor?" And the next thing she knew, she heard herself saying, "Of course, I wouldn't mind bringing dessert."

She dared a glance at Joe, who looked as though he wasn't quite sure what had hit him, either.

"I don't know how long we can stay, though," he said. "I've got a ton of specs to go over before Monday."

"I understand completely," Dawn said. For somebody who'd spent more than a decade in New York, she was laying on the sweet country gal act as thick as Arliss Potts's banana-mint cream cheese frosting. "But like I said, this isn't anything fancy. Whenever you get there, we'll just toss a few burgers on the grill." Then she grinned at Seth. "Now you make sure your brother doesn't back out, you hear?"

"Yes, ma'am," the boy said, and Jordy called out that their orders were ready to go, so Joe picked them up and paid for them, and a second later, everybody's hormones floated back to earth. Somewhat.

Taylor waited until Maddie and Jenna had gone to the ladies' room before she turned on Dawn. "Tell me you didn't plan that."

Dawn blinked as innocently as the snoring two-ton baby in

her arms. "Oh, come on, Taylor—even I'm not that good. Swear to God," she said, lowering the baby into his carrier and strapping him in, "I had no idea the man was coming in here."

"Maybe not. But you sure as hell jumped on an opportunity."

"Sweetie, I'm a lawyer. Jumping on opportunities is what I do." Then she winked. "Something you might want to keep in mind. For later."

Taylor crossed her arms. "It's that married lady thing, isn't it? The minute a woman gets a ring on her finger, she becomes obsessed with trying to fix up every single woman she knows."

"Not every single woman." She patted Taylor's arm. "Just you."

Taylor dug out a tip from her wallet and plopped it on the table. "For heaven's sake, Dawn. Did it ever occur to you that maybe Joe and I wouldn't work together? Or that maybe neither one of us is interested?"

"Uh-huh," she said, stuffing a million and one baby things back into the bag. "Neither of you is interested. Right. I was just imagining the lustful gazes zinging back and forth between the two of you."

"Lusting after something doesn't mean it's good for you."

"Doesn't necessarily mean it's not, either. After all, there are many paths to the same goal. Ryan and Maddie got there through sympathy, Jenna and Hank through Blair, Cal and I…" She stroked a knuckle down Max's cheek, then straightened up. "Honey, Max is here because that man and I couldn't keep our hands off each other. Still can't," she added with a grin. "And for a long time, I wanted to believe that's all we had. Chemistry. But if chemistry got us where we are now…" Her shoulders hitched. "Who am I to say?"

Taylor blew out a breath. "Now's probably a good time to tell you I set myself on fire in chem lab in college."

"Which means you were an active participant, not somebody who let her lab partner do all the work."

"You're terrible."

"No argument there," Dawn said, swinging the baby bag up

onto her shoulder. "But at least I admit it. Unlike some people I know," she said, more gently, "who won't admit they're lonely."

"What?"

"And so is that man," she went on, ignoring Taylor. "Okay, I finagled things so two lonely people who are obviously already interested in each other have a shot at being in the same place at the same time. So sue me. Maybe nothing will happen. Or maybe the two of you will decide to enjoy each other for a few weeks. Or maybe..." She shrugged. "You never know."

The others reappeared, thankfully cutting off any further discussion. But, honest to Pete—anybody who believed that small-town life was simple had clearly never spent more than twenty minutes in Haven.

Chapter 10

Joe glanced across the front seat as they drove back from Tulsa, savoring a quiet burst of tenderness for his sacked-out baby brother, his skinny little face smushed into Joe's wadded-up denim jacket tucked between his face and the window. Kid'd talked nonstop for the first fifteen minutes or so of the return trip, only to suddenly pass out like he'd been hit with a tranquilizer dart. Just as well he caught a few winks now, though, or he'd be too tired to enjoy himself later.

Of course, that brought a cloud down around Joe's thoughts, because frankly he felt about as much like going to this shindig tonight as he did eating a hornet's nest. His head was throbbing, his stomach felt like he *had* eaten that hornet's nest and his mind-set at the moment was a lot closer to murderous than sociable.

And a good part of his murderous mood stemmed from his encounter with Taylor in Ruby's this morning. Not that she'd done anything, or said anything— Had they even talked? He couldn't remember—but that was just it. Just the *awareness* of her was driving him crazy. One glance from those knowing green eyes and he'd feel stripped bare, connected in some way that was far more intimate than any sex he'd ever had.

Was it any wonder he'd gone out of his way to stay out of hers, for not putting himself in the path of those see-everything eyes? Hell, he didn't even trust himself to talk to her about Seth, even though that meant giving up hearing her say it was going to be fine, just give it a chance, be patient. Sure, he could say the same things to himself—and God knows, living with a grieving eight-year-old gave him plenty of opportunity to do just that—but it wasn't the same as hearing it from her.

That he wanted her wasn't an issue. Hell, yes, he wanted her, so badly he was beginning to hallucinate what it would feel like to feel her skin gliding along his, to slowly, painstakingly taste every inch of that skin, to hear her cries as he drove her to the same brink of madness she brought him to with those damn eyes of hers. But he'd wanted before. Maybe not this intensely, but he'd wanted. And he'd dealt with it, one way or another. However, *want* wasn't the same as *need,* and that's where things could get hairy. Because if Joe wasn't careful, he was going to start thinking he needed Taylor McIntyre. And that could be a real problem.

A problem he did not need on top of whatever the hell this was going on with Wes Hinton.

Oh, his boss had made good on paying Hank back, just as Joe figured he would. And none of his other checks had bounced, at least not on either of Joe's two projects. However, there were other things, things more worrisome than bounced checks.

For one thing, Joe had never known Wes to sub out to anyone but the best. In fact, his reputation for quality was one of the things that had made him so successful, first in construction and then, over the past several years as a developer. People could trust him to get the job done, on time, at a fair price, and know they weren't going to have to come back in a year or two and fix things. But there were some weird things going in with this Tulsa project. For instance, this framer Wes had hired was for the birds. Half his crew looked like they weren't sure which end of the hammer they were supposed to be using, and the foreman couldn't read plans worth spit. Fortunately, Joe had caught a couple of problems before they happened, but this morning he'd discovered one whole wall had been set a foot off, which of course had to be completely redone. When he'd called Wes and told him they needed to find another sub, his boss had gotten real quiet, then mumbled something about the bid being so good.

"A low bid is worthless if the work is, too," Joe had said. "We gotta can this guy, Wes, before he screws up any more than he already has."

Wes had finally, if reluctantly, agreed, which only solved half the problem. The other half—finding a reputable framer who wasn't booked clear to Christmas—was a headache Joe didn't need on a project with an already tight schedule. It was so unlike Wes, though, going on the cheap like that. What was the man thinking—

"Where are we?" a sleepy voice said beside him, followed by a huge yawn.

"About halfway between Claremore and Haven," Joe said, taking in the wrinkled face, the blinking eyes, and he realized—with a mixture of mild panic and profound relief—that, even though they still hadn't gotten down and dirty about the heavy stuff, somewhere along the way he'd grown pretty damn crazy about his little brother. Guess cluelessness didn't preclude love. Smiling slightly, he looked back out the windshield. "Have a good nap?"

"Yeah..." Another yawn. "I guess. I can't wait to get to Dawn's. I'm *starving*."

Joe chuckled as another trickle of relief shimmied through him, somewhat dissipating his bad mood. If all it took to jolt Seth out of his shell was the promise of a grilled burger and a horseback ride, he supposed they weren't doing too badly. As if he'd read Joe's mind, the boy strained against the seat belt to fish the plastic shopping bag out from behind Joe's seat and from that came a pair of the cheapest kid-sized cowboy boots Joe could find in the western clothing store. Dawn hadn't exactly told Joe the boy needed boots to ride; she'd just pointed out his feet might slip out of the stirrups if he wore athletic shoes. Seth, apparently, was entranced.

"These are so cool," he said for at least the tenth time, carefully inspecting one tan leather boot. "I'm gonna be tall as you in 'em!"

"Those heels aren't but an inch high, bud. The view won't be a whole lot different."

There was also a new pair of jeans, which the kid already had on. Joe had drawn the line at the cowboy hat, though, pointing out that he was only going for a ride, not doing the rodeo circuit.

"I can't wait to show Taylor," Seth now said, and more hornets took off in Joe's stomach. He wasn't so out of the loop that he couldn't tell when some serious matchmaking was going on. Or that three very happily married ladies were bad news for anyone who wasn't. So it was a good thing, he told himself, that Taylor had looked every bit as disgusted about her friends' meddling as he felt.

A damn good thing.

A few minutes later, they cut off the highway onto a shady road that, in turn, led to a dirt road flanked by two pastures. Seconds later, Cal's horse farm came into view.

"S'that it?" his brother said, wriggling in his seat to get a better look.

"That's Taylor's truck out front, so yeah, I guess so."

"Where are the horses?"

Joe chuckled, pulling the Blazer up behind Taylor's truck. "I don't imagine they let them roam the place, like chickens."

There were, however, dogs. At least three or four—it was hard to tell from the quivering mass of lolling tongues and wagging tails accosting them the minute Joe and Seth got out of the car. For a second, Seth plastered himself against Joe's legs, only to let out a giggle of delight as he tried to pet them all at once. The muscles at the base of Joe's neck eased somewhat as he sucked in a lungful of air laced with the earthy-sweet scents of animal and flowers and dirt...and the Pavlovian-response-inducing aroma of seared meat.

"There you are!" he heard from the porch of the unpretentious brown-and-white single-story house. He looked up to see a grinning Dawn striding toward them in sandals and a straight, slippery looking dress that skimmed her body almost to her ankles, its colors rivaling those of the dozens of rose bushes in heavy bloom edging one side of the lawn. "Cal's already got the first round of burgers on the grill, so come on around to the back. Mooner, for heaven's sake..." On a laugh, she grabbed the collar of a mutt of indiscriminate parentage who'd appointed himself Seth's best friend. "Give the kid some breathing room."

The moan of a screen door brought Joe's head around, and suddenly Seth wasn't the only one needing breathing room.

Her arms full of Dawn's baby, Taylor came to the edge of the porch, where the late day sun scythed through a nearby cottonwood, dusting them with quivering drops of gold. As usual, she was in a what-you-see-is-what-you-get getup—baggy shorts, a plain white tailored blouse, her hair caught in a couple of clips like she couldn't be bothered—but then, it wasn't the magic of the picture that sent longing arcing through him, it was the genuineness of it.

The baby was asleep, slumped heavily against her chest, but she clearly was in no hurry to put him down. She smiled when Seth noticed her, then put a finger to her lips as he took off for the porch to give her a hug. Another spurt of yearning sang through Joe's bloodstream—not only for her, but for things that seemed to get further out of his reach every day.

And if her smile said "That's close enough" when he approached the steps, he should be grateful, right? Except her eyes told a completely different, eyes chock-full of promises he wondered if she even knew she was making. Full of promises he had no right to expect her to make in the first place, let alone keep.

"Where's the horses?" Seth asked Dawn as she carefully peeled her son from Taylor's arms.

"Most of 'em are out in the back pastures this time of year," she said, "but there's a couple in one of the paddocks close by the barn. You wanna see?"

Seth nodded and showed off his boots, which both ladies enthusiastically made over before Dawn herded the boy and a dog or two into the house, leaving Joe and Taylor by themselves.

Of course, he could have followed Dawn and his brother.

But then, Taylor could have, too.

Then a smile flickered across her mouth as a scrap of hair teased her long, pale neck. "I know where they keep the beer," she said, and he said, "Those are the sweetest words I've heard all day." She laughed and led him into the kitchen, where an older woman with Shake 'n Bake colored hair wearing a T-shirt that said These Aren't Hot Flashes, They're Power Surges came at him like a heat-seeking missile.

"I'm Ethel," she said, holding out a spotted hand with a surprisingly firm grip. "I come with the place. You must be that Joe Salazar everybody's talking about."

Joe shot a glance in Taylor's direction, but he got the distinct feeling she was enjoying this far too much to interfere.

"And why is 'everybody' talking about me?"

"'Cause we're sick to death of talking about ourselves, for one thing," the old woman said. "And because now that the Logan boys're all married, us oldsters are sorely in the market for somebody new to drool over. And looks to me like you fit that bill real nice." Sharp brown eyes took their sweet time raking him from head to toe and back up again. "Oh, yeah…*real* nice." A thousand wrinkles scampered out of the way as she grinned. "You want a beer?"

Finally. "Please."

Seconds later, an ice-cold Coors landed in his palm and Ethel bustled outside with a bowl of something. And Joe's gaze stumbled into Taylor's and he saw her breath catch and a flush bloom in her cheeks. Then she whirled around, heading for the patio door as well. He should have let her go, if he'd had any sense he would have let her go, but a man's control can only be stretched so far before it snaps. And Joe's snapped so hard he could feel it writhing around inside him like a downed, and very much live, electrical wire, driving him to grab her hand and yank her back around. The startled look on her face only lasted for a second before she burst out laughing.

The unexpected sound was like throwing water on that still-flailing wire, and the sizzling and popping and blinding showers of sparks jolted him awake, jolted him alive, and he smiled down on her, nearly consumed with an all-consuming need—to get back at her.

Brandishing the ice-cold can of beer in one hand, he smoothly tucked their linked hands behind her back, jerking her close enough to make her gasp. Gasping was good. Gasping meant he had her right where he wanted her.

And, he thought as her cheeks went red, right where she wanted him to have her, too.

"You threw me in Ethel's path deliberately, didn't you?" he said, letting the beer can hover tauntingly close to her bare neck.

Her chin lifted, a show of bravery totally blown when her mouth quivered, barely six inches below his. "Maybe."

He tugged her closer. Close enough for their body heat to mingle, to see her pupils darken, blossom. To feel her breath on his face. "Any particular reason?"

"Other than this perverse streak I can't seem to shake?"

"Other than that, yeah."

Her voice gentled. "This might be way out of line, but you looked like you could use a little…loosening up."

Confusion short-circuited his thought for a second as he frowned into her eyes. Eyes filled, not with teasing, or the blatant sexual hunger of a moment before—had he imagined it?—but a deep concern, and kindness, that were far more dangerous.

He slowly lowered the beer can, let her go and backed away. *Save it for the kid,* he wanted to say. *Save it for somebody who needs saving.*

"We should join the others," he said quietly, lifting the can to his lips.

"Joe—"

"Don't. Okay? Just…don't."

"Don't what? Call it the way I see it? Joe…" He'd turned away; she only tromped around to get in his face. "You look like a truck ran you over. Like you're carrying the weight of the whole damn world on your shoulders—"

"Taylor, I appreciate your concern, but I can't change my life just because some busybody female's worried about me."

If he thought—hoped—his rudeness would offend her, he'd been dead wrong. Instead of tucking her tail between her legs and scurrying away, she scowled at him. "Yeah, I figured that's how you'd see it. And you're right, it's none of my business. After all, it's not as if we're part of each other's lives or anything. But it *is* Seth's business, and at the moment he's part of *both* of our lives. If you don't want me to worry about you, fine. I won't. You wanna work yourself into the ground, you go right ahead." Her eyes narrowed. "But if you think that child isn't picking up on how overworked and exhausted and stressed you are, you'd better think again."

Instead of answering right away, he took another slug of beer. Not because he was trying to dull the pain—exactly—but to stop him from shooting off at the mouth. Even so, the alcohol sliding down his throat only seemed to exacerbate the frustration and helplessness flaring, raging inside him. Finally, he realized she wasn't going to go away until he said something. So he swung his gaze to hers.

"Okay, I'll admit I'm going through a rough patch right now, which is making me a little…tense—"

She snorted.

"—but it's nothing I can't handle."

"Then you'd better damn sight tell that to Seth. Because he's worried, Joe." She laid her hand on his arm. *Bad move, honey.* "A lot."

He frowned down at her fingers, pale against his darker skin, her pretty long nails all glossy and pink. Told himself it was just a trick of his imagination, that a single light touch could make him that hot, that fast. But dammit, his *ears* were burning. "He tell you that?"

"Not in so many words. But he went through it with his mother, after his father left. He worried about her, and he's worried about you. I can see it in his face."

Just as he could see it in hers. Their gazes tangled for a moment before he pushed out a sigh. The woman was aggravating as hell and far too honest for his comfort, but staying mad at her simply was not possible. How could he, when all she was doing was going to bat for the kid?

Joe dragged a hand over his mouth, then shook his head. "Thanks," he said to his shoes before looking back up at her. "For telling me about Seth. He still won't talk to me much. I mean, I keep telling him he can, but…" His mouth thinned. "And I guess I'm not real good at reading kids."

"You're probably a damn sight better than most," she said gently. "And I know you want what's best for him, which is half the battle. It's just…his losing his parents is still real fresh. So if he thinks he might lose you, too…"

"I get it." He blew out a breath, then said, "Okay, I'll admit I could use a vacation right about now. Or at least a good night's sleep." For some harebrained reason, he reached up to slide a knuckle down her cheek, its coolness soothing his heated skin. "But I'm not on the verge of keeling over, I swear."

Her eyes had widened, almost imperceptibly, but she didn't flinch. In fact, she went as still as a rabbit sensing danger. From outside, they heard a burst of laughter; neither of them reacted.

"You wouldn't be thinking again about kissing me, would you?" she said.

He smiled. "You do realize that no matter how I answer that question, I'm in trouble?"

"Yeah. So?"

Damn her.

He opened his mouth to say…well, he wasn't sure what he was going to say. Except then a couple of brain cells bumped into each other and he thought, maybe if he made her think he was some disgusting pig who was only after her body, she'd hightail it in the other direction and everybody would get through the summer and this…whatever it was would die a natural death.

"Honey," he said, his gaze fused with hers as he deliberately let his hand trail south, his fingers skimming her jaw…her neck…tracing the gentle ridge of clavicle before dipping farther to cup her breast, his thumb rasping over one hardened nipple, "I'm thinking about doing a helluva lot more than kissing you."

Her eyes lowered, taking in her breast in his hand, then lifted again. Except for a faint blush, there was nothing in her face to indicate her reaction. Other than her pupils practically swallowing up her irises.

"I really hate to tell you this," she said, "but if this is where I'm supposed to slap the daylights out of you…you blew it."

Then she backed away, leaving his hand feeling lonely and bereft, and walked outside. Joe took another pull of the beer, then got up from the stool, wondering if anything was ever going to go the way he'd planned, ever again.

Great. Now she was hornier than ever and Joe had just made it abundantly clear that he was trying to scare her off, which he might have had a better chance of accomplishing if he hadn't groped her, because—she now lamentably remembered—she really liked the feel of a man's hand on her breast and it had been way too long since one had been there.

But this went way beyond hands on breasts and Taylor's enjoyment thereof. This was about her having a real problem with people…men…*Joe* putting up that brave I'm-da-man-I-fix-everything front when it was patently obvious how much he was hurting, and how she couldn't stand seeing anything hurting and how patently unfair it seemed that someone as good and generous and selfless as that man *should* be hurting. In fact, the more she thought about it, the more ticked off she got. Because...because, dammit, here was somebody who deserved to be loved, and she had all this love just lying around and going to waste, but trying to get this *idiot* man to take it would be like trying to sell snow skis to a Tahitian.

Which made the sudden silence which greeted Joe's and her reappearance all the more irritating. Dawn's brows slid up a triumphant notch or two, Ethel was practically quivering with curiosity, and even Cal, who was the most laid-back of the three Logan brothers, was wearing a why-you-old-dog grin when the two men shook hands after Dawn introduced them.

"So...what happened?" Dawn whispered the first chance she got.

"Nothing," Taylor whispered back, stabbing a piece of celery into a bowl of onion dip. "What?" she said, crunching. "Did you expect us to go at it in your kitchen?"

"It wouldn't be the first time that kitchen's seen action."

"You know, you are the Queen of Too Much Information."

Dawn shrugged and took enough potato salad to feed three people. "I'm a newlywed, I'm allowed to be obnoxious."

Taylor snorted.

"You know," Dawn said, "for somebody who just had 'nothing' happen to her, you sure are...distraught."

"Not the word I would use." Taylor ripped a hunk out of the celery.

"Oh."

"Yeah. Oh." Taylor glanced over to see Joe talking to Cal, looking like a man whose body was going through the motions but whose mind was a million miles away. A pang swept through her, a bizarre mixture of sympathy, annoyance and regret. Then, as if he could hear her thoughts, his gaze swerved to hers, and she saw pretty much the same mixture in his eyes. Especially the regret.

And Taylor thought, that much of a masochist, she wasn't.

"I'm sorry," she said, giving Dawn's arm a squeeze, "but I'm not feeling well. I think I'd better just go on home."

"You are such a liar."

"Believe me, honey, I am *not* feeling well right now. Give my regrets to Cal, wouldja?" she said, then made tracks around the side of the house, feeling like a prisoner making a run for it. Only she obviously wasn't running anywhere because guess who had parked behind her?

She let out a PG-13 cussword and trooped back around the house to find Joe. "You're parked behind me, you need to move your car."

"Where're you goin', Taylor?" Seth asked.

"I've got a headache, sweetie," she said with a strained smile, "so I think I'm just going to go home and lie down."

"But you won't get to see me ride a horse!"

"Maybe another time, okay?" She looked at the boy's brother, deciding she didn't have the energy to read his expression. "So if you wouldn't mind…?"

"No, of course not," Joe said. "Stay put, Seth, I'll be right back."

He waited until they were well out of earshot before saying, "There's no headache, is there?"

"Oh, I've got a headache, all right," she said, wrenching open her truck door. "And his car is currently blocking mine."

"Taylor—"

"What? This is what you wanted, isn't it? To scare me off? To put as much distance between us as possible?"

Confusion darkened his eyes. "I didn't think I had. I mean, yeah, that was my intention, but…I thought it hadn't worked."

"If you thought you were going to offend me by doing exactly what I wanted you to do, no. That didn't work worth squat. It's what you don't do, or won't do, or can't do that's doing the trick. Now would you please—"

"You don't understand, Taylor!" Although his voice was low, the words howled with frustration. "I can't get involved with you! Or anybody else!"

"Why?" she demanded, crossing her arms.

"Because when the hell would I fit it in?"

Her breath left her lungs in a silent *oh* as his agony melted her anger. Her hand lifted to his face of its own accord, tracing the hard lines of his cheekbones, the proud set to his jaw. But as she looked into his eyes, she saw a warning flash in their dark depths:

Don't pity me. Don't you dare pity me.

And suddenly, with lightning-bolt clarity, she understood something else: That she was willing to risk everything for a shot at something, anything, with this man. This proud, stubborn, impossible man who loved so hard, so completely, he'd forgotten how to *be* loved in return.

Okay, so maybe she *was* that much of a masochist. But, hey—at least she was a masochist with a sense of purpose.

"Surely you could find an hour or two for yourself," she said softly, then let her hand drop, deliberately, slowly, tracing the contours of his hard chest, feeling his stomach jump as her fingers trailed lower, one knuckle rasping gently over the bulge in the front of his jeans.

With a ragged sigh, he grabbed her hand. "I wouldn't be enough for you," he said, and she laughed.

"First time I ever heard a man admit that."

A ghost of a smile touched his hard mouth. "Not what I meant."

"Then prove it," she whispered. "Anytime. My dance card is wide open." She climbed up into her truck. "And all I'm asking for is one dance—"

"Joe! Where *are* you?" Seth popped around the corner of the house, bristling with excitement. "Cal said I can ride one of the horses now!"

"Be there in a sec, buddy," Joe called out, then swung his gaze back to Taylor. "You sure you don't want to see this?"

She hesitated, then said, "I'd love nothing more. But this is a perfect opportunity for you to bond with your brother. Without me. Now go move your damn truck so I can get out of here."

His eyes danced with hers for another second or two before he finally walked away and climbed into the Blazer, started the engine. A minute later, she was headed for home, trying to remember where she'd last seen her mind.

Joe settled in at his desk in the cabin, hoping to get in a couple hours work before calling it a night. They'd gotten back to the cabin a little before nine; not ten minutes later, right in the middle of a sentence, his brother had conked out. The boy had opened up a little, on the ride home, about what things had been like with their father, who apparently hadn't been much more "there" for Seth than he had been for Joe, about how Seth's mom had had to work so hard because his father never seemed to be able to hold down a job.

Yeah, that sounded familiar. But then, Joe had hardly expected his father to change his stripes simply because he'd had a new family. That his old man had walked out on that family the same way as he'd done on his first was no surprise, either. The social worker had said Seth's parents had apparently been separated for a couple years, but hadn't gotten around to getting a divorce. Knowing his father, Joe figured Jose had probably been too lazy to do anything about it. Or maybe Seth's mom, Andrea, had been hoping for a reconciliation. Nobody knew. Just as nobody knew why the couple had been together when Jose lost control of his car and went flying across the median, straight into the path of a semi.

Joe's stomach knotted. And not just at how horrible the accident must have been. One day, he supposed, he was going to have to work past the resentment, the anger. But for now—for the past fifteen years—that anger and resentment had fueled his drive to be the provider his father had never been, even before he'd left them. Whenever he was tempted to slack off, all Joe had to do was remember the sound of his mother weeping over a pile of bills on the kitchen table, the pained look on her face after a phone call from a creditor.

Now, all he had to do was look into his little brother's hopeful brown eyes to know what really mattered. And it wasn't Joe's comfort.

Except Taylor's words tonight had rattled him.

Surely you can find an hour or two for yourself.

For himself. Not *her.*

He spread out the new plans for the main building—Wes had thought it would make sense to turn the whole thing into a restaurant and gift shop, but Hank was adamant about leaving at least a half dozen rooms for guests that didn't need or want a whole cabin, so now they were working from new plans that needed to adhere to the original budget—but Joe was having a real hard time concentrating on electrical layouts and window elevations.

...an hour or two for yourself...

He had no right to accept her offer. Or even be thinking about it.

...an hour or two...

He could see in her face, in those eyes, her need for a real family, for babies of her own, for a husband who could devote more than bits and pieces of his life to her...

All I'm asking for is one dance...

Joe looked up, staring across the room.

When was the last time he'd danced?

Damn.

If it hadn't been for Oakley making such a racket, Taylor would have never heard the rap on her door. Poking her wild hair behind one ear, she padded barefoot through the living room, her shortie robe clutched to her chest. Damn dog was snuffling at the bottom of the door, butt in air, tail wagging a mile a minute, "talking" to whoever was on the other side.

"For God's sake," she heard coming through the partially open window, "you're gonna wake her up, you dumb mutt!"

Taylor's heart catapulted into her throat. She shoved the dog out of the way and opened the door, blood whooshing in her ears. Among other places.

She wasn't sure which of them was having a harder time believing Joe was here. But there he was, yep, leaning one wrist on her doorjamb with his other thumb hooked in his jeans pocket, his expression a blend of lust and profound sorrow.

"I take it you're not here to borrow a cup of sugar," she said.

"Depends on where you keep the sugar," he said.

Chapter 11

He came inside, shoving the door shut with the heel of his hand. "And if there's anything in particular you don't like," he added, lifting his T-shirt over his head as he walked toward her, "tell me now, because I do not want *anything* to interrupt the flow."

She froze, thinking, *Oh, man, that is* some *chest,* then gathered a wit or two enough to say, "Not much into chains and whips, but other than that, I'm good."

"I just bet you are," he said. A second later, she'd met him halfway, her heart racing, her fingers fumbling with his belt buckle as he yanked out a string of condom packets from his pocket and tossed them on the table by the front door.

Hmm, she thought, then looked up at him. "You can't be serious."

"Oh, believe me, honey," he murmured as his hands threaded through her loose hair, his touch on her scalp sending her into immediate overdrive. "I couldn't be more serious." Their mouths crashed together, their first kisses tripping over each other, clumsy and frantic, until Taylor wasn't sure whether she was more desperate to give or take, at which point some part of her yelled, *Hey! No thinking allowed!* Only then, some other part of her yelled back, *Are you nuts? Get every bit of this down, sister!*

What was this, sex by committee?

Anyway...his mouth—which she was delighted to discover wasn't just for show—was burning a damp, hot trail along her neck when, somehow, a question peered through the haze of arousal.

"How did you—?"

"Blair. We've got until midnight. Is this good?"

"Cheesecake is *good*," she managed through the gasps. "This is...um... remember the dry kindling th-thing?"

"Oh, yeah," he said, then kissed her again.

Hands roamed, breathing hitched, exquisite aches blossomed in places she'd almost forgotten existed. She was in more danger than she'd ever been in her life and thank heaven for it. Joe's zipper gave way—somehow—and she shoved his jeans and boxers past his hips, took a second or two to marvel, then cupped him. "This is going to be one helluva ball, Prince Charming," she murmured, and he chuckled, and she saw something in his eyes that made her heart melt. She kissed him again, her palms cradling his face, worrying his lip between her teeth, soothing it with her tongue as his scent invaded her senses, making her think wild, crazy, libidinous thoughts. Can't have too many of those, boy.

He growled, clamping his hands to her bottom through the thin cotton of her robe and yanking her to him. They kissed some more, and he finished undressing and yanked her to him again, at which point various body parts were obviously thinking about getting real cozy. By this point, well, her entire body hummed with songs of praise and wonder, is what. Vaguely, she registered Oakley wandering by as she heard a mantra spill from her lips of *touch me, please, please, yes, like that, that feels wonderful, yes,* with lots of little groans tossed in for good measure.

He backed her against the wall, his chest heaving, touching his forehead to hers. "I don't think I can hold off much longer—"

Her laugh was borderline hysterical. "Joe." She closed her fingers around him, marveled for another second or two, then said in what she hoped sounded like a husky, sexy voice, "This. Inside me. Now."

His mouth found hers again as he fumbled on the table for the condoms…then fumbled some more, then finally broke the kiss to jerk his head around, only to let out a "What the hell—?" followed by, "Oh, for God's sake!" Then Taylor was all by her lonesome, the wall the only thing keeping her from collapsing into a puddle of lust on her floor. Through a *this-close*-to-orgasm haze, it registered that a naked, and extremely aroused, man was now storming across her living room and yelling obscenities at the dog. Who had the strip of condoms clamped between his enormous paws and was happily gnawing on same. At Joe's approach, however, the beast leapt to his feet, prize firmly clenched in his jowls, and took off to the other side of the room.

"Dammit!" Joe yelled and went after him, dodging furniture as the dog zig-zagged around it with amazing agility for such a large animal. Thinking, *This could only happen to me,* Taylor lost it, stumbling across the room and collapsing onto the sofa, howling harder with laughter every time dog and Joe zipped past.

"You could help, you know!" Joe threw out on one of their passes, and she finally grabbed a breath and bellowed, "Oakley! *Drop it! Now!*"

The dog scudded to a stop, gave her an "Aw, maaaan" look and spit out what was left of the condoms. Muttering under his breath, Joe snatched them up off the floor. *"You,"* he lobbed at the dog, shaking the condoms at him, "are gonna be the death of me yet!"

Oakley plodded over, tail wagging, ears dragging, and collapsed in submission at Joe's bare feet.

Taylor cleared her throat and squeaked out, "How many did he get?"

"Three," Joe said on a sigh, sinking onto the sofa beside Taylor, only to let out another curse. He stabbed one hand underneath him, hauling out a nasty, half-eaten rawhide bone the size of his forearm from between the sofa cushions.

In imminent danger of hyperventilating, Taylor fell over onto her side, laughing so hard there were tears.

Only to shriek when Joe yanked her legs out and planted himself on top of her, warm and heavy and looking extremely chagrined. And feeling extremely…impressive.

"Did I really just chase a dog naked around your living room?"

"Uh-huh," she got out on a strangled laugh. "Damn shame I didn't have a video camera…Oh!" Joe swiped aside her robe to nuzzle her breasts, the tip of his tongue teasing first one nipple, than the other. "Just help yourself," she murmured, and he said, "I already am." Taylor linked her hands behind his neck, shut her eyes and let him have at it until he leaned back, his head in his hand, to trace one aureole with his fingertip. And sighed, his warm breath chilling the damp tip, snapping it to attention.

"These are even prettier than I'd imagined."

She opened her eyes, peered down to check, then looked up at him. "Just your average set of 34Bs, nothin' special." Then she cocked one eyebrow. "Hold on…you've been *imagining* them?"

"Oh, yeah." The grin grew more deadly as he grasped a nipple between his thumb and forefinger and gently squeezed. She nearly jumped out of her skin. "Wanna make something of it?"

"Mmm, um…w-who, *me*?" she said on a gasp, only to let out a yelp of startled delight when suddenly his mouth was *everywhere,* and she was laughing all over again, her fingers tangled in his thick, soft hair, the committee cheering her on as she all but purred from the delicious torment of his lips and tongue while his fingers…did things, the things your mother told you only bad boys did because she didn't want you *to find out.*

Then, as if that wasn't bad—or good—enough, he took one nipple into his mouth and started suckling her like there was some kind of elixir in there, and all she could think was Ohhhh… (the committee having apparently gone silent). What she said was "Harder," and Joe, being the obliging sort, tugged her so high she was afraid to open her eyes for fear her eyeballs would pop out…and then she was floating, swirling in the sheer luxury of having a damn good time, and things continued in this fashion for a nice long while until she felt the welcome slide of him inside her, filling her, claiming her, even if only for these few minutes, just for tonight.

As if reading her thoughts, Joe suddenly stilled, his gaze on hers, *in* hers, bringing to mind a scene from one of those fantasy martial arts movies where the action is suspended midair, heightening the anticipation of the completed move.

"What?" she whispered, searching his face, hearing her heartbeat in her ears, feeling a sweet echo between her legs, embracing his hardness.

His smile gleamed in the dim light, like a blessing, as he shushed her, smoothing her hair from her face.

"You're incredible," he said, almost in wonder, his mouth meeting hers in a kiss so tender she nearly passed out. Then she wrapped herself around him to bury her face in his salty, damp neck, giving whatever comfort she could.

Whatever comfort he'd allow himself to take.

Then, slowly, he began to move inside her, encouraging her with whispers and murmured praise—not that she needed it, but still—lifting her knees so he could reach places inside her she hadn't even known existed.

But, oh, was she ever glad to meet them.

Each thrust was slow…deep…delicious, allowing her to hold him, savor him, before he withdrew, then pushed himself inside again, slower, deeper…so deep she felt as though he was truly reaching her soul, taking her past pleasure, past sensation into a realm where words failed, time was outlawed and there was nothing left but pure, undiluted emotion.

Then, on a scream of triumph, the first spasm flashed through her, followed by another and another and another and another, pushing and shoving each other out of the way like a horde of children just let out of school. And Joe was with her, each thrust demanding more tremors, and more still, until she couldn't get her breath and began to think if she survived this one, it would be a miracle.

And if she didn't, she thought as Joe let out his own hurrah, she wouldn't much care.

Then, finally, the shock waves settled down into little pulsing echoes, as the committee applauded and cheered...and she burst out laughing.

Joe propped himself up on his elbows, his brow furrowed even as a grin teased his mouth. His beautiful, wonderful mouth.

"Have I mentioned that you're one very strange woman?"

"I'm sorry, it's just..." She swallowed down a giggle. "I didn't know they came that big."

He glanced down at where their bodies were still joined. Taylor swatted his shoulder.

"Not *that*. What I just did."

Sure enough, that got a nice, cocky grin.

"Yeah?"

"Yeah." She skimmed one finger over his shoulder, then smiled into his eyes. "Somebody's had a lot of practice."

His features clouded; then he carefully lifted himself off of her and went into her bathroom. Taylor slipped her robe back on and followed him, figuring since he hadn't closed the door, it was no big deal. She found him with his hands braced on either side of her sink, frowning at his reflection, completely unselfconscious about his nakedness. Of course, if she had a butt like that, she wouldn't be, either.

She leaned against the door frame, her arms crossed. "What?" she said softly, for the second time in ten minutes.

In the mirror, she saw his mouth harden. "You scare the hell out of me."

"Gee, thanks."

He turned, then held out his hand, beckoning her back into his arms. "I've never had a woman come apart like that on my watch, either," he whispered across her temple. "I was beginning to wonder if you'd ever stop."

"You're not the only one." She pressed her lips into the springy mat of hair on his chest, then snuggled her cheek back into it. "Really? I mean about me being the first time that's happened to you, too?"

"Really."

"Huh." She reared back to look at him. "Got any theories as to why?"

"Yeah. 'Cause I never cared enough to take that much time to make sure she did."

"I see." Splaying her hands on his chest, she said quietly, "Does this mean we have another problem?"

Joe slipped his hands up to her shoulders and set her a little apart, and what she saw in his eyes broke her heart. "You make me want to feel things I've got no business feeling," he said softly, lifting her tangled hair away from her face. "Make me want to believe in things I stopped believing in a long time ago."

"And this is bad…*why?*"

His mouth torqued into a sad smile. "You know why."

No, actually, I don't, she wanted to say, but figured this wasn't the best time to press the issue. Whether he realized it or not, a huge chunk of his defenses had just come crumbling down. But she imagined only in the areas not strengthened by the rebar forged by fear and false assumption. Their gazes wrestled for several seconds before she lifted a hand to his stubbled cheek. "And if you think that's my cue to send you on your way, you're crazy. I've got another…" she glanced at the little clock over the medicine chest "…hour and thirty-five minutes left on my dance card, buddy."

"And if this is the only night we ever get to dance? Taylor…" He cradled her head in his hands, his thumbs skating over her cheeks as his dark, agonized gaze bore into hers. "I don't want to hurt you. Or lead you on."

She steeled herself against the sensation of having just swallowed one of Oakley's rawhide bones, slobber and all, even as she closed her fingers over Joe's hands, so strong, so gentle. Like him. Common sense—the pittance she had left—told her she should nod, say, "I see. Well, thanks for a good time," and send him on his way. But doing that would be giving up…on him.

Because she knew, in a way she'd never felt before, that this man needed her. Maybe only for now, true—she wasn't deluding herself—but never had anyone made her feel more important, or desired, or necessary. And damned if she was going to walk away from that. From him.

So she girded her emotional loins and said, "You just gave me the time of my life, buster. And if you really feel you need to leave, right now…if you really believe making love to me again would *hurt* me, then fine. There's the door. It's been a blast, no hard feelings, see ya around." She slid her hands down to link with his, feeling some small measure of triumph when his fingers tightened around hers. "Then again, you could think of this as, I don't know…a vacation. You know going in it's going to end, but you can still have a great time. In fact, you can enjoy the experience even more *because* you know it's temporary, right?"

Joe looked at her steadily for several seconds, then let out a short, dry laugh, shaking his head. "I don't know…"

"Neither do I, Joe. Neither do I. But I think fear of what *might* happen is kind of a lame excuse to avoid something that could do both of us some good, you know?" She smiled. "And the clock is ticking, bud. While we've been in here yakking, ten minutes have passed. And for heaven's sake—who has talks like this in the bathroom?"

He laughed, then lifted his hands to her face to kiss her, long and slow and deep. Then he took her hand and led her to the bedroom, at which point Taylor figured she'd pretty much won that round, at least.

Joe got back to his cabin a few minutes before midnight to find Blair just ejecting a DVD from the player. She looked up at his entrance, grinning, the light from the kitchen overhead spilling into the living room, making her braces sparkle.

"Good timing. Cool."

"I'll run you home, then—"

"No, that's okay," she said, pulling her cell phone out of her pocket. "Dad said he'll come get me so you don't have to leave Seth...yeah, s'me," she said into the phone. "Uh-huh, I'm ready."

Guilt nudged Joe's gaze to Seth's closed bedroom door. "Did he wake up?"

"N'uh-uh," the teenager said, poking her phone back into her shorts. "Out like a light the whole time. You get everything done you needed to do?"

Heat warmed his face. Damn—when had been the last time he'd blushed, for God's sake? But then, when was the last time he'd had to sneak off to have sex? Good thing the light wasn't real bright in here, was all he had to say. "Yeah, I did," he said, tugging his wallet out of his jeans and thanking God for an excuse not to have to look Hank's daughter in the eye right away. "Sorry, I have no idea what the going rate for baby-sitting is these days..."

Blair wrinkled her freckled nose. "How's ten sound?"

"Let's make it fifteen." Joe handed her a ten and a five just as they heard Hank's truck pull up in front of the cabin. With a grinned *thanks,* she slipped out the screen door and down the porch steps. Joe followed, waving back when she did from the passenger seat of her dad's truck.

Blair was a good kid, he thought. A *regular* kid, with almost infinite possibilities open to her—

He caught himself, shut his eyes, pushing out a breath of frustration, and irritation, and melancholy, as the reality of his life swept away the past two hours like sand castles in the tide. He knew better than to compare Blair with his sister; he knew it wasn't right and, God knew, it was pointless. But sometimes it just seemed so unfair. Looking at Blair, knowing she'd probably be popular in high school, go on to college, have a career, maybe get married and have children of her own...

All he wanted for Kristen was for her to be happy. But after fifteen years, he'd seen just how elusive happiness could be for someone on the wrong side of the invisible fence that separated "different" from what the world considered "normal." But then, he thought as he went back inside, it wasn't always easy defining happiness when you were part of the so-called "normal" world, either.

He went into the kitchen to pour himself a glass of milk, feeling…shredded. Now he knew why he never let his impulses govern his actions. He should never have gone over to Taylor's tonight, never made love to her, never let down his defenses. Because now that he had, how the hell was he ever going to get them back up? If he'd left after the first time, if he'd torn himself away from all that openness and generosity and humor while he'd still had some control, it might've been okay. *But nooo,* he had to go along with all that vacation crap and take her back to bed, lose himself inside her again, and now…

Now he was screwed, because now he knew what he'd be missing if he gave her up.

When he gave her up.

"Joe?" came the soft voice from across the room. Joe looked up to see Seth standing in his T-shirt and boxers, flushed from sleep and blinking in the light, and a whole bunch of feelings laced themselves around his heart. And squeezed.

"Hey, squirt…whatcha doing up?"

"I heard a car or truck or somethin' outside. Was somebody here?"

"That was Hank, coming to get Blair. I needed to go out for a couple hours, so I had her come stay with you." He smiled. "You didn't even know, did you?"

Seth shook his head, then padded over to the counter and climbed up on a stool. "C'n I have some milk, too?"

"Sure."

Joe poured some into a plastic glass and handed it to his brother, who frowned up at him and said, "Where'd you go?"

Why did the idea of telling the kid the truth make him feel slightly sick?

"Just out. Nowhere important. Come on, finish up your milk so you can get back into bed before you keel over."

The kid gulped it down; Joe handed him a napkin to wipe his

mouth, then herded him back to his room and tucked him in, only to have a pair of wiry little arms thread themselves around his neck and pull him down for a hug. His heart turned over in his chest, even as the very air in the room seemed to hum with the boy's neediness. But when he lay back on his pillow, a tiny crease had settled between his dark brows.

"You smell like Taylor's," he said, accusation peering out from behind his words.

Joe started. Even though he'd taken a fast shower before he left, leave it to Seth to have a nose as keen as Oakley's. "I do?"

"Yeah. Is that where you went?"

"Okay, yeah, that's where I was. She, um, wanted to talk to me." He ruffled his brother's hair. "About you."

"What about me?"

"Just about how much better you seem to be doing. Stuff like that."

"Oh." The frown deepened. "So how come you didn't just say that to begin with?"

Oh, boy. "Because…I don't know." He tried smiling for the kid. "Maybe because I didn't want you to feel you'd missed out on something, you know?"

"Oh. What's gonna happen? When the summer's over, I mean?"

Joe's heart knocked against his ribs. He hadn't been able to think beyond getting these two projects done, beyond the next several weeks. Now Seth's question smacked him with the realization that he really didn't know what came next. Especially if he didn't get the promotion. Which, as much as he wanted it, as much as he knew he deserved it, wasn't a given. Nope, whatever came after the end of the summer stretched in front of him like a long, black, endless tunnel.

Especially if Taylor wasn't in it.

But Taylor couldn't be in it, he reminded himself. Because while maybe she was okay with an hour or two of his time while he was here, he doubted seriously she'd be okay with that for the long haul. After all, even vacations got old, after a while, because they weren't real life. Because they weren't meant to last forever.

"I don't really know," he finally answered over the cold, hard knot in the center of his chest. "Guess we'll just have to wait and see how everything works out. And now you need to go back to sleep, okay?"

"Okay," Seth said after a moment, then gave Joe a little smile that pierced his heart. "Today was really cool, goin' to Tulsa with you and then to Cal's and riding the horse. Except I wish…"

"What?"

Tears flooded the kid's eyes. "I really wish Mom could've seen me ride."

Battling a tightness at the back of his own throat, Joe scooped his brother into his arms and held on tight. "I bet she would've been real proud," he said, then laid Seth back on his bed and pulled the sheet and summer blanket back into place, suddenly feeling awkward. He got up from the bed, nodding toward the bedside lamp. "You want me to leave the light on for a while?"

Seth gave a vigorous shake of his head. "No, why would I want that?"

Joe smiled at the kid's bravado. "Well, okay. 'Night."

"'Night, Joe."

But when he closed the door behind him, he felt like he was pulling a door shut on his own heart.

After Joe left, Seth got up and turned the light back on, then sat down on the scratchy, oval rug beside the bed to look at his new boots some more, scratching a mosquito bite on his leg and thinking about how, all in all, he really liked it here. He was starting to get to know some of the kids at camp, like Wade Frazier and Noah Logan, for one thing. And there was Ruby's—she was so nice! And Taylor, of course. And then, going out to Cal's ranch had been so cool, he'd thought he'd bust. The horses were awesome, their noses so soft and stuff when he petted them. He even liked the way they smelled. Oh, yeah, he'd be real happy if he could stay here forever.

But that wasn't gonna happen, so he should probably just forget about it, 'cause they'd be going to live in Tulsa, Joe said, once he was finished with these projects. Seth'd never been to Tulsa before today. It was okay, he guessed, but it was still a city. He'd lived his entire life in a city, and he liked the country a whole lot better.

Bet he couldn't ride horses in Tulsa.

With a sigh, he got back in bed and turned off the light before Joe noticed it was on. Jeez, there were so many thoughts in his head, he felt like they were gonna crash into each other. He'd really, really wanted to tell Joe he loved him, but he didn't know how Joe would take that, so he didn't. Maybe brothers weren't supposed to say things like that. Or maybe Joe would get all weird like Dad used to, when Seth would say it. 'Course, he'd stopped saying it a long time ago, since it didn't feel right telling somebody you loved them when they never said it back. And maybe Joe wouldn't feel like saying it back, either, and that would totally suck.

What really sucked, though, was how Joe thought Seth was too dumb to figure out that he'd gone over to Taylor's because he liked her, not because he wanted to talk to her about Seth. But if he wanted to be with her, how come he wouldn't let them stay for dinner the other night? Why did he act like he didn't want to be around her when he obviously did?

Grown-ups were peculiar, that's all he had to say.

Then something else occurred to him, something that made him almost sick to his stomach, and that was, if Joe did like Taylor, but thought maybe Seth was keeping him from being with her, then maybe Joe would decide Seth was more trouble than he was worth. Dad had sure felt like that, always getting mad whenever Seth came into the room when he was kissing Mom and stuff. "Don't you have someplace else to be?" he'd yell, or "What the hell do you want *now?*"

His mom had loved him, sure. And Taylor always smiled for him and made him feel like she really liked being with him. But maybe that's because they were women. Maybe men weren't made that way, maybe having kids around made them nervous or something.

Except Cal Logan hadn't acted that way around Seth. And he'd seen Sam Frazier hug his boys and stuff when he'd pick 'em up from day camp. So he guessed that wasn't it, either. Maybe… maybe it was just the way *some* men were. Like his father. And Joe? Seth wanted to stay with Joe more than anything in the world, but he'd wanted his dad to stick around more than anything in the world, too, and look how that had turned out.

Seth scrunched his pillow up under his cheek and thought about that. Strangely enough, he didn't feel sad as much as kinda relieved, like maybe he'd figured something out. It was like Mom always said, you gotta know what the problem was before you can solve it. So Seth laid there, his forehead all in a knot, contemplating a whole bunch of ways that would maybe solve his problem. And Joe's, too.

And after a real long time, he thought maybe he had an answer.

Chapter 12

The woman was driving him nuts.

In the five days since Joe'd paid that little late night visit to Taylor's house, she hadn't done or said a single thing to indicate anything had changed between them. Which, if he were being logical, he should be happy about, right? Because he didn't need the distraction and all. That he wasn't happy one bit did not bode well, speaking to a side of his character from which he'd done everything in his power to distance himself ever since he could remember.

Because he was still distracted, he thought as he walked up to her front door to pick up Seth. Oh, boy, was he distracted. By memories so vivid he could almost catch her scent mixed in with the tang of sawdust and pressure-treated wood, hear her soft—and not-so-soft—cries of pleasure even over the whine of a power saw. Oh, yeah, the woman sure did know how to enjoy herself. He felt like an alcoholic who'd gone off the wagon, agonized with recriminations, more agonized by the temptation to do it again…

She met him at the door with a pleasant expression.

…only somebody had locked up all the booze.

"I suppose you heard," Taylor said with a perfectly normal smile, "that Maddie had her baby?"

"Uh, yeah, Hank told me." Joe leaned one hand against a porch post, smelling her. Aching for her. Visualizing all too clearly those cute little breasts hidden away beneath two layers of cotton, and coming about as close to hating himself as he ever had. Her hair was loose, a thousand shades of red tumbling over her shoulders, and he wanted to plow his fingers through it and bring his mouth down on hers and let her take him to that place where there was nothing but them and hot, mind-numbing sex. But instead he stayed where he was and said, "A boy. Over nine pounds or something?"

She laughed, the sound a siren call, beckoning, teasing. Tempting. "Yep. Noah's over the moon at finally getting a brother after two sisters."

Reality—his reality—elbowed back into his thought, and he looked at her, feeling his brows pull together. "And…everything's okay? With the baby?"

The green, knowing gaze gentled, as if she understood. "Yeah, Joe," she said softly. "He's fine. I got over to see him last night. Kid's got a set of lungs on him like a tornado siren." Her eyes met his for a moment, then skittered away. "Let me go see what's keeping Seth," she said, walking over to the door and hollering at him to get a move on, Joe was waiting. Then she turned around, her hand resting lightly against the door latch, as Oakley dragged himself over and flopped down at her feet with a groan, taking up half the porch.

"So," she said. "Your mom and sister are coming in tomorrow, right?"

Now reality flat-out blew a whistle, instantly clearing the place of all thoughts involving sex and escape and temptation. But aggravation lingered, huddled in one corner of his brain where reality couldn't see it, that not once had she even hinted at getting together again. And whether it made any sense or not, considering the situation, considering everything *he'd* said to begin with, for crying out loud, her not bringing up the subject was plain beginning to spook him. Especially since he'd never yet met a woman who didn't use sex as a reason to lay claim to a man.

"Tomorrow evening, yeah." He glanced away, his face heating, knowing the logical thing to do would be to suggest they all get together at some point. But the words backed up in his throat where they got hopelessly tangled in the guilt and confusion already there.

"Joe?"

He met her gaze, warily, petrified of being sucked in. Even more petrified of *wanting* to be sucked in.

"It's gonna be okay," she said, her mouth tweaked up at the corners. He didn't even know what the hell she meant by that—if she was talking about his family being here or how Seth was going to react or even, maybe, if she was talking about them—but suddenly he felt like his head was going to explode because she was being so damn reasonable about a totally unreasonable situation.

"Dammit, Taylor—why are you acting like this?"

Her eyes stayed fixed on his, her face betraying nothing. "Acting like what?" she said mildly, infuriating him even more.

He took a step closer, slapping his hat against his thigh. "You know damn well *what*."

"Oh..." she said on a slowly released breath, then crossed her arms. "You mean, because I'm not acting all clingy and demanding?"

"Well...yeah."

Brows lifted. "You *want* me to act all clingy and demanding?"

"Well, no, but...it's just confusing."

"Joe." She glanced behind her to make sure Seth wasn't there, then said quietly, "The other night was amazing. But I'm a big girl. I don't play the game unless I understand, and can live with, the rules." Underneath her crisp white shirt, her shoulders hitched. "What else is there to say? So," she said, her voice higher, brighter, "how's the Double Arrow coming along?"

"I don't want to talk about that," he growled.

"Uh, yeah. You do." She nodded behind her to indicate she heard Seth coming, then shoved her hair out of her face, exactly the way she had when she'd straddled him, that last time, her breasts silvered in the moonlight stealing across the bed, her nipples glistening from his mouth. A shudder streaked through his blood, settling right smack in his groin. "And there's not much point in discussing the other, is there?"

No, there wasn't. Not if either of them was even remotely interested in being logical. If he were being *logical,* he'd chalked this up to a cross between infatuation and lust. Except he and lust had more than a nodding acquaintance, it seemed to him, at least enough to know that the overwhelming tenderness, the pure joy, that had swamped him when she'd fallen apart in his arms—*each and every time*—had never been part of the deal before. Yeah, he wanted her naked again so badly he could hardly think straight, but he also wanted the laughter and the sighs and the smiles and the holding each other afterwards, the precious silence filled with something so damn good he couldn't even define it.

The feeling of sanctuary when he was with her.

Even if that feeling was something he could ill afford.

Seth appeared, slapping back the screen door and grinning for him, driving home at least some of the reasons why Joe should be grateful Taylor wasn't demanding a single thing of him.

"The Arrow's coming along good," he said, hooking one thumb in his belt loop. "Just putting the finishing touches on the cabins, then the demolition crew's coming on Monday to start gutting the old motel."

"And the project in Tulsa?" she said, sliding one arm across his brother's chest. Joe's eyes slipped to her hand, to those slender, long-nailed fingers he could still feel soothing his skin, inflaming it, before his gaze slid back up to her face.

"Found a new framer, so we're back in business."

"Oh, good." She smiled, hugged Seth and sent him off to the car. And Joe just stood there, his entire body tightening when Taylor's eyes edged to his. Never in his life had he wanted to give more to a person than he did her; never in his life had he felt he had so little to give. His mouth fell open: he should say something, *anything,* only God knew what that would be. "Taylor—"

"Go on, Seth's waiting for you," she said quietly, opening the screen door and disappearing inside.

She stood at the door, watching Joe stride back to the car, her heart aching at the burden of pride so precariously balanced on those broad shoulders, the male arrogance propelling those long legs away from her. It wasn't until the Blazer was out of sight, though, that she let go of the breath she'd been holding.

The past five days had been a bitch and a half.

Patting her leg for Oak to follow her and keep her company, she wandered into the kitchen to drag out a frozen dinner from the freezer, even though she felt as much like eating right now as she did lassoing skunks. Playing cool had that effect on her. But no way was she going to complicate things more than they already were by giving her emotions their head, or let on that it was killing her not to touch him, how every night when he dragged himself up onto her porch, looking beat, it had taken everything she had not to wrap her arms around him. No way was she going to let on that just thinking about that night set assorted places on her body to tingling so badly she half expected them to catch fire, significant if for no other reason than her body parts were not prone to tingling for just any old person who happened to cross her path.

And no way was she going to let herself think that what had just happened indicated a weakening on Joe's part. Not in any substantial way, at least. Oh, if his hormones put up a big enough stink, he might figure out how to carve another hour or two out of his life to be with her. And she wouldn't fight it. She wagered ninety-nine percent of the world's women never had a man make love to them the way Joe had her, and for sure she wasn't enough of a fool to turn down the opportunity to repeat the experience, should the occasion present itself. But she was long since past believing a woman could will, or nag, a man into changing. And even longer past thinking she had the energy to try.

A fingernail gave way as she ripped open the box to the frozen dinner and yanked it out. She folded back the little corner, plonked the dinner into the microwave, shut the door and set the timer before she realized she had no idea what was in the tray.

And if that wasn't a sad comment on her life, she didn't know what was.

Scouring her brain for what scraps of pride she had left, she tramped back into her bedroom to file down the broken nail, before gathering up two weeks' worth of clothes to wash. Oh, no…no way was she gonna force the issue. She didn't want to be one more thing for Joe to worry about.

Which had nothing to do with how much she worried about him.

Grumbling, Taylor batted back the clothes hanging in the closet to get to a stray pair of shorts *somebody* had flung into the far corner, only to run smack into the stupid blue dress. She blew her hair out of her face and glowered at the thing. Then she yanked it off the rack, hauling it out of the closet like an errant child and planting herself in front of the cheval mirror in the corner, molding the glittery fabric to her body as if to say, *And what do you have to say for yourself?*

And what the dress said was, *Hey. Nobody told you to buy me.*

Just as nobody had told her to fall in love with Joe Salazar.

Except, as she dimly recalled, the last time she'd been in love, she'd felt relatively happy about it. This time, if felt more like a chronic case of menstrual cramps.

On top of the flu.

Taylor tossed the dress on the bed, grabbed her laundry basket and stomped back to the little utility porch off the kitchen. Once she'd stuffed a load of whites into the washer, she pulled her dinner out of the microwave. Salisbury steak, as it happened. Her mouth scrunched up, she peeled off the top, took one sniff and set it on the floor for the dog, who gobbled it down in two point five seconds and was clearly thrilled.

"At least one of us is," Taylor muttered. Then her gaze swung over to the phone. Where it hovered, waiting for her brain, then her hand, to catch up. She plucked it off its stand and punched her mother's auto-dial number.

"You've reached the McIntyre residence. Please leave a number after the tone."

Not that Taylor had expected anything else, but still.

"Hi, Mom, it's me, Taylor. Everything's fine, just called to check in. I'll…talk to you later."

With a sigh, she dropped the phone back in the stand. Five seconds later, she was scarfing down what was left of the chocolates (after unearthing the almost empty box from where she'd hidden it from herself), while Oakley rattled the empty plastic dinner tray from one side of the kitchen to the other.

The next afternoon, Joe stood in the center of the living room in one of the new cabins, hands on hips, feeling pretty doggone pleased, overall. Even though it was a real scorcher outside, cool air hummed through the vents as speckled sunlight danced over the plank flooring. It had been Jenna's idea to partially furnish the new cabins with pieces from estate sales and such, which gave the place a much homier feel than one usually encountered in your average resort. Cherise, Hank's head of housekeeping, had just left after personally making up the beds for Joe's mother and sister (leaving behind a healthy dose of her perfume), and Blair had filled a bunch of vases with wildflowers—whites and yellows and deep purples and oranges—which she'd set here and there around the cabin.

Yeah, Joe thought on a rush of pride, it all looked real inviting. Peaceful. Hank'd do real well with the place, he imagined, only to frown as the oddest sensation settled into pit of his stomach. If he didn't know better, he'd peg the feeling as almost proprietary. Of all the projects Joe'd worked on over the years, he'd never become personally attached to any of them. When they were done, he'd gone on to the next, never giving the old one a second thought. But this one…this one felt like it might be a little harder to walk away from.

His forehead knotted, he stepped out onto the porch, just about the time his mother's white Taurus nosed into view, setting off a whole new slew of conflicted feelings fighting for squatting rights in his brain.

"Joe! Joe! Joe!"

The car had barely come to a stop before his sister shoved open the passenger side door and clambered out, flying over to him. Laughing, he bent over and closed his arms around her, inhaling the mingled scents of floral shampoo, potato chips and fabric softener. Then he held her at arm's length to admire her fancy T-shirt, bright pinks and purples with all manner of glittery designs on it. Picking up on her cue, Kristen spread out her arms and slowly twirled, her dark hair gleaming in the sun.

"I look…hot, huh?" she said, giggling, then pushed back her hair to reveal tiny gold studs.

Joe whistled, then grinned, his hands on his hips. "Hot is right! And is that eye shadow? And lipstick?"

"Uh-huh," she said, pulling off her thick-lensed glasses to show him the pale lavender shadow already creasing in her lids. "But Mama said only on…special oc-casions. And I hafta…keep my ears clean." She pointed to the studs. "I have holes now. Like Mama."

Speaking of whom, Danielle had joined them, her smile as bright as the embroidery on her billowing white cotton dress. Her affectionate gaze washed over her daughter for a moment before she, too, pulled Joe into a surprisingly strong hug for someone a good foot shorter than he was. "Damn, it's good to see you," she whispered in his ear, then held him back much the same way he'd done to Kristen a few moments before, her dark eyes unnervingly astute underneath a head of thick, short salt-and-pepper hair brushed back from an angular face. A face currently creased into a frown. "You've lost weight."

"It's this shirt," he lied, plucking at the loose-fitting khaki work shirt he wore tucked into his jeans. "I picked up an extra-large by mistake, was too lazy to take it back."

The straight set to her unlipsticked mouth told him she wasn't buying it. But then she turned back to Kristen, who was standing there grinning.

"Doesn't she look great?" Danielle said, giving her daughter, who barely came up to her shoulder, a one-armed hug, then smiled at Joe. "She did the makeup all by herself!"

"She looks terrific," he said with another smile for his sister, even as a pang swept through him at how much his mother read into every accomplishment, no matter how minor.

"Is it…four o'clock yet?" Kristen asked.

"What does your watch say?" Danielle asked, pointing to the pink-strapped watch on Kristen's wrist.

His sister lifted her wide, short-fingered hand, frowning at the face for several moments before she stuck her tongue between her teeth and carefully said, "Three…four…six." Then she looked up. "Is it time for my show?"

"That's three *forty*-six," Danielle said patiently, then said, "Yes, that's close to four o'clock, but…" Tucking fingers underneath Kristen's chin, she looked into her eyes. "We talked about this before, remember? That they don't have the same TV shows everywhere, especially in the afternoons?"

"Why not?"

Joe saw his mother take a breath, knowing she'd probably explained this to his sister many times before. "Because…during the day, each TV station decides what programs it wants to put on. Remember when your class took a trip to the TV station last year?"

Kristen's heavy brows drew together; then she slowly nodded. "Where they had all the big cords on the floor, like snakes?"

"That's right! Good girl!" Danielle beamed. "Anyway, that's where the TV shows come from. So they might not have the same shows here they have in Kansas."

"Actually," Joe said, "we might." Both his mother and his sister turned to him; he pointed to the satellite dish up on the roof. "Just installed, free satellite TV. There's a schedule in the drawer underneath the TV," he addressed his sister. "Look right in front of you when you walk in, and you'll see it."

"Then bring it out here," his mother said, "and we'll check it together."

With a grin, off she went, her trundling gait little improved from what it had been as a child.

"Oh, my God, Joe…"

He turned to find his mother standing at the edge of the lot, her hand visoring her eyes as she took in the same view that had stolen Joe's breath away a few days before. "This is incredible! I had no idea it was so beautiful."

Joe crossed to the Taurus to unload the trunk, wishing he could jettison the uneasiness that refused to give him a break, even for a moment. About Kristen, about Taylor, about whatever was going on with Wes. His boss had been late again paying another sub, this time on the Tulsa project. And this time, when Joe had called the office—because Wes had apparently turned off his cell—he'd gotten that Madison character, who, instead of simply taking Joe's message, started making noises about how he had the new job in the bag…news which had settled in Joe's stomach like ground glass….

"Joe? Is something the matter?"

The trunk yawned open in front of him as he realized that's as far as he'd gotten. He grabbed a piece of luggage and smiled for his mother, hoping to ease the concern on her face.

"No, everything's fine. Just got lost in thought for a moment."

Danielle laughed. "Honestly. I would have hoped you'd have outgrown that by now. Remember how we used to find you standing in the kitchen, having no idea why you were there?"

Yeah, well, he was no less lost these days. He hefted several cases of various sizes from the trunk, lowering them to the ground as his mother, who always had switched subjects with carefree abandon, said, "I knew this would be a good idea! Bringing Kristen here, I mean. It's been so long since she's seen you…she misses you, Joe."

He slammed shut the Taurus's trunk and then glanced anxiously toward the cabin. "I wonder what's taking her so long?"

"She probably had to use the bathroom," his mother said calmly.

"Are you sure it's okay?"

Danielle looked at him, brows raised. "Why shouldn't it be? Or does the toilet work differently than any other toilet?"

"No, but…"

"Then she's fine." On a sigh, she looked back over the vista. "You always did worry too much about her."

Only because you never worried enough.

The thought shot through him with enough force to make him flinch, following closely by intense shame. Considering his mother had lived every minute of her life with Kristen, *for* Kristen, how could he even think such a thing?

After the luggage was all inside and his mother had duly oohed and aahed over the place, she went into the kitchen, opening and closing cupboards and nodding in apparent satisfaction. Kristen had indeed used the bathroom, regaling them both about the experience upon her return. Then Danielle prompted her about washing her hands, and off she went back to the bathroom.

"I thought Seth might be here," Danielle said, locating a glass, inspecting it, then filling it with water from the sink.

"No, he's still at camp. I thought I'd go get him while you and Kristen rest up from your trip."

She managed to both bat at him and shake her head as she drank, then set down the glass and said, "Nonsense! We're fine! We'll come with you!"

"Ma…I'm not sure that's such a good idea."

"Why on earth not? And this way, we can get a glimpse of the town! It looked charming, from what we could see of it. Besides, Kristen's been talking my ear off for the last two hundred miles about how she can't wait to meet her new brother! Isn't that right, honey?" she added as the girl reappeared.

"Uh-huh," she said with one of her heart-stopping grins, then pressed her hand to her stomach. "I'm ex-cited. Mama says I have but-terflies in my sss-stomach, but I think she's just kidding me."

Joe shot a look at his mother, but she was too busy fixing Kristen's twisted-up shirt to notice. Maybe Kristen was ready for this meeting, but Joe wasn't all that sure he was. And he had no idea what Seth thought, since all the kid had said when Joe'd reminded him that his mother and sister were coming today was, "Oh, yeah."

"Ma."

Finally, his mother glanced in his direction.

"I really think it would be better for them to meet here."

Kristen had wandered over to the TV set in an entertainment center along one wall and turned it on. *Power* was one of the first words she'd been able to recognize. As the applause and bells of some game show filled the cabin, Danielle's eyes darted toward her daughter, then landed back on Joe.

"Because Kristen has DS, you mean?"

Yeah, he knew that was coming. "I don't get the feeling Seth's been around many kids with DS," he said, his gaze locked with his mother's. "I'd just like to make this as easy as possible for everyone."

"For everyone? Or you?"

Annoyance ripped through him. "I meant exactly what I said, Mother," he said softly. "Or don't I count as part of 'everyone'?"

Her head actually jerked back slightly at that. Then she let out a sigh, as though realizing how she'd sounded. That didn't mean she'd back down, though. Not if Joe knew his mother. And sure enough, she said, "I'm sorry. Of course your opinion counts. It's just…" Another quick glance at her daughter, then: "It just seems to me the less of a big deal we make out of this, the less trouble we'll have down the road. With them adjusting to each other and all." Tilting her head, she touched Joe's arm. "Don't you think?"

After a brief standoff, Joe lifted his hands in surrender. "Fine. If that's the way you want to do this, that's what we'll do."

But if it backfired, he thought grumpily as he herded the two of them out to the Blazer, guess who'd have to clean up the mess.

Chapter 13

Taylor had spent most of the day being so damn chipper she probably scared people, beginning with a long, sweaty run with Jenna first thing in the morning, during which Taylor did her level best to ignore the blonde's you're-not-fooling-anybody glances. Then, swarming with exercise-induced endorphins, she'd bounced into day camp, actually eager to take a dozen little boys on a hike into the woods adjacent to the church. Of course, Seth being one of the little boys made her be-happy-or-die-trying vow a mite harder to keep, but she managed. Especially since she noticed how well he was beginning to get on with some of the other little boys who were close to Seth's age.

Only then, she got to thinking about how he'd be leaving, after struggling all summer to find his footing in a new environment, and how much she'd miss him. That knocked a chunk or two out of her good mood. Or would have, if the good mood hadn't been as fake as a claw machine gold necklace to begin with.

Which by the end of the day had begun to severely tarnish. So much so that when Sam Frazier came to pick up his boys—all five of whom were in camp this summer—even watching the gentle farmer's exuberant hugs for his gaggle of rug rats couldn't fully restore the shine.

"Hey, Taylor," the tall, almost gangly widower said with one of his sunny smiles, only to feign having the breath knocked out of him when Wade, the eight-year-old, caromed into his thighs. "Got a few extra kids you'd like to send home? Hey, Frankie… whatcha got there?" A blue-and-red plaid shirt stretched across Sam's leanly muscled back as he crouched, the first-grader hugged backward to his chest, to look at a painting the child had made that day. As Frankie talked about the painting, Sam gently corrected the boy's speech from time to time, the result of his not hearing too well out of one ear. Then he told everybody to make sure they had their lunch boxes or whatever else they'd brought with them; as they scattered in what seemed like a hundred different directions, Sam grinned down at his youngest, Travis, then plucked the four-year-old off the floor and swung him high in the air, making the little one shriek with laughter.

Her arms crossed, Taylor smiled, her insides warmed at the obvious affection between this man and his children. She'd come to Haven nearly a year after Sam's wife had died. Word was that, despite his own grief over a woman he'd apparently loved since he was a teenager, he'd never withdrawn from his kids or let them believe their lives were over simply because their mama's had ended way before it should have. And yet, despite the man's goodness and intelligence, despite his being pretty good-looking, actually, with those pale eyes and light hair against summer-browned skin, and despite his having six kids, which was not the obstacle for Taylor it might be for other women, she'd never been even remotely attracted to him. Nor he to her, if her intuition was even remotely on target. A turn of events she knew disappointed many in town who'd probably thought, "Aha! Have we got a man for you!" before she'd even finished unpacking.

Which only went to show, she thought as her heart starting doing an Irish clog dance when she caught sight of Joe walking in the door, how little logic had to do with falling in love.

Then she realized he wasn't alone. The petite, iron-haired woman with the miss-nothing eyes would be his mother, she guessed. And the girl, shorter than her mother, somewhat heavy-set, her thick, dark hair glimmering in the overhead lights, must be Kristen.

Taylor lifted her eyes just in time for Joe's gaze to snag hers, sending a jolt through her. Not only of sexual awareness, although heaven knew that was part of it—in spades—but of something else, something she wondered if he even realized. Especially when his eyes tore from hers to scan the room, looking for Seth, she presumed.

Her breath backed up in her throat—she'd lay odds this was not the way he'd intended for his siblings to meet, in a public place. In front of Taylor. And he wasn't at all happy about it. But why? What was the big deal?

Taylor only half heard the Frazier kids' "See ya Monday, Miz Taylor!" as they filed out the door, her gaze following Joe's until it lit on Seth, sitting across the room at a table with Blair, the boy's expression just this side of shell-shocked. Kristen made a beeline for one of the tables, still littered with construction paper, ribbons, feathers and glue bottles from a recent arts and crafts project, plopping herself down in one of the little chairs and diving into all the goodies, her face beaming.

"Kristen?" Joe's mother said in a level, but brook-no-argument voice. "Did you ask permission to do that?"

Even though Taylor instantly understood she had no business interfering in whatever discipline strategy the mother had implemented for the girl, she couldn't help the prick to her heart when Kristen's bright smile instantly dimmed, her entire face crumpling into a scowl. Then short arms clamped across her chest.

"I wasn't…hurting any-thing, Mama! I was just playing. See?" She unfolded her arms to grab two pieces of ribbon off the table, holding them up, her expression both pleading and defiant. "Okay?"

The few people left in the room were now engrossed in the

little drama playing out in front of them. Terrific. Taylor sucked in a deep breath in a futile attempt to relax. She'd worked with children with Down syndrome before, when she'd taught in Dallas, but only with the two or three who'd been mainstreamed into her classes. Even so, she knew how radically different one child with DS could be from another; the last thing she wanted to do was base her judgment on how to handle the situation on assumptions that might be way off base.

Then she felt a gentle, brief squeeze on her shoulder as Joe brushed past her and over to his sister and mother, where he squatted down beside the girl. Taylor couldn't hear his words, only the soft rumble of his voice, a sound she realized had become very precious to her.

A sound apparently also very precious to the still glowering young woman seated at the table. At first she sat stiffly, glaring mutinously at the table, her hands dangling at her sides. But as Joe talked and rubbed Kristen's back, Taylor watched the tension slowly leak from the girl's body. Then she leaned into her brother's chest, nodding, sparing a glance now and then at Taylor through her thick glasses.

"Okay?" Joe said, giving her a quick hug. "Can you do that?"

"Yeah, Joe," Kristen said. "I can do that." Then she sat up and said, "Is it o-kay if I play with some of this, Miss Taylor?"

"Of course you can, Kristen," she said with a smile. "For a few minutes anyway. Since we're about done for the day, we have to clean up soon."

The girl smiled back. "I can help clean up. I'm good at that."

"I'm sure you are."

Then Joe's eyes met hers again, and she flinched, startled at the frustration and guilt she saw in them. "Well," he said, straightening up. "Guess it's time Seth and Kristen meet each other, huh?" Only this time, instead of his voice being soothing, she heard the strain of somebody plumb worn-out from trying to make everybody happy. And she was nearly overcome with the urge to tell them all to leave the poor guy alone, for crying out loud.

She could just imagine how well that would go over. Especially with Mr. I-Can-Do-it-All over there.

"You must be Taylor?" she heard beside her. She turned to meet an extraordinarily bright smile. "I've heard so much about you," Joe's mother said.

And Taylor thought, *Oh, yeah?*

Joe was halfway across the room to Seth when he noticed his mother move in for the kill. When he couldn't do a damn thing to stop her, of course. That was the last time he mentioned a woman, he mused irritably, only to then think, *And just what other women do you think you'd be mentioning, or not, anyway?*

There was a heart-stopping thought.

In any case, Taylor—who he now knew was tougher than she looked—could probably hold her own with his mother without coming out too bloodied. His little brother, on the other hand, looked like he didn't know which end was up. Joe's heart turned over—it was one thing to hear about Kristen, quite another to deal with her in person. There seemed to be little middle ground for his sister, emotionally—she was either giddy with joy or having a hissy about something. Fortunately, the happy times generally outweighed the unhappy times, but Kristen had never taken kindly to any attempt to thwart her exercise of free choice.

"That's her?" were the first words out of his brother's mouth after Blair left them alone.

"Yep. That's Kristen. And the lady talking to Taylor is my mom Danielle."

The boy nodded, saying nothing. But the apprehension and confusion in his eyes tore Joe up inside.

"Seth?" A beat or two passed before the kid turned to him. Joe laid a hand on his shoulder, dipping to see into his brother's eyes. "What's going through your head?"

Under his palm, his brother's muscles tightened. "Nothing."

"Seth, you can tell me the truth."

"That *is* the truth! Jeez, it's not like I can say something that's not there."

As if Joe wouldn't know hot air when he heard it.

"So, are you ready then? To meet your sister?"

"Yeah, sure." He got up, banging the chair up against the table so hard it sounded like a gunshot. Then he looked over at Kristen and said, "Will she understand? Who I am, I mean?"

"She knows our father had another child after he wasn't living with us anymore. And she understands what it means to have a brother. So yeah, I think she'll understand who you are."

"She needs a lot of help, doesn't she?"

"Yeah, she does," Joe said with a kick to the gut. Especially, Joe thought as they walked back to where Kristen was sitting, gleefully cutting construction paper into strips and gluing them into circles, to make sense of a world so out of sync with the one that damn extra chromosome had trapped her in.

Then again, he doubted she felt nearly as trapped as he did, he thought with a shudder of guilt. And again, as it had a few weeks before, the urge to shuck off the burden of responsibility swamped him, seduced him with promises of how much easier life would be if he just…

He would not, could not let himself complete the thought. Even when Taylor's calm, strong gaze caught his, her compassion and understanding a balm to his conflicted, tormented soul.

A balm…or a temptation? Because one glimpse into her beautiful face, a single remembered sigh or burst of laughter, and everything—*everything*—inside him screamed for surrender. To seek refuge in her arms, in her heart and mind and body, not just for a couple hours, or a few weeks, but for the rest of his life.

But to yield to that temptation—to run, to hide, to forget—would make him the most selfish bastard on the face of the planet. He broke his very unsteady gaze from her curious one—did she somehow sense what he was thinking?—letting it wash over his mother, his sister and little brother, tentatively checking each other out. People who'd already been let down by one man who didn't have the balls to live up to his responsibilities.

"Joe?"

He looked down, somehow not surprised to find Taylor standing there, concern beetling her brow, softly edging her questioning smile. His heart thundered inside his chest, at how much he'd grown used to having her in his life.

He tried a smile. "You survived my mother?"

"Oh, she's okay. Hey, at least she's there for her kids. Which is more than I can say for mine." Then she shook her head, as if refusing to let the obvious disappointment and bitterness gain a foothold, and said, "This is really hard on you, isn't it?"

He crossed his arms, legs spread, not giving a damn that she'd see straight through his macho posturing. "Nah, I'm fine." He smiled, feeling like his cheeks were about to crack. "It was a little awkward there for a second, but I think we're through the rough part now."

"Oh, Joe," she said on a sigh. "How clueless do you think I am?"

Then she walked away, and Joe watched her, ached for her, thinking, *Clueless?* She didn't even know the meaning of the word.

Seth stretched out on a patch of warm dirt in front of the cabin where Joe's mom and sister were staying, staring up at the sky and watching the clouds change shapes, something that had always made him feel better, for some reason. Kristen and Dani—Joe's mom had asked him to call her that—had been there for two whole days, and Seth still felt like he was playing some weird game where he didn't know the rules. Oh, Joe's mom was real nice and all. And she was a far better cook than Joe, that was for sure. But she was almost *too* nice, like the people behind the desk when you went to the doctor's or dentist's office. Like the more they smiled and laughed, the less it would hurt.

He'd been reading inside, but Kristen had been pestering him until he was about to go crazy, so he'd escaped. Joe was working—so what else was new?—so Joe's mom said he might as well spend the afternoon with her and Kristen, if that was okay with Joe. Seth had really hoped Joe would say no, but he didn't. In fact, he looked pretty relieved, and since Joe didn't look relieved a whole lot these days, Seth figured it wasn't to his advantage to add to Joe's worries.

He thought maybe a lot of Joe's problems had something to do with his work, but he didn't know what, only that whenever his brother talked to Hank or somebody who had something to do with his job, he didn't sound happy. A couple of times, Seth asked what the matter was, but Joe always said, "Nothing for you to worry about, buddy," with that tired smile that grown-ups never thought kids couldn't see straight through. So after a while, Seth stopped asking, since it was obvious he wasn't going to get an answer anyway.

But even worse than Joe's work problems—in Seth's opinion, anyway—was whatever was going on between him and Taylor. Jeez, Seth couldn't even bring up her name without a cloud coming over Joe's face, like it hurt to think about her. If you asked him—not that anybody was, but still—Joe and Taylor were in love with each other but didn't know what to do about it. Seth had watched lots of those stupid romance movies with his mom, where people were all the time acting dumb because they actually liked each other, so he figured he pretty much knew the signs. However, Seth also figured nobody would be much interested in hearing a kid's take on the issue—if he'd had any advice to give to begin with, which he didn't—so he kept quiet about that, too. After all, in most of those movies, everybody eventually stopped acting dumb and just went ahead and admitted they loved each other, so everything turned out okay in the end.

Except even Seth knew that life wasn't like the movies, and that, more often than not, things don't turn out in the end. And anyway, even if things *did* turn out okay for Joe and Taylor, where would that leave Seth?

A big, fat, fluffy cloud right over him started changing from a dog to a dinosaur. Kinda like a tyrannosaurus, but without the teeth. Seth folded his hands behind his head and kept his eyes fixed on the cloud, like if he stared hard enough, he could float right up there with it, where he didn't have to deal with Joe being grumpy or wondering what was going to happen at the end of the summer or trying to be nice to Joe's mom and especially his sister, which was turning out to be a lot harder than he thought it would be. That made him feel bad, because he knew it wasn't Kristen's fault that she was slow doing lots of stuff or that Seth couldn't always understand what she was saying.

"Whatcha doin'?"

Oh, brother. Or in this case, *sister.*

Seth looked up at Kristen, grinning down at him, and that bad feeling came over him again. He really wanted to like Kristen, but he didn't know how. Or if he could. Yesterday, in fact, they'd been in the supermarket with Dani and Kristen had thrown her arms around Seth and given him this huge hug and embarrassed the life out of him, not to mention nearly knocking the breath out of him, too. And then he'd felt all guilty about feeling embarrassed when all she was doing was showing how happy she was to have him in her life now.

Anyway, here she was, all happy and stuff, and here he was, not happy at all. But it wasn't like he could say, "Go away," because that would be mean and hurt her feelings—and he'd already learned that Kristen's feelings hurt real easy—or even, "I'd like to be alone," because he didn't know yet if that would hurt her feelings, too. So he was stuck.

"I'm watching the clouds," he said.

"Yeah?" She looked up, squinting through her glasses.

"Yeah. You ever do that?" he added, just for something to say.

"Uh-uh." Her gaze lowered to his. "C'n I lay down beside you?"

"Sure, I guess."

With a grunt, his sister lowered herself to the ground and said, "If I get dirty, I'm telling Mom it's…your fault."

Well, he hadn't expected that, and to tell the truth, it made him laugh. Maybe there was more going on in her head than you could tell unless you knew her. Kristen laughed, too, a loud, "HA! HA! HA!," that was going to take some getting used to, but Seth figured he could do that. He pointed up at the tyrannosaurus, which was now changing into something else.

"That one kinda looked like a dinosaur a minute ago. But now…it looks like an elephant. See the way that piece coming off the side looks like a trunk?"

Kristen looked hard at the cloud for several seconds, breathing loudly through her mouth, then said, "Uh-uh. It's a man, running." Her chubby fingers jabbed at the sky. "There's his…legs, see? And one arm…is behind his back."

Seth angled his head a bit, then grinned. "Yeah, I see it."

Kristen moved her head to look at him, then looked back up at the sky, tucking her hands behind her head, too. Imitating Seth. "This is fun, Seth." She had to say his name slowly because the *th* sound was hard for her. At first, it irritated him; but he was getting used to it, so it wasn't so bad now. "Like watch-ing TV, huh?"

He chuckled. "Yeah, I guess. Except quieter."

They laid there for some time without saying anything, just feeling the warm earth underneath them and listening to the leaves swishing in the breeze and the buzzing of a bee a few feet away, and Seth shut his eyes, feeling a little more relaxed. Then he remembered something Taylor'd said, about how she wasn't close to her sisters because they didn't really have anything in common, except for having the same parents. That got Seth to thinking about how, on the surface, Kristen and him didn't have anything in common, either. But they both liked to lie and look up at the sky, and for sure they both loved Joe. And something told him she also knew what it felt like to never really fit in anywhere, even if maybe she couldn't put it into words. It wasn't much to build on, but it was better than nothing, he guessed. Because, after all, he did need to keep his options open….

"Joe! Joe!"

Seth jerked—he hadn't even heard the Blazer pull up because

he must've dozed off or something. Kristen, however, who'd gotten to her feet awfully fast for somebody with such short legs, was nearly over to the car by the time Seth pulled himself together. She was going on to Joe about how they'd been seeing pictures in the clouds, and Joe looked over and grinned for Seth as if he were real proud of him, which made Seth feel all warm inside and kinda sad at the same time. Then Dani came out onto the porch and said the enchiladas were just about ready, and sure enough, Seth got a whiff of green chili that made his stomach growl. So for the moment, things weren't too bad.

But even he knew better than to trust in the moment.

Joe had to admit, a bellyful of his mother's enchiladas and homemade sopaipillas went a long way toward mellowing him out. At least enough to make him tolerable in polite company for a little while.

"So," Danielle said, covering the leftover enchiladas with foil, "you thought any about where you and Seth are going to live after you finish up here?"

So much for feeling mellow.

"Not as much as I should have," he admitted, leaning back in his chair in the dining area. On the other side of the room, Kristen and Seth were watching one of the *Spy Kids* movies, both on their stomachs on the floor and their chins propped in their hands. "Although I should probably think about looking for a house since my apartment's only a one-bedroom."

"In Tulsa?"

"Where else?"

"If you get this promotion, you mean?"

"I'll get it, don't worry."

"I'm not worried," his mother said mildly, stacking plates in the dishwasher. "Whether you get it or not. But don't count your chickens, *mijo.* Although a house would be nice. Someplace with a big yard, so Seth could have a dog, maybe." Then she slipped in, "Maybe we could find a house together."

Joe knew he should say, "Sure, why not?" or something equally agreeable, but the words refused to budge from his brain.

"It's not that outlandish an idea," Danielle said when he didn't respond, sparing him a glance as she opened the refrigerator to put the enchiladas inside. "I could help you with Seth. And it would be good for the kids, giving them time to get to know each other—"

"Seth's not your responsibility," Joe said, then lowered his voice. "And you've got your hands full with Kristen as it is."

She looked at him oddly, but then she shrugged. "It was just a thought," she said, and then his cell rang, cutting off anything further she might have said.

"J-Joe?"

"Taylor?" Instantly, every nerve cell went on full alert. "What's wrong?"

"Oh, God, Joe—something's the matter with Oakley, he can't move his hind legs! I—I went to call him to go for a walk with me and he couldn't get up! I'm so sorry to bother you, but he's too heavy for me to get into the truck to get him to the vet and I tried everyone else but nobody's home—"

"I'll be there in two minutes," he said, already halfway to the door.

Chapter 14

Joe pulled up in front of Taylor's and bolted from his car, leaving the engine running and his door open as he ran around to open the hatch. Taylor was sitting on the porch next to the prone dog, holding his huge head in her lap and crooning, "You hang on, you overgrown fleabag, you hear me?" over and over, periodically swiping at the tears streaming down her face. Joe'd never seen her look so completely destroyed, and it ripped him wide-open inside.

"If you can just put him in the truck for me so I can get him to the vet—"

He shot her a quelling look, then squatted down to stroke the dog's side. "Hey, you old pain in the butt," he said softly, "what the hell'd you do to yourself?" The dog made a funny noise in his throat, then lifted his head to schlurp a sloppy kiss across Joe's chin. "Yeah, I love you, too," he said, hefting the enormous beast into his arms and starting back toward the Blazer. "Only pardon me if I don't kiss you back, okay?"

"What are you doing…?"

"He'll be more comfortable in the Blazer."

She didn't argue. Not that it would've done her any good. "I already c-called the vet's emergency number," she said, and he guessed from her voice she was shaking real bad inside. "He's m-meeting us there. It's out on the highway, about halfway to Claremore."

"Yeah, I know where it is," Joe said, gently laying the dog onto the old blanket he always kept in the car, hearing the passenger side door slam shut in tandem with his closing the hatch. After he got in and gunned the accelerator, he said, "It's gonna be fine, honey, you'll see—"

"And maybe it won't!" she said, her gaze jerking to his. "Not everything can be fixed, you know!"

Despite knowing it was her worry talking, and not her, Joe couldn't help the bolt of pain that lanced through him. "I'm well aware of that," he said stiffly, "but predicting a bad outcome isn't gonna do any of us a lick of good, is it?"

She yanked her head back around. "I'm sorry, it's just…"

"You're scared, I know. It's okay." Dusk was rapidly giving way to dark; Joe put his headlights on, their straight beams' piercing the gloom a comfort, somehow.

"Where's Seth?" Taylor asked suddenly, like maybe he'd forgotten him somewhere.

"With my mom and sister. We were over there for dinner. And we were long since done," Joe said in a voice meant to cut her apology off at the pass, although whether it worked on Taylor or not remained to be seen. "He wanted to come, but I thought it was better if he didn't."

"No," she said after a couple of beats. "Especially if…" She stopped.

Joe glanced over, his insides cramping at the expression on her face in the murky light. "You got any idea what the problem might be?"

She shook her head. "He was fine at dinnertime. At least, I thought he was. I'd taken him out with m-me when I went for a bike ride this morning, so I guess I just thought he was worn out from that, although…" She rammed a hand through her tangled hair, let it drop, then shifted in her seat as if she couldn't get comfortable. Finally, she unlatched her seat belt so she could twist around to touch the dog.

"Put your seat belt back on, Taylor," Joe quietly ordered. "I don't need to be worrying about you as well as the dog."

Out of the corner of his eye, he thought he saw her give him an odd look before sitting around again and clicking her shoulder harness back into place.

"You probably think I'm crazy, getting so worked up over an animal."

Joe frowned. "Why would I think that?"

A shrug was her only reply, giving Joe the impression she was having a struggle with hanging on to her emotions.

"Honey," he said, not looking at her, "only a fool wouldn't understand how much of a friend Oakley is to you. When he hurts, you hurt. That's just logical."

"Never mind that you called him a pain in the butt."

"That's because he is." He looked over, so she'd be sure to see he was smiling. "But in my experience, most family members are pains in the butt. Doesn't mean we don't love 'em anyway."

She contorted herself as much as the seat belt would allow to look back at the dog for a moment, then faced front again and said, "You ever have a dog as a kid?"

Joe shook his head. "Nope. My father thought they were too much trouble. But then, he seemed to think his kids were too much trouble, too."

His own response caught him off guard, although not nearly as much as it would have a few weeks ago, when he would have rather cut out his tongue rather than letting anybody see inside his head. But somehow, around Taylor, it didn't seem right keeping everything all bottled up inside the way he usually did. Except she didn't comment, which was unusual for Taylor, he thought. He looked over to see she'd turned her head.

"Go ahead and cry, if you want," he said. "I can take it."

Something like a laugh burbled from her lips before she said, "I'm not c-crying."

"Well, that's okay, then. But should you want to, don't feel you have to hold it in on my account."

She sat stone still for a couple of seconds. Then she yanked open her purse and rooted around in it until she unearthed a package of tissues, barely getting out, "You may regret saying that," before the floodgates opened.

One hand firmly clamped around the steering wheel, Joe reached over and cupped the back of her neck, letting his fingers tenderly massage that sweet little hollow under her skull, as if he could take all her sorrow and fear into himself, somehow, and bear her burden for her. Because while he'd been telling the truth about not being one of those men who got all weird when a woman cried, that wasn't the same as not being profoundly affected by a woman's tears. This woman's tears, in any case. It was just his nature to want to fix things. But like she'd said, not everything was fixable, a fact which wasn't always easy to accept.

By the time they got to the vet's a few minutes later, though, her tears had more or less dried up, and she was more or less back to being the tough little thing he knew. The vet, a big, burly gray-haired guy of about fifty or so, came right out the minute they pulled up, swiftly removing Oakley from the back of the Blazer and carting him inside and on back to the exam room. After asking Taylor several questions, he then said he had a few ideas but needed to take some X rays to be sure. He said they should go back to the waiting room and he'd be out to talk with them as soon as he knew anything.

Joe led Taylor out to the bare-bones waiting area; on a Sunday night, they had the place all to themselves. He steered her over to a padded bench, pulling her down with him and wrapping one arm around her shoulders. She seemed to think over the wisdom of this for a moment or two, then leaned into him. Other than the occasional dog yapping or plaintive, questioning meow from the back, the place was almost eerily quiet.

"Now, see," Joe said quietly, "would you have been able to do this—" he squeezed her shoulder "—with any of those other people you'd tried to call?"

She let out a little muffled laugh. "Probably not. Since their wives might not have understood. Well, I did try calling Sam Frazier, but we don't have that kind of relationship."

Silence descended like a lead curtain, trapping on the other side all those unspoken questions both of them were dying to ask and neither was about to. Taylor suddenly pulled away to snatch a dog-earred—as it were—copy of *Dog Fancy* off the low table in front of them, madly flipping through the pages like she were going be tested on the contents in the morning. Joe calmly—on the outside, anyway, since anything having to do with relationships rendered him decidedly not calm—tugged the magazine from her fingers and said, "So what kind of relationship do *we* have?"

"When I figure that out, I'll get back to you, 'kay? So give me back my magazine—" she plucked it back out of his hand "—so I can keep both my mind and mouth occupied before I get myself into any more trouble."

Joe leaned over and riffled through the other mags, finally settling on a five-year-old *U.S News & World Report.* Some time later, Dr. Harrison came out, looking relieved.

"X rays look good, no apparent spinal trauma or arthritis, so I went on a little search-and-destroy mission and found this." He held up a vial containing something that looked like a grape with legs. Taylor visibly recoiled.

"Ohmigod. *That's* what got my dog?"

"Tick poisoning is rare, but it does happen," the vet said. "For some reasons, a few of the buggers secrete a toxin that causes paralysis. And possibly death, if not caught in time. You were smart to get Oakley in to me as soon as you did."

Her hand went to her throat as she visibly paled. "I check him for ticks every single night in warm weather...how on earth did I miss one that size?"

"With all those skin folds?" Dr. Harrison chuckled. "Don't beat yourself up. Took me nearly twenty minutes to find it, too. And we doused Oak with tick spray, too, just in case the critter brought buddies to the dinner party." Then he went on to say he'd given the dog a painkiller and some antibiotic, he wanted to keep Oakley overnight but that the dog should be up and moving again within hours. So Taylor was to go on home and put her mind at ease since, in all likelihood, the dog was going to be just fine.

"You're sure?" Taylor said, and Joe could see it was going to take some convincing to get her to leave, but the vet smiled and said, "I imagine you'll be cussing him out again in a day or two at the most," which seemed to assuage her enough for Joe to at least get her outside and back into the truck. But she kept her eyes on the clinic until they were too far away for her to see it anymore. Then she turned around and sighed.

"I really am pathetic," she said, and Joe got irked with her and told her if she said that again…well, she just better not, was all.

Got a little laugh out of her, though. Then she remarked again about the grossness of the swollen tick, and Joe—knowing full well what he was doing—said it was a shame, though, the vet hadn't popped it so they could've seen the blood spurt all over the place. Sure enough, she let did this whole shuddering, *"Ick! Ick! Ick!"* thing, her hands waving wildly in the air, which he found every bit as entertaining as he'd hoped. Then they both laughed, her with her hand over her mouth, shaking her head, and she may have mumbled something about men never growing up. Since she didn't seem unduly perturbed, however, he didn't take her comment too seriously.

Even though it was closing in on ten o'clock, he figured he'd better call his mother and Seth and let her know what was going on. Except Danielle said Seth had fallen asleep on her bed a half hour before and under no circumstances was Joe to disturb him.

"You just leave him be," she said when he tried to protest anyway. "I'll sleep out here on the sofa bed. Then I'll take him on over to camp in the morning." Then she lowered her voice. "Kristen's been asking me if she could go, too, but I didn't know if it would be okay or not, so I didn't say anything. But since you're with Taylor, could you ask her?"

"Ma, it's for little kids."

"Your sister wouldn't care. And you know, the more she gets out and interacts with people, the better it is for her."

By now, Taylor was whispering, "What is it?" so he finally told his mother to hang on and asked her about Kristen coming to day camp.

"Oh," Taylor said. She thought things over for a second or two before saying, "I don't see why not. We have visitors all the time."

"I heard," Danielle said. "Tell her thank-you and we'll see her tomorrow," then she disconnected the call without saying good-bye, which was nothing unusual for his mother.

"Seth fell asleep over there," he said, slipping his phone back in his shirt pocket. "So it looks like I don't have to rush back to get him." Which he realized could have definite…overtones. Now the question was…did he want them to?

He felt her gaze on the side of his face and glanced over. "What?"

"How long have you been beating yourself up for not being able to accept your sister's condition?" she said gently.

He nearly drove off the road. Feeling his jaw tighten as he reclaimed control of the vehicle, he said, "I have no idea what—"

"Joe. This is me you're talking to."

The odometer clicked over another mile. Then he said, "A long time."

"Because it's something you can't fix?"

"Maybe. I never stopped to analyze it, you know?"

She laid a hand on his wrist and said simply, "It's okay," and then promptly changed the subject. "You really shouldn't talk on your cell while you're driving, you know."

He looked at her as long as he dared, and not because of the cell phone comment, then smiled and looked back at the road. "That wouldn't be you being worried about me, would it?"

"You? Heck, no. I'm the one sitting in the death seat."

"Never mind that it's been a good five minutes since we've passed another vehicle."

"There are other things to worry about. Like deer, and..." She made a circular motion with one hand. "And cows...and...things that, you know, appear unexpectedly. From out of nowhere."

"I'll be sure to keep an eye out," he said, not even trying to hide his smile. "But in any case, I wouldn't worry if I were you." He nodded toward her side of the dash. "Airbags."

"Ah. So what you're saying is, if we crash because you're distracted on a phone call, I might still end up with two broken legs, not to mention nasty airbag burns, but hey, I'd still be alive."

Joe actually considered keeping his thoughts to himself, but apparently, thinking about it and actually following through were two different things, because he heard himself say, "Honey, believe me...as long as you're sitting beside me, distraction-wise, the cell phone is the least of your worries."

"Oh," was all she said, but Joe figured there was a lot more where that little word had come from.

A few minutes later, they pulled up in front of her house, the atmosphere was suddenly—well, not so suddenly, actually—charged between them. The air was thick and sultry and honeysuckle-scented, the kind that clung to your skin. Crickets chirped and peepers peeped and neither of them made a move. Or said anything for some time. Until finally he heard the sharp intake of her breath, followed by a breathy half laugh.

"The place seems so...unfinished without Oakley." She looked out the window. "Like half the porch is missing."

Slowly, Joe reached over and skimmed a knuckle down her cheek.

"I don't have anywhere I have to be tonight," he said softly.

She turned to him, smiled and said, "Oh, yes, you do."

Thank you, Lord, Taylor thought as Joe followed her into the dark, still house, *for letting Joe be the one to suggest he stay. And not just because I'm thinking about sleeping with him again,* she hastily added, *but because I really don't feel much like being alone right now.*

She could practically hear a voice from above going, *Uh-huh. Right.*

Okay, so if things went in that direction, she certainly wouldn't mind, but it was true. She didn't want to be alone, and Joe was who she wanted to be with, but there was no way she was going to do the needy female bit. So Joe's taking the lead had been a profound relief.

Of course, she had no clue what was going through his mind, she pondered as she went through the living room and into the kitchen, turning on lights along the way. Then she looked over at him, leaning in her kitchen doorway with one hand tucked in his front pocket and fairly radiating carnal thoughts, and she thought, *Who am I kidding?*

"I'm starving," she said, finding herself dragging out a baking pan and the fixings for corn bread. "How about you?"

Joe got a funny tilted smile on his face. "That wouldn't be you sidestepping the issue, would it?"

"And what issue might that be?" she asked, goading him. At his raised eyebrow, she said, "Ohhhh…I suppose you mean whether or not we have sex tonight?"

"That would be the one, yep."

Taylor stooped down in front of a lower cabinet to get out plastic bins of flour and cornmeal that she used on rare occasion, hauling them up onto her counter. "No, that would be me being hungry and having a sudden craving for corn bread." She scanned the recipe she kept inside the cornmeal bin, then went about gathering the oil and baking powder and eggs and what-all as if she actually knew what she was doing, all the while aware of Joe's inordinately curious stare from a few feet away. "Do you like corn bread?" she asked, fully aware she hadn't yet answered his question.

"Who doesn't?"

"Well, that would be my take on it, but you'd be surprised at the number of people who do not, in fact, like it at all." She started measuring and tossing ingredients into a big glass bowl, cracking an egg on its edge. "But I've loved it ever since I was little and Mama used to make it every single Sunday." A knot formed in the center of her chest as the freed egg slithered down the side of the bowl, settling onto the dry ingredients, bumped from behind by a second egg like kids on a Slip 'N Slide too impatient to wait their turns. "'Course," she said, taking a fork to the mixture and mushing it all together, "it's been a long time since Mama made corn bread. Or anything else. All the cooks and maids we had, and not a single one of them knew how to make corn bread, do you believe it?"

The tears came out of nowhere, and for no good reason that she could tell. But when Joe took her by the shoulders and turned her around, enfolding her in his arms with his chin resting atop her head, she was not about to protest. She cried for a minute or so, then slid a hand over her cheek and mumbled, "I don't know what's wrong with me tonight," and he said, "Nothing's wrong with you," his voice all rumbly underneath her ear. She sighed and snuggled closer, smelling him and feeling him and wishing…

No, not wishing for anything. Just enjoying the moment. Then she leaned back to look up at him, sniffling a little, her fingers curled around the soft folds of his shirt, and said, "I'm not sidestepping anything. I definitely want sex. With you," she added, blushing a little. "But not until I've had at least three pieces of corn bread."

His mouth stretched into one of those smiles a woman knows is meant only for her, that makes her brain take a hike, and he slowly forked one hand through her hair, making her scalp sizzle and everything else snap to attention. Then he dropped a kiss on the top of her head and whispered, "Deal," and the word *life-altering* came to her.

Taylor pulled away to finish up getting the corn bread batter into the pan and then put it in the oven, setting the timer for twenty-five minutes. When she turned around, Joe was leaning against the fridge, hands shoved into his front pockets, flat-out gaping at her. With anyone else, she might have felt self-conscious, but not with Joe. At least, not anymore.

Self-conscious, no. Steamy, however…hooboy. She pushed up the kitchen window a little higher, then opened the kitchen door. A moth fluttered in and started pinging around the overhead light, casting spooky, darting shadows over the room.

"Is it my imagination," she said, "or are you picturing me nekkid?"

"Actually," he said, his gaze roaming where it would, "I'm picturing you in an apron."

"Let me guess. And nothing else, right?"

He grinned. "Can't get anything past you."

"Well, I hate to break this to you, but I don't *do* the role-playing thang."

"Party pooper."

"Whatever." She reached into the cabinet to get out two glasses. "Actually, I tried it once, with my husband when we were first married." Toting the glasses to the table, she shook her head. "I just felt silly. Not exactly conducive to getting in the mood."

"Unlike watching a naked man chasing a dog with condoms in its mouth."

"Exactly."

"Like I said. Strange."

"Aw…bet you say that to all the girls."

"No, ma'am. Since I've never met anybody as strange as you."

"Boy. You really don't get out much, do you?" she said, and he got this funny look on his face, after which he pushed himself away from the fridge and walked out into her living room. Taylor followed to find him looking at the framed family photos she'd put up on the far wall.

"Mom and Dad, when they were first married," she said, pointing to each one in turn. "Then later, when I was about six.

My sister Erika with her husband and kids. And that's Abby, the 'baby,' with her husband."

His gaze swung back to the more recent photo of her parents. "I see where the red hair came from."

"Daddy's hair started going gray shortly after that. I don't really remember him with red hair."

Joe looked at her. "You loved him, didn't you?"

"I adored him."

He slung one arm around her shoulders and led her back to sit on the sofa. He propped one foot on her coffee table, positioning her so her back nestled against his side.

"So tell me about him," he said.

"You don't really want to hear about any of that."

"I'm not asking to be polite, I'm asking because I'm nosy."

She laughed. And started talking.

By the time the corn bread scent filtered in from the kitchen, she'd told him about how her father had gotten screwed over by his business partner when she and her sisters were still small, how he'd determined to start over, bounce back.

"And did he?"

"Yep. By the time I was eight or so, we had the big house in Houston, the pool, the new cars every two years, the whole nine yards. We just didn't have Daddy." The oven buzzer went off; she reluctantly untangled herself from his arm, draped across her front, and scurried into the kitchen to get the corn bread. Overbaked corn bread was the pits.

"Smells great," Joe said, coming in behind her.

"You want milk?"

"What else?" he said, his face falling when he pulled the carton of skim milk out of the refrigerator. But he gamely carried it to the table, only to laugh when she unwrapped a stick of real butter and plonked it on a butter dish. "Real butter, but skim milk?"

"It's a girl thing," she said, setting the hot corn bread on a trivet in the center of the table.

"Huh. Maybe I could stir some butter in the milk and make it taste like milk again."

"Whatever floats your boat." She set two plates on the table and started cutting the steaming bread. "Anyway, to continue the saga of Taylor's dysfunctional childhood…after my father died, the family totally fell apart. Or should I say *more* apart. We all lived in the same house, but that was about it." She lifted out a square of corn bread, setting it on Joe's plate.

He sliced his bread in half, then slipped in a pat of butter. "And now?"

"Now I talk to their voice mail a lot," she said brightly, buttering her own bread.

"That sucks."

"Pretty much my take on it, yeah. What's wrong?" she said as Joe groaned.

"Only that this is the best damn corn bread I've ever had."

"Yeah?" she said, beaming.

"Yeah." He took another crumbly bite, wiping his hand on a napkin, then locked their gazes. "Now tell me about your ex."

Taylor shrugged. "Not a whole lot to tell. I married a man who I guess reminded me of Dad. You know, driven to succeed and all that fun stuff. But after six months, I wondered why I'd bothered. Or why he had. I figured it was time to get a divorce when I realized cobwebs were collecting on his side of the bed. Not to mention—" she took a sip of milk "—in certain parts of my anatomy."

She somehow didn't think Joe's choking on his milk was entirely due to its low fat content. When he recovered, he said, "Did you love him?"

That was worth a moment's reflection. "I was dazzled by him. By his energy and focus. But love?" She shook her head. "I was never much into the whole long-suffering wifey thing. So what about you?" she said, licking buttery crumbs off her fingers.

"You mean girlfriends?"

"Or wives, whatever."

He glanced down, his mouth twitching. "No wives. And no one I'd call a real girlfriend. There've been lovers, though."

"Well, duh. Anyone serious?"

"Not really, no." Amazing, the loneliness packed in those three little words.

"Anyone *recent?*" she asked, even though she knew better.

"One," he said, taking another bite of corn bread.

Great. Now she had to deal with the post-nasal drip sensation of jealousy trickling through her. "Yeah? How recent are we talking? Exactly."

Joe grinned into her eyes, his own darkening with intent. "Ten days."

She threw a greasy, balled up napkin at him, which landed in his plate. He laughed. And started to unbutton his shirt. Right at her kitchen table. She stared, fascinated, as the words, "You done with your corn bread?" dimly registered in her hormone-drunk brain.

"Mmm-hmm," she managed.

"Good," he said, tossing his shirt…somewhere. Then he stood, planted his hands on the table, and leaned over to lick a corn bread crumb from the corner of her mouth, which led her to seriously rethink the whole apron fantasy thing.

Seth woke up with a start, confused for a couple seconds until he remembered where he was. Yawning, he pushed back the light blanket somebody'd put on top of him and got up, padding out to the living room in his bare feet. From behind the closed door to the other bedroom, he could hear Kristen snoring. Joe's mom was sitting up on the pulled out sofa bed, watching TV in a short-sleeved robe with little pink flowers all over it. She jerked a little when she realized he was standing there, then smiled at him. "Hey, *chico*…how come you're awake?"

He shrugged, still half asleep. "Where's Joe?"

"Oh, he called after you'd fallen asleep, so I told him just to let you stay here. You want something to eat?"

Seth shook his head, then remembered why he was there to

begin with. Almost afraid to hear the answer, he asked, "Is Oakley okay?"

"The dog? Yes, they think he'll be fine. Something about a tick poisoning him, can you believe it?" Seth shook his head, even though he didn't think she really expected him to answer her. "Anyway, Joe said they were keeping him overnight at the vet's, just as a precaution. So I'm taking you to camp tomorrow. You and Kristen, actually, since Taylor said it was okay for her to come visit."

Although Seth was glad Oakley was going to be all right, he still got a funny feeling in the pit of his stomach, like something was out of whack but he couldn't quite figure out what. Part of it had to do with Kristen coming to day camp, because he didn't know if that meant he had to watch out for her while she was there or what, but that wasn't all of it.

"So where's Joe? Is he still with Taylor?"

Joe's mom looked back at the TV. One of those boring old movies in black-and-white, it looked like. "They got back from the vet's a long time ago," she said, like he wouldn't know she hadn't answered the question.

"So how come he didn't come get me?"

"I told you," Dani said, facing him again, "you were already asleep. Which you need to be again or you'll be all draggy tomorrow, and you don't want that, do you? So come on," she said, pushing herself off the bed. "Let's get you tucked in again, okay?" She waved to him, clearly expecting him to follow, so he did. This time, she pulled back the bedspread and suggested he take off his T-shirt and shorts so she could wash them for the next day in the little washing machine in the bathroom. So he did—underneath the sheets, so she wouldn't see—and handed them to her. Then she leaned over and kissed him on the forehead, like his mother used to do, and left him.

All he had to say was, the inside of his head felt like a bunch of Legos without the instructions—no matter how hard he tried to put the pieces together, they just would not go.

* * *

The first Joe was aware of the phone ringing was when his skin suddenly cooled from where a warm, naked woman had been a second before. Vaguely thinking *Come back,* he opened one eye to register that she was sitting on the edge of the bed, all luminescent bare back and lush bottom. As his brain cells began to slowly regenerate, he took in the odd sensory impression—rumpled, soft sheets smelling of sex, Taylor's sleep-roughened voice, a glint of light in her tangled hair. He rolled over to press a kiss at the base of her spine, making her voice hitch. She twisted around, grinning; light leaking in from the living room glanced off the curve of one breast, highlighting an already hardening nipple. His mouth said, "Gimme," as tenderness roared through him.

He was a goner.

And not because of the sex, even though there was nothing to complain about in that department. Because…because when they were together, all he could think was, *Oh, yeah.* And because she *got* him. Understood him. Because—he thought back to her comment about Kirsten in the car—he knew he could bare his soul to her without fear of her somehow using it against him. Even though they still hardly knew each other, he'd already grown to trust Taylor more than he trusted himself.

And if that wasn't confusing the hell out of him, he didn't know what was.

"Yes, Dr. Harrison," he heard her say, relief shining in her voice, "I'll come get him around lunchtime, if that's okay…. Thanks so much!" She clicked off the phone and set it back in its stand; Joe tugged her back against his chest. "Oakley's okay," she said, her hair tickling his nose.

"I knew he would be," he said, then flipped her on her back, nestling between her warm, blessedly receptive thighs. *Someone should write a sonnet about these thighs,* he thought, only what he said was, "I think this calls for a little celebration, don't you?"

"No arguments here."

"No cobwebs, either," he murmured, and she laughed. But when she reached for him, he grabbed her wrist. "Not so fast. I've got plans for you."

"Plans are good," she said, shutting her eyes, then giggling as he nuzzled her neck. Then he kissed the base of her throat, before moving to her breast. "I especially like those plans," she whispered as his mouth closed around that cute little nipple.

"Yeah, me, too," he said, and she said something about not talking with his mouth full, so he decided to stop talking—since he wasn't much into multitasking, anyway—and concentrate on suckling. Which, judging from her whimpering and arching and moans, was an inspired move on his part.

"More..." she said, and he said, "Not to worry," and shifted to the other breast where he tugged and nipped and messed around until she bucked underneath him.

"If you touch me, I'll..."

"...scream?" he said, reaching between her legs, smiling when they fell right open. Never one to turn down an invitation, Joe let his fingers do the...walking, her slickness inciting a riot in his groin as he dawdled here and lingered there until he heard her gasp.

Now, bringing her to climax at this point would have been a no-brainer, since he figured she was about a millisecond away. But Joe wanted more, wanted to give her more, wanted to do something for her he'd never been much inclined to do for another woman. But first he was going to confuse her a little, because a confused Taylor was truly a joy to behold.

So he raised up to kiss her on the mouth, his hands cradling her face, letting his lips and tongue convey all the stuff in his head he wasn't sure he could put into words. And sure enough, when he lifted up to look into her eyes, she was one confused chick.

"What are you doing?" she asked, breathing kinda heavy.

Joe just grinned.

He grabbed a condom, watching her watch him as he rolled it on, then began a leisurely stroll down her body, revisiting her breasts for a few seconds because it seemed a shame to bypass them when there they were, just begging for a little attention, before continuing south over her belly, her hips, that delectable spot where her smooth skin gave way to soft, warm curls. It was long about this point that she apparently caught on to his intentions because she made a funny little noise in her throat.

"Open for me," he whispered.

She made another funny little noise and said, "Are you sure?"

"Well, since I'm in the neighborhood and all, I thought it might be fun."

He thought she might have muttered "Thank you," but he wasn't all that sure she was thanking *him*.

Not that he cared.

What he cared about, he thought as he kissed her where she was hottest, was making her as happy as he could, for as long as he could. Not that this was a chore, by any means—she smelled of some girly soap and sex and woman and damn, he was having a good time, nibbling and nuzzling her up…up…up…until she spasmed under him on a high, thin cry.

He rose up and plunged inside her, catching her orgasm on its descent and yanking it up again on the current of his own release, startling an "Ooooohhhh!" from her mouth, so close to his ear, even closer to his heart, pounding an inch from hers.

Afterwards, they lay panting in each other's arms, still joined. Then he heard the muffled giggle in his ear.

"You're just full of surprises, aren'tcha?" she said.

Joe hefted himself to his elbows to smile into her eyes. And kiss a nipple while he was at it. "Is this a bad thing?"

"No-no-no, not at all. But damn, you're gonna spoil me."

"You deserve to be spoiled," he said.

Too many seconds passed before she whispered, "So do you," and he thought, *Yep. Total goner.*

Chapter 15

Mary-Jo, Wes's secretary, was on the phone when Joe got to the office the next day, but she smiled for him anyway, yanking open her middle desk drawer to get his pay envelope. By the time Joe pocketed it, though, she was done with her call and was in the mood to chat. She asked about his mother and sister and how work was going on the two projects, the way she always did. Except anybody with half a brain could hear the worry fringing her words. Before he had a chance to ask her if everything was okay, she said, "You talk to Wes lately?"

"Actually, I was just about to ask you if he was in. I take it he isn't?"

Her mouth pulled tight, like a smashed pair of red licorice sticks. "That man has not set foot in this office but three times in the last two weeks. And half the time I try to reach him, I either get his machine or his cell phone's turned off. So I was wondering if you know something I don't." Now the licorice sticks got all droopy at the corners. "Judging from your expression, I assume that's a 'no.'"

Joe shook his head. Even though Wes didn't have a problem with delegating responsibility, Joe'd never known him not to keep close tabs on every detail of his business. In order to preserve what little was left of his sanity, Joe had told himself the glitches over the past several weeks had been an aberration, but if Wes was even staying out of Mary-Jo's way…

"I asked Riley, too, and he doesn't know any more than anybody else. Oh, Joe, what am I going to do if… if something happens? I can't afford to lose this job. Not with my mother ailing the way she's been and Medicare only picking up part of the tab. And you know it's not easy for a woman my age to find another job at the drop of a hat."

"And maybe we shouldn't jump to conclusions," Joe said gently, handing the now weeping brunette a box of tissues from the corner of her desk. "He's been paying his bills, hasn't he?"

Mary-Jo honked into the tissue, then let out a shaky sigh. "He took the bookkeeping away from me a couple weeks ago, said his wife wanted to do it, she needed something to keep her occupied now that the girls were away…" She dabbed at her eyes, leaving black smears on the tissue. "I don't know, Joe. I just don't know. But I've got one of my feelings, and that's not good."

No, it wasn't. Especially since Mary-Jo's "feelings" were rarely off the mark. But then she got a phone call—from her mother, sounded like—so Joe took the opportunity to escape, since she was clearly looking for words of comfort and Joe was fresh out at the moment.

The sun lanced through his shirt when he stepped outside, much the same way all these unsettled thoughts were burning a hole in his brain. He was beginning to feel like he was walking blindfolded down an unfamiliar path, unsure whether his next step might send him hurtling over the edge of a cliff. It was not a pleasant feeling.

Since his bank's drive-through line reached clear to the next county, he parked and went inside to deposit his check. He'd just finished his transaction, politely sidestepping the dimple-cheeked little teller's attempt to flirt with him, when he heard "Joe Salazar? Is that you?" from a few feet away. Slipping his billfold back into his jeans, he looked over, breaking into a grin for Mitch Carlson, a contractor who'd worked off and on for Wes over the years. Joe'd always liked Mitch, a good ole boy in fancy boots and a white cowboy hat with a laugh that registered a good 6.5 on the Richter scale. After a minute or so of truncated answers to the requisite "whatcha-been-up-tos?", Mitch folded his arms across his padded stomach and gave Joe a speculative look.

"You still working for Wes, I take it?"

"Yep."

"You happy?"

Figuring this was one of those times when a smart man played his cards close to his chest, Joe said, "Can't complain. Why?"

"As it happens, I've been meanin' to give you a call. Don't know if you're aware of this, but I hooked up with a local architect to develop a gated community south of town. And since neither of us intends to be a one-trick pony, we figure this is just the beginning." A sly grin crossed the other man's face. "I know your work, Joe. Haven't run into anybody yet who's worked with you who didn't have good things to say. So, you know, if you're looking for a change…" Huge shoulders shrugged, followed by an eyeball-to-eyeball stare. "I'll match whatever Wes is paying you, plus throw in an extra ten percent."

Joe's eyebrows lifted even as the air swooshed out of his lungs for a second. "Gee, Mitch, I'm really flattered…"

"Okay, fifteen percent."

Grinning, Joe slipped his hands into his back pockets. "Like I said, I'm flattered. But Wes was there for me when I really needed a leg up, and I've been with him ever since. Wouldn't seem right to throw him over just because."

"Twenty percent, then," Mitch said, and Joe laughed outright.

"You're making it damn hard to keep sayin' no."

"That was the idea. Joe…" Blue eyes speared through him, all serious, as he lowered his voice. "I know your family situation. You can't tell me the extra money wouldn't come in handy."

"And I won't insult your intelligence by saying it wouldn't. But sometimes, money isn't the only issue."

After a moment, the older man nodded, then clapped Joe on the shoulder. "I admire your loyalty, son. Which, ironically, is one of the reasons I was so hot to have you come on board. So I'll say no more. Except…" He tugged his wallet out of his back pocket and extracted a business card. "You ever change your mind, you let me know. And I mean that. *Anytime* you want to come work for me, you just give me a holler." Then he put out his hand, they shook, and the big man clomped off through the small bank and on out to the biggest, meanest, blackest four-by-four Joe'd ever seen.

Joe got back in the Blazer, but instead of starting up the engine, he sat there, trying to sort out his thoughts. To say he felt torn in two didn't even begin to cover it. It hadn't just been loyalty keeping him from expressing more interest in Mitch's offer, although that was a large part of it. Whatever was or wasn't going on with his boss, after everything he'd done for Joe he deserved better than to be left twisting in the breeze at the first sign of trouble. But more than that, Wes'd been around a long time, weathering fluctuations in the economy with barely a burp. However, while Mitch Carlson had always been a reliable contractor, putting on a builder's hat was something else again. There was a big difference between buying a piece of land and actually making a profit on the investment, not to mention still being in business five or ten years down the road. Job security meant everything to Joe, and to the people who depended on him. Going in with an unproven entity was just too risky.

Except there was that little matter of Mary-Jo's "feeling."

A feeling which he might have been tempted to believe had more merit than he wanted to give it, had Wes not picked that moment to call.

"Hey, there." His boss's voice rang in his ear. "Bet you were thinkin' I'd fallen off the face of the earth!"

"You might say," Joe said, revving the engine and pulling out of the bank parking lot. Steering with the flat part of one hand, he pulled into traffic. "Mary-Jo's worried sick 'cause she hasn't been able to get hold of you."

"Now, she knows I've gotten back to her after every single message she's left me, even if I haven't been available at the precise moment she's called. Had trouble with the cell service for a while, you know how that goes. Got tied up, too, with some unexpected personal matters that've kept me from sticking my nose in as much as usual. But I figured you and Madison had things in hand, am I right?"

Stopped for a red light, Joe leaned back in his seat, glaring out his window at the silver pickup pulsing with eardrum-shattering hip-hop. "Mary-Jo said you took the bookkeeping away from her."

After a slight hesitation, Wes said, "Yeah, Carmela wanted to go back to doing the books, like she used to when I first started the business. I didn't figure Mary-Jo'd mind since she's still getting the same salary for less work, right? Anyway, so I thought maybe I'd get up to Haven in the next day or two, see how that's coming along. Hank's been pestering me, and he's right, I should probably see where my money's going. He said your mom and sister are staying in one of the new prefab cabins? How's that working out?"

Joe couldn't detect a single thing in the man's voice to set off any alarms. So why was he feeling so damn jittery? Maybe it was the heat. Or Mary-Jo's paranoia infecting him. Or maybe, just maybe, it was all the other stresses in his life ganging up on him, causing him to hallucinate bogeymen in every shadow?

By the time he got off the phone, he'd decided to go with that. Not that there was any comfort in that decision, but at least it made sense.

What didn't make sense, however, was the almost overpowering urge to talk things over with Taylor. Confide in her, get her take on things. For all her emotionality, she was still one of the most clear-headed people he'd ever met.

And if that wasn't a warning sign that he was losing it, he didn't know what was. Okay, fine, so they couldn't—and were no longer going to—keep their hands off each other. He wanted her, she wanted him, and staying away from each other was downright inhuman. But sharing your problems with a woman…hell, even he knew that was a one-way ticket to disaster.

Especially when they started doling out advice you didn't want to hear.

"Hi, Miss Tay-lor!"

Reveling in the frosty air billowing out of the frozen foods case at the Git-n-Go, Taylor turned to catch Kristen Salazar's big, bright smile.

"Well, hey, Kristen," she said back, grabbing a pint of Ben & Jerry's Chunky Monkey and dropping it into her basket, even as she waited out a little ache of need brought about by Kristen's appearance. On the surface, she'd been fine with Joe and her not being able to be together the rest of the week while his folks were here. It was what was going on under the surface that was a problem. Because way down deep—okay, maybe not so deep—she missed him with an intensity that made her head spin. And maybe this was wishful thinking on her part, but she had a real strong feeling Joe's thoughts were running pretty much along the same lines, given the looks she'd catch him lobbing her way whenever she happened to catch his eye.

But it was about all these people and obligations and circumstances piling up higher and higher between them….

"What're you doing here?" she finally asked Joe's sister.

"Ma-ma's over there, get-ting milk for din-ner. We ran out. Did you walk here? We walked. Mama says it's good for me to walk a lot."

"It's good for everyone to walk," Taylor said with a smile. "I walked, too."

"Yeah? Cool. That looks good," Kristen said, pointing to the ice cream. "I like ice cream. But on-ly if it doesn't have stuff in it."

"Not even pieces of chocolate?"

The girl grinned. "I guess that would be okay," she said, and Taylor laughed, even though *she* needed those pieces of chocolate like a hole in the head.

"Oh, there you are," Danielle said—a little breathlessly—to her daughter as she appeared. "But then," she said, chuckling, "I should have known you'd follow your ice-cream radar. Why don't you pick something out for dessert?" she said to her daughter, then turned to Taylor, her gaze just assessing enough to make Taylor shiver slightly. "I've been meaning to tell you how much Kristen enjoyed being at camp. Thanks for letting her visit."

"No problem," Taylor said with a nod. "It's been great having her."

An awkward silence followed while Danielle helped Kristen find her favorite kind of ice cream and Taylor stood there wondering what came next.

"It's a shame we have to leave tomorrow," Danielle said, starting for the register.

Taylor followed, muttering something brilliant like, "Yes, it is."

Danielle unloaded her groceries onto the checkout counter as Kristen drifted over to the magazine rack and started leafing through a bridal mag. Joe's mother glanced over at her daughter, her expression a mixture of love and concern, and then gave Taylor a speculative look that nearly made her jump.

"Is something the matter?" Taylor asked, half smiling as the skinny gum-chewing girl behind the counter rang up Danielle's purchases.

"No, no. It's just…" She frowned. "Are you in a hurry, or could we talk for a minute?"

"Sure, no problem," she said, even as, *This can't be good,* flitted through her brain.

After Taylor paid for her groceries, they left the store, Kristen striking out a little ahead of the two women. "She likes to walk by herself," Danielle said. "Helps her feel more independent."

"You've done a great job with her," Taylor said, and Danielle laughed.

"Believe me, I worry about her far less than I worry about my son."

"I can see why," Taylor said softly.

Danielle was quiet for a moment, then said, "You care a great deal for Joe, don't you?"

"Not much point in denying it."

"But…?"

She met the shorter woman's kind gaze. "But…it's not just up to me."

"Ah. In other words, Joe's being mule-headed."

Taylor laughed. "That's one way of putting it. He…" How could she put this diplomatically? "He…takes his other responsibilities very seriously."

"Kristen and me, you mean?"

"Yes."

Danielle sighed. "Just for the record? This isn't coming from me."

"I didn't think it was. Just for the record."

They shared a smile, then Joe's mother shook her head. "We don't need his money, Taylor. Not anymore. Between what I make and what we get from the state, we're fine. But pride is a very hard habit to break."

They came to a stop at Taylor's turnoff; Danielle touched her arm, catching Taylor's gaze in hers. "I don't know much about whatever other relationships Joe's had before this, but I sense he feels something very different for you. Something *real.* And I can see why," she added with an amused smile. But then her brows drew together. "I don't mean to sound melodramatic, but you might be his last chance. To shake him out of whatever this is that has him so convinced he can't have his own life. I'd like to know I can leave him in your hands, that you'll be there for him."

Taylor's gaze strayed down the road to Kristen, who was singing to herself as she walked. "I *am* here for him, Danielle," she said, then looked back at the older woman. "But he has to meet me halfway."

"And if that's not enough?"

Taylor let out a dry, *I'm doomed* laugh. "Then...I guess I have to go a little further?"

The other woman smiled. "Right answer, *chica,*" she said, and set off down the road after her daughter.

There was a reason Taylor decided to pay a visit to Maddie Logan on Saturday afternoon, and it wasn't just to bring her manicotti. The doctor's wife, her new—and *enormous*—baby son hiked up on her shoulder, greeted her with both delight and suspicion, her light brown brows dipping slightly as she took in the towel-shrouded casserole. "What is it?"

"Uh-oh. Someone looks like she's had a recent close encounter with Arliss Potts."

"Lord, yes," Maddie said, leading Taylor through the high-ceiling foyer and on into the cluttered living room, chock-full of original-to-the-house furniture, baby stuff and country music. In her sleeveless blouse and baggy shorts, the woman looked more like her baby's big sister than his mama, even though there was nothing even remotely childish about Ryan's wife. "She's taken to putting canned peas in her tuna casserole."

"Oh, no." The Baptist minister's wife's cooking "skills" were legendary. "With the chili powder or instead of it?"

"*With* it."

Taylor laughed, even as she said, "I'm so sorry, honey. But this is baked manicotti. No peas, no chili powder. I made two batches last night."

The baby deposited on his back in a nearby bassinet, Maddie came over to lift a corner of the towel. "Oh, my," she said on a sigh. "You know what? Forget the fridge, there's no room in there anyway. Just go on ahead and put that right in the oven. And go on and get yourself some tea or whatever you want while you're at it. How's that for bein' the gracious hostess?"

"Sounds good to me," Taylor said with a chuckle, heading into the equally chaotic kitchen, the refrigerator all but obliterated with drawings and recipes and kids' photos, the dining table piled with whatever projects the other kids had been working on last. Her heart twinged, a little, as it always did whenever she came over here. It was hard, sometimes, being in the midst of other peoples' happiness. Even if she knew how hard-won that happiness was, for both Maddie and Ryan. Which was part of the reason she was here.

So she put the baking dish in the oven and turned it on, then found a clean pair of glasses and poured them both some tea. "Should take about a half hour," she said, coming back out into the living room and handing one glass to Maddie, who smiled her thanks from where she'd collapsed on the sofa. "Where're the rest of the kids?" she asked.

"Ry took 'em over to Dawn's and Cal's so I could get some rest," Maddie said with a weary laugh. "'Cept I ended up spending all day cleaning." She took a sip of her tea and glowered at the room. "Although you could never tell it."

"Hey," Taylor said, sweeping a pile of dolls off a nearby chair and sinking into it. "Kids live here. Go with the flow."

"Yeah, except one day the flow's gonna carry me right outta here. Anyway, talk to me. About anything other than babies and breastfeeding. So Joe's mom and sister left?"

"Yesterday, yeah."

"Didi tells me Kristen visited camp a few times."

"She did."

"How'd that work out?"

"All in all, pretty well. And it was good for the other kids, too. To tell the truth, there was some serious staring going on the first day or so, but by her last day there, I think most of them had stopped seeing her as 'different' and just related to her as another kid. But..." She blew out a breath. "It was so hard watching her struggle to do things kids half her age had mastered years ago."

"How's her family deal with it?" Maddie asked, as if reading Taylor's thoughts.

"Her mother's one of the most upbeat women I've ever met, which I'm sure is the main reason Kristen's made as much progress as she has. Seth, of course, is still coming to terms with having a sister, let alone one with Down syndrome. He hadn't said anything much to me about it, but while I think he was glad to meet her—to satisfy his curiosity, if nothing else—I think he's glad for some space to absorb it all."

"Makes sense to me," Maddie said, then snuggled down into the sofa, leaning her head back against the cushions. "And Joe?"

Taylor poked at the ice cubes in her tea—no way was she about to betray his trust by discussing his confession of sorts from a week ago. So all she said was, "He's about to bust something trying to make everybody happy."

Maddie set her tea down on the end table and crossed her arms, her feet perched on the edge of the coffee table in front of the sofa. From the bassinet, the baby made little going-to-sleep snuffling sounds. "Does 'everybody' include you?"

Mirroring her friend's pose, Taylor met her gaze. "That's a leading question."

"That was the idea." Then her eyebrows disappeared underneath her bangs. "Ohmigosh—you two are foolin' around, aren't you?"

Since this was her real reason for being here, Taylor had no choice but to nod. Maddie's grin collapsed. "Is this good news or bad news?"

Taylor lifted her hands in a "beats me" gesture, then said, "The man is the most generous, selfless, noble man I have ever met in my entire life. Well, except for your husband."

Maddie grinned. "But…?"

"But selfless, noble men are major pains in the butt."

"Tell me about it," Maddie muttered, then regarded Taylor steadily for a moment. "But if you love him, then you just gotta deal with that, right?"

"I didn't say—"

Maddie laughed. Taylor glowered.

"But how? How am I supposed to deal with it when the man

won't let me into his life?" She leaned forward, pushing her hair behind her ear. "How did you get Ryan to let you into his?"

She grinned, a cute little three-corner number that was equal parts innocence and don't-mess-with-me grit. "I don't think he let me into his life as much as he finally figured out I'd already burrowed my way into his life deeper than the tick on your dog."

"Yeah, except that tick paralyzed Oakley, remember?"

"Okay, so maybe that wasn't the best analogy I could've used. But really, sometimes all you can do is to just keep lovin' 'em until they realize they can't live without you."

"If only it were that simple," Taylor said on a sigh.

"I know, honey," Maddie said, her expression sympathetic. "I know."

Ryan and the kids returned at that moment, which more or less put the kibosh on any further conversation since the kids climbed all over their mother until she looked like one of those storyteller dolls from New Mexico. But for the rest of the day, and the day after, as Taylor tended her flowers and went grocery shopping and trekked clear up to Bartlesville with Jenna to some estate sale to pick up some more pieces for the new cabins, Maddie's words kept replaying in her head. The thing was, much as she wanted Joe to know she loved him and was there for him, being thought of as a tick did not appeal.

Go figure.

Joe managed to get Taylor alone for about two seconds when he dropped Seth off on Monday morning, although since he couldn't touch her, let alone kiss her—or do anything else—he found the encounter somewhat less than satisfactory. But at least he had her smile all to himself for those two seconds, and while that wasn't nearly enough, it was something.

"Who's that?" he asked as Seth made a beeline toward a knot of noisy little boys in the center of the room, where he started gabbing up a storm with a scrawny blond kid with big ears and a bigger grin.

Taylor turned, her shirt collar shifting to reveal the fading love bite he'd given her more than a week ago, causing various and sundry parts of his body to stir with interest. And his mouth to tingle with wanting to freshen the bite up a bit.

"Oh, that's Wade Frazier," she said, then turned back to him with a smile. "One of the Frazier brood. I think Seth and Wade have become best buds." Considering the way the boys were currently shoving and poking at each other, he'd say Taylor's assessment was dead on. "So I hear your boss finally put in an appearance last week?" Taylor asked, recapturing his attention.

"Yep. He seemed pleased."

"So life is good?" she said, her eyes twinkling.

He felt his mouth stretch into a slow, sexy grin. And said, knowing there was far too much noise in the room for anybody to hear except the one person who counted, "Not as good as I'd like it to be."

Something he couldn't quite figure out flitted across her features, but then she said, "Yeah. I know what you mean," and he thought—hoped—maybe he'd just imagined it.

Then he said, "I gotta go," and she said, "We'll see you later," and he walked out feeling about as mixed up as a man could feel without the guys with the nets coming after him. In many ways, his life was better than it had been in, well, a very long time. Seth seemed to be coming around, the crisis with Wes seemed to have been averted, he had a lover—even if the loving part didn't happen nearly as often as he might like—and yet, he couldn't seem to shake this sense of foreboding, like the feeling animals got right before an earthquake.

A sense that stayed with him all the way into Tulsa, when he walked into Wes's office to find Mary-Jo next door to hysterical.

Chapter 16

Joe had never seen Hank flat-out furious before. It was not a pretty sight.

Of course, since Joe was every bit as furious, he didn't imagine he was any too pretty a sight, either.

They were standing outside, staring at the crater in the ground where the swimming pool was supposed to go. Behind them, the original motel had been reduced to little more than walls and roof. As hot as it was, Joe could feel Hank's anger rolling off him from two feet away.

"And you had *no* idea this was about to happen?"

There was little point in revealing to Hank all the little, and not so little, signs that Joe had chosen to ignore over the past couple of months. He honest to God thought Wes would come through whatever this was, that he wouldn't be the kind of guy to leave his secretary of twenty years with an envelope with five hundred bucks in it and an apology that it couldn't be more. And then, for all intents and purposes, vanish from the face of the earth. His phones had been disconnected, his house was empty, his accounts closed.

"I'm as flabbergasted as you, Hank," Joe said, then turned to look at the other man's hard-edged profile. "You saw him yourself, when he came up here a couple days ago. Did he sound like a man about to throw in the towel to you?"

Hank glared at the hole in the ground for another second or two, then blew out a breath and shook his head. "No. And I thought I was pretty good at readin' people." Then he looked over at Joe. "Now what?"

Yeah, he knew that question was coming. Too bad he had no answer.

To say Joe was reeling was an understatement. He'd *trusted* Wes, dammit. Had gradually let himself believe he could count on him at a time when counting on people wasn't exactly an easy thing for him to do. And now he'd been lied to—left hanging—exactly like before.

He hadn't thought it could hurt this bad, not a second time, not after all these years.

He'd been wrong.

But there was no time for self-pity, no more now than there had been then. So he looked at Hank and said, "First off, do you want to finish the project?"

That got a dry, humorless laugh. "I maybe have enough cash to pay the people Wes left in the lurch, but unless I can swing a loan, or find another partner..." He muttered an obscenity, then said, "And here I thought bein' a cop was hard."

They stood there for several moments, staring at that hole in the ground, trying to figure out how where to go from here when Hank said, "But what about you? You got any options?"

He thought about Mitch's offer, wondered if the other man had gotten wind of something about Wes Joe hadn't known about. "Yeah, actually. As it happens, another Tulsa developer approached me last week."

Hank glanced over at him, then back at the hole. "I take it the money'd be good?"

"Supposedly."

"And you'd have that security that's so important to you."

Joe snorted. "There's an illusion for you."

"Hey. You said it, not me." Several beats passed, then he said, "So I guess that means you wouldn't be interested in goin' in with me?"

Joe's head whipped around. "Me?"

"Yeah, you." Hank's gaze was unnervingly steady. "Give me one good reason why not."

He could give him plenty of reasons. Yet, the only one that came out of his mouth was, "I'd already made plans to move back to Tulsa, to be closer to my mother and sister."

"So bring 'em here."

"My sister—"

"—can go to school in Claremore and get all the services she needs. But what am I saying? We'd probably have to take out a loan to get this done, and I have no idea whether that's something you could even do. Or would want to do."

Joe knew how much it would take to finish the work. He also knew he had the money. Or could easily get a loan with his portfolio as collateral. More than a dozen years of socking it away had built up quite a nice little nest egg, a nest egg he'd always intended to use for Kristen. But he wouldn't have to use all of it, after all….

"And I bet we could do a lot of the work ourselves," Hank was saying. "Not pouring the pool, stuff like that, but the cabins are more or less done, it's just a matter of redoing the lodge. If I can start taking reservations again on the cabins, that'd bring in a few bucks so at least we wouldn't starve."

Joe turned to face the man he realized he thought of as a friend. But enough of a friend to trust again? "It's a big risk," he said, and he wasn't just talking about the money.

"Yeah. It is. But hell, Joe, *life's* a risk, you know?"

With a vague promise to think it over, Joe went back to his cabin, where he spent the rest of the day making about a million phone calls, assuaging subcontractors, doing what he could to link up the various people Wes had left in the lurch, including letting Mitch know there was a half-finished strip mall in Tulsa he might be interested in getting his hands on. And a secretary who desperately needed a job. In turn, Mitch reiterated his offer, telling Joe he could start work for him anytime, just let him know.

Why Joe didn't immediately jump at the job, he didn't know. Certainly, there was nothing keeping him from taking it now. Except, when it came time to say, "Okay," the only thing that came out was, "Can I get back to you on that?"

Mitch probably thought Joe was several sandwiches short of a picnic. Hell, so did Joe. Especially as up to this point, life had been pretty black-and-white, you know? Decisions had been clear, if not always easy. But now…now his head felt like somebody'd stuffed it with old socks.

It was nearly six by the time he got to Taylor's to pick up Seth. She met him at the door, her face crumpled with concern. There was something peculiar about the house his muddled brain couldn't decipher at first, until he realized he was smelling something cooking.

"I do a mean roast beef," she said.

"With gravy?"

"How else? And there's one of Maddie's peach pies, and potatoes which Seth helped mash."

He looked deep into those compassionate green eyes and said, "You know?"

"I ran into Jenna at Ruby's," she said, and took him by the hand and brought him inside, where he gathered her close and held on tight.

Seth floated on his back in the aboveground pool at camp, watching the clouds and wishing the icky feeling inside him would go away. But no matter how hard he tried, it just stayed there, like a dog that wouldn't go home.

Joe and Taylor had acted weird the whole time they'd been at her house for supper last night, talking in whispers whenever he left the room, clamming up the minute he'd come back in. A couple times, he'd come right out and asked what the matter was, but they'd both said, "Nothing," with these funny looks on their faces, like he was too dumb or little to figure out they were full of it.

Actually, they'd been acting strange all week whenever they were together, so he pretty much figured it had something to do with sex. Not that he was real clear on the particulars, but he'd heard enough here and there to get the general idea. Which meant his original hunch had been right all along—that Joe had what some of the older kids called "the hots" for Taylor. Whatever it was, he'd sure felt like odd man out last night, boy. Even when Joe'd put him to bed, he'd smiled at Seth like he didn't really see him....

Water splashed in Seth's face, scaring the bejeebers out of him and making him sputter and choke until his feet touched bottom. As he swiped water out of his eyes, he heard Wade Frazier giggle. Since he'd done the same thing to Wade the day before, he guessed he couldn't get too mad.

"Are we even now?" Seth asked, squeezing his nose until the stinging went away. Since the pool wasn't but three feet deep, he hadn't been in any danger of drowning, but Blair and Wade's sister Libby and them got mad anyway if they horsed around too much.

"Yeah, we're even." The kid grinned, water droplets sparkling in real short hair practically the same color as his head. "You okay?"

"Yeah, 'course."

"Let's get out now, I'm bored."

"Yeah, me, too."

They got out of the pool and wrapped themselves up in their towels, then went to sit in the grass, in a sunny spot so they'd dry off quicker. They compared fingers and toes to see whose were wrinkled the most, then Wade poked Seth in the arm and said, "Hey—maybe you could over to my house for supper tonight."

Seth was kind of surprised at this, since although he and Wade played together a lot at camp, this was the first time he'd suggested they hang out together afterwards. The icky feeling began to go away, a little. "You sure?"

"Oh, yeah. Daddy won't mind." Wade grinned, showing off two of the biggest front teeth Seth'd ever seen. "He says we've already got so many kids, a couple more don't make any difference one way or the other."

Seth smiled, wrapping his towel tighter around his shoulders since the sun had gone behind a cloud. But he felt so good inside he didn't care. Deciding maybe him and Wade were best friends now, which meant they could talk about stuff that bothered them, he said, "C'n I ask you something?"

"What?"

"Were you sad for a real long time after your mama died?"

The other kid seemed to think about this for a while, his almost invisible eyebrows pushed down so hard that there were three bumps of skin over his nose. "I guess maybe I was," he said, poking a corner of his towel in his ear to soak up the water, then pulling it tight around his shoulders again. "But it was a long time ago. I was real little. Like in kindergarten. So I don't remember too much about it." He made a funny face. "I don't really remember Mama all that much, to tell you the truth, but I don't let on to Daddy."

"So you feel okay now?"

"Most of the time, yeah."

That sounded pretty good to Seth. Even though he wasn't sad all the time anymore, it still kept coming back. Especially whenever Joe was grumpy about something or other. "You ever think about gettin' a new mom someday?"

Shoulders even skinnier than Seth's popped up, then back down. The sun—which had come back out—flashed off his pale head. "Sometimes, I guess. But I don't think Daddy's much interested in gettin' married again."

Seth perked up at that. "Yeah?"

"Yeah. I heard him on the phone once telling somebody women just weren't worth the bother. That Mama'd been the only woman he needed, and now that she was gone and we'd all 'justed to her not being here, there was no sense upsettin' the apple cart by tryin' to train up somebody new."

His friend's words playing in his head, Seth stretched out his towel on the grass and laid on his back to do some more cloud watching. He wasn't sure yet, but he thought maybe some of those Lego pieces in his brain were finally beginning to click into place.

"You sure you don't mind taking Seth?" Joe asked Sam Frazier that evening as the two boys—as well as several others of assorted sizes—barreled past them, Wade yelling, "You c'n sit by me!" to Seth. "Looks to me like you already have your hands full."

Sam gave a low chuckle, his face creasing into a smile. "Which means I'll never notice one more. There's always extras at my place, anyway." Sam told Joe he'd swing Seth back home around nine, if that was okay, winked at Taylor, who was standing nearby, then followed his kids out to an old Econoline van parked out under an elm tree.

"He winked at you," popped out of Joe's mouth before he even knew he was thinking it.

"Sam winks at everybody," Taylor said with an amused expression as she started to clean up a nearby table cluttered with books and stuff. Straightening, she lifted one eyebrow. "Jealous?"

He lifted one right back at her. "Should I be?"

"Unfortunately, no," she said on a sigh, carting the books across the room to toss them into a bin. "I don't think there's a woman alive who could break through the wall that man has put up around his heart."

Joe frowned. "Why? He seems friendly enough to me."

"Friendly's not the same as being open to love." She got her purse out of a nearby desk drawer, hollered goodbye to Didi on the other side of the room, then headed outside. Joe followed, blinking in the glare of the late day sun.

"Why do I get the feeling we're not talking about Sam anymore?" he said when they got to their vehicles, parked right next to each other.

She looked over at him, but all she did was tuck a loose strand of hair behind her ear and say, "You make any major decisions today I should know about?"

"I think that's called a non sequitur."

"Not in my mind, it wasn't. Well?"

They'd talked for a long time last night about his options. While she never once tried to tell him what she thought he should do, if she'd said "But what do *you* want?" once, she'd said it a hundred times. As if that made his decision any easier.

"Still…trying to figure out what's best for everybody."

"That may not be possible, you know."

"Yeah. I know."

"You haven't told Seth yet, have you?"

Joe shook his head. "Until I have something concrete to tell him, there doesn't seem much point. Same with my mother. I don't want her to worry."

Taylor looked at him for a long time, then said gently, "Don't take this the wrong way, okay? But maybe you're not giving her enough credit."

"I just don't want to let her down."

"I know," she said softly, then cocked her head, a knowing smile teasing her lips. "You know, it sure looks to me like somebody could use another…vacation."

On a half laugh, he shook his head. "Whatever happened to being practical?"

"Because you *might* walk out of my life, you mean?"

"Yes."

Over her truck's hood, her gaze was unwavering. "Are you absolutely, positively sure you *will* walk out of my life?"

The thousand and one reasons why he should say "yes" filtered through his brain before his mouth opened and he heard himself say, "No."

"That's good enough for me," she said, getting in and slamming shut her door.

But was it? Joe wondered, even as he climbed into his car and followed her home.

Despite her promise to Joe's mother, despite Maddie's suggestion to just keep loving him, Taylor had no illusions that convincing Joe they had a future was about as dicey as her riding a bicycle across a tightrope over Niagara Falls. Blindfolded. But she suspected that part of Joe's reticence stemmed from his never having had anyone there for him the way he'd always been there for everyone else. Since she loved the guy and all, she figured she didn't have a whole lot to lose. Well, other than her dignity and peace of mind, but they'd been shot to hell some time ago anyway.

They'd had dinner—steaks on the grill and corn on the cob—and were just getting down to the "vacation" part of the evening when Joe's cell rang. Of course, Joe's attention being somewhat diverted at the time, she had to say, "Joe! Your phone!" several times before he actually heard it. He grabbed the phone off the nightstand, but apparently didn't recognize the number right off, answering with a slightly annoyed, "Yeah, this is Joe." Then: "Sam? Is Seth okay?"

He sat bolt upright, grabbing his shirt off the chair by Taylor's bed and attempting to shrug it on one-handed, which in turn prompted Taylor to go on a bra hunt. There was a pause, then Joe said, "What?" in such a way as to send a cold chill streaking down her spine. She pulled herself back together as well as she could and lowered herself to the chair by the bed, anxiously watching Joe's expression as he took in whatever Sam was saying to him. Then he buried his face in his hand, letting out a soft groan, followed by a "No, it's okay, thanks for letting me know…yeah, I do, too. I'll be there in a minute."

"Joe?" Taylor gently said after he hung up. "What is it?"

He forked a hand through his hair, then stood, buttoning his shirt and ramming the hem back into the waistband of his pants, which he hadn't yet gotten around to removing. When he finally spoke, it was with the voice of someone who can't quite believe what he's saying.

"Seth asked Sam if he could come live with him. Permanently."

"*What?* Why?"

He dug in his pocket for his keys. "That's what I'm about to find out."

"Wait, I'm going with you—"

"No!"

Never had a single word flattened her so hard and so fast. Except then, on a harsh breath, Joe cupped her face in his hands, his brows drawn as if trying to commit her features to memory. "Whatever this is, it's between Seth and me, okay?"

She lifted a hand to cover one of his, wishing like heck she could knock some sense into his thick head. But it would be like arguing with a rock. So all she said was, "It's going to be all right," because that's what people said at times like this. He kissed her, his mouth hard against hers, then turned to leave. But she'd apparently lost her battle with sanity because she followed him out into the living room, heard herself call him back, heard the words "I love you," spill from her lips, where they hung in the air between them as if, now that they were free, they had no idea where to go.

Joe gave her a sad smile, then walked out the door. Taylor looked at Oakley, who wore the woebegone expression of the terminally depressed, although that probably had more to do with the fact that she wouldn't give him the second steak bone than Joe's leaving.

"It *is* going to be all right," she told the dog, even though she didn't really believe it.

Chapter 17

Joe waited until Seth got in the Blazer, then slammed shut the door and stormed around to his side. When he got in, Seth said in a tiny voice, "You mad at me?" and Joe let out a long, worn-out sigh before looking over at his brother.

"No, I'm not mad at you. But you and I got a lot of talking to do. Now get your seat belt on so we can go back to the cabin and do just that."

The boy nodded and clicked his seat belt into place. Rain clouds plunged the landscape into premature darkness, a pathetic little drizzle dotting, then blurring, the Blazer's windshield. Joe turned the windshield wipers on low, their thunk-thunking an irritating counterpoint to the sound of his heartbeat hammering inside his head.

If Joe lived to be a hundred, he'd never forget the rejection in Taylor's eyes when he left. And he wished—oh, God, he wished!—he'd had the words to make it better, to fix it so all the damn pieces of his sorry life would somehow fit together, that *she* could fit at least reasonably close to the center of his life, not way out there on the edge where the best they could manage were occasional glimpses of each other as Joe zoomed by, like he was on the merry-go-round from hell.

For a split second, he thought he'd only imagined her saying she loved him. But she had, and there was no doubt in Joe's mind that she'd meant those words with all her heart, words that for the first time in his life echoed in his own, begging for release to mingle and mate with hers. But he'd kept them imprisoned, lifers without hope of parole, because he knew Taylor, knew that once he admitted he loved her, too—no, not just loved, but *craved* her, adored her, needed her more than he could have ever imagined needing anyone—she'd only come up with a hundred and one reasons why they couldn't let anything get in the way of what they felt for each other. As long as she thought her feelings were one-sided, though, he had a chance, a small one, of coming out of this mess in one piece. As did she.

The tightness at the back of his throat stung like bad whiskey, but without the anesthetic benefits. Because while walking away was the only way to save Taylor, it was Joe's one-way ticket to hell.

And yet, while he could curse the gods up one side and down the other about the crappy hand they'd dealt him when it came to his love life, all he had to do was look at the confused little boy beside him to remember what *real* pain was. And why, ultimately, there was only one choice Joe could make. He didn't have to question Seth about his motives for asking Sam to let him come live with them, because he already knew. Oh, boy, did he know. After all, even though Joe's father hadn't really left until Joe was nearly grown, Jose Salazar's presence in their lives had been an ephemeral, unreliable thing, like a ghost…thrilling, scary and too insubstantial to put any real faith in. Obviously, Seth's experience had been a carbon copy of Joe's.

And like Joe, Seth wasn't about to let history repeat itself if he could help it.

A clap of thunder split open the skies as they pulled up in front of the cabin; they both made a dash for the porch, bullet-hard raindrops stinging through their clothes. The porch floorboards thundered underneath their feet as they reached sanctuary a second before Joe heard the zing and pop of lightning striking nearby, followed by another thunderclap that shook the house and sent Seth jumping back from the porch railing, where he'd been watching an instant river snake through the dry earth.

Joe chuckled softly, shaking water off his hat. "You okay?"

"Yeah. I guess."

Rainwater sluiced off the porch overhang in a solid, silvery curtain, pounding the ground below. "You wanna go inside or stay out here?"

That got a shrug, but no reply.

"Then have a seat," Joe said, plunking his butt onto the porch swing. After a second or two, Seth followed suit, skootching back into an Adirondack chair nearby, his legs crossed underneath him. Joe's heart constricted at how small and lost his brother looked, at how much he obviously needed and how little he'd asked for. "I find it's sometimes easier to talk when you can't see the other person, anyway," he said gently. "So who's gonna start?"

Another shrug.

Joe waited out a spurt of frustration—and half a wish he'd taken Taylor up on her offer—then said, "Okay. I'll go first." The swing groaned as he pushed with his heels, taking a second or two to gather his thoughts. Except he realized if he was waiting for exactly the right words to say, they'd be there forever. So he sucked in a deep breath, then said, "You know how I said I wasn't sure I'd be much good at this? Taking care of a kid, I mean?"

He sensed more than saw the kid's nod.

"Well, what I guess I should've said was that I was hoping you'd help me out. You know, let me know if I was making a mistake or doing something all wrong." He glanced over and saw the pointed little chin jutting straight out as Seth watched the rain. "Like you," he said softly, "I didn't exactly have the greatest example to learn from. So if you've got a problem, you've got to tell me, Seth. Flat out. No beating around the bush."

After a moment, his brother said, "I was afraid you'd get mad."

"I won't get mad, Seth." When the boy looked at him, Joe put his hand over his heart. "I swear. But if you act like you're happy when you're not, I might get the wrong message..." Then he caught himself and roughly exhaled. "Or I might decide it's easier to let myself believe you're happy instead of really paying attention and trying to do something about it."

He saw Seth glance at his face, then turn back around.

"So," Joe said, "why don't you tell me what's really going on?"

Lightning flashed again, followed by much softer thunder. The storm was already moving on. "I was scared that if I was too much trouble, you'd send me away," Seth said at last, so softly Joe almost couldn't hear him over the rain.

"I see." Except Joe didn't see at all. Good Lord, how did people do this parenting thing on a full-time basis? "So...you decided to farm yourself out before I got a chance to, is that it?"

Several seconds passed. Then Seth finally nodded. Joe patted the space beside him. "C'mere, goof," he said, and the little boy scrambled out of the slanted chair to come sit beside him. Joe draped an arm around his brother's skinny shoulders and hugged him to his side.

"That wasn't going to happen, Seth. And it isn't. Ever. Because I love you, and there is nothing you can do that would make me send you away. You got that?"

Seth looked up at him. "Really?"

"Yeah, really. You think I'd lie about something like that?"

His brother scratched his leg, rubbed a finger under his nose, then finally said, "I thought you were only puttin' up with me because you had to. I could tell you'd be a lot happier if I wasn't around."

"That's not true—"

"Guys don't like it when kids get in the way," the boy pushed out. "When they want to be with a girl, I mean."

Joe shut his eyes, trying to control his breathing. When he felt more or less sure he wasn't going to let out a word Seth shouldn't be hearing, he said, "Is that what our father said?"

He listened to his brother's slightly ragged breathing for several more seconds before the kid said, "When Mom and Dad still lived together, he'd all the time get mad if I came into the room when he and Mom were talkin' or kissin', especially if Mom paid attention to me. Then, after he left, I was supposed to go stay with him on the weekends. Only then he got a girlfriend and he wanted to be with her more'n me, so I couldn't go over there much anymore. Not that I wanted to much. It wasn't much fun."

"No, I imagine not."

After another long silence, Seth said, "I heard Mom and Dad arguing once, about how Dad hadn't even wanted me to be born, but Mom had gone ahead and had me anyway. That it was just supposed to have been the two of them, then I had to come along and ruin everything."

Joe swallowed down a wave of nausea, then hugged his brother tighter. "Okay, don't you dare repeat me, but that's a load of crap, Seth. Did your mom love you?"

"I guess. I mean, she told me she did."

"Then that's all that matters. Because our father was a real piece of work. I never did understand how his mind worked—if it worked at all—but I can promise you that whatever his problem was, it had *nothing* to do with you. Besides…" He pushed back to look down at him. "If you hadn't been born, I wouldn't have a little brother to hang out with."

"Except if Mom and Dad hadn't died," Seth said in a small voice, "you might not've ever met me."

"We don't know that. But in any case, we know each other now. And I don't know about you, but I think it's pretty cool."

After a long moment, Seth said, "So how come last night, whenever you an' Taylor were talking and I walked in, you stopped? And every time I tried to ask you what was going on, you made out like it was none of my business?"

Joe stilled, realizing how their secretiveness must have looked to a child used to being shut out of his parents' lives.

Or at least, his father's. "Because I lost my job yesterday," he said quietly. "And I didn't want to say anything to you until I figured out what I was going to do. I didn't want to worry you."

"But you were talking about it with Taylor?"

"She's…a friend. Sometimes it helps to talk things out with a friend. You talk things over with her sometimes, don't you?"

"That's all she is?" he said, sidestepping Joe's question. "A friend?"

"She doesn't mean more to me than you do," Joe said, doing some sidestepping of his own. Because admitting the truth to the boy might destroy the fragile trust just beginning to blossom between them.

Because admitting the truth to himself would likely destroy *him.*

"I thought you liked Taylor," Joe said evenly.

"I do. I like her a lot. But…" He could feel the confusion radiating from the small body, and suddenly Joe thought maybe he understood what Seth couldn't put into words—that he felt like he was competing with Taylor for Joe's attention. Whether it was true or not was beside the point to a little kid who'd always felt last in line.

"It's okay," Joe said. "You don't have to try to explain. And this past little while's been rough, I know. But from now on, I'm gonna figure out some way to spend more time with you. I promise."

"Don't say that."

"Don't say what?"

"That you promise. 'Cause grown-ups never mean it."

"I mean it, Seth. No, I do," he added when the boy snorted his disbelief. "I don't break my promises. You can ask Kristen, the next time you see her. Or my mother. When I say I'll do something, I'll do it. In fact…" Pain lanced through him. "I think you just helped me make a decision."

"'Bout what?"

"About what comes next. With my job, I mean. As it happens, I got an offer from somebody else in Tulsa a little while back.

Pay's good, and I'd be staying in one place, so I'd be around for you more."

"Oh. So…you're not stayin' here and helping Hank run the Arrow?"

Joe flinched. "How'd you know about that?"

"I heard Blair talkin' about it with Libby, Wade's sister."

Damn small towns. And big ears.

"I thought about it, yeah…but I don't think that's the best choice. For any of us," he added as another tremor of regret shuddered through him. Even if he could justify the financial risk, he now knew there was no way he could stay here and stay away from Taylor. And Seth obviously wasn't in a place where he could deal with that. Not now, in any case. Yeah, Joe could reassure him from now to kingdom come that his place in Joe's life and affections were secure, but words meant squat without the foundation of trust. And the only way Joe was going to earn the kid's trust was to *show* him he had nothing to fear. Maybe someday, the kid would be ready to share Joe…but Joe knew all too well that "someday" had a nasty habit of staying just out of reach.

"So. We'll get a real house in Tulsa, and you'll have your own room, and a yard for a dog, if you want one." He gave Seth's shoulders a squeeze. "How's that sound?"

"Okay, I guess."

"So are we clear on a few things? That I *want* you with me? And that nobody's going to make me change my mind about that?"

A second or two passed before Seth nodded, then flung his arm around Joe's middle and gave him a hug…and let out a huge yawn. Joe hauled his brother up into his arms, despite sleepy protests about not being a baby, and got him into bed, sitting beside him and rubbing his skinny little back until his deep even breathing told Joe he'd fallen asleep. Then he got up and tiptoed out of the room, noiselessly shutting the door behind him so the boy wouldn't hear him make the last phone call in the world he wanted to make.

* * *

Taylor barely saw Joe at first, waiting on the porch steps, his hands linked between his knees. The rain had stopped; moonlight sliced across the clearing, the silvery glow enough to see the pain in his eyes, a pain which seared right through her.

She didn't imagine this would be a very long conversation. She also could pretty much guess the outcome.

"Well?" she said softly, sitting on the damp step beside him, not sure whether to touch him or not. But Joe reached for her hand, the tension in his fingers vising her heart.

"He figured I was too busy to take care of him. That I'd be happier if I didn't have him to worry about."

Taylor wasn't sure which broke her heart more—the devastation in his voice, or the weariness. "Oh, Joe…he's just a little kid. I'm sure he didn't mean it the way it sounded."

His eyes met hers, hard and black. And in a weird way, unforgiving. "He's a little kid whose own father made it quite clear he was a mistake. An annoying burden he wanted little or nothing to do with."

"So…you think every time you're not around, he's reading it as your not wanting to be with him? Because his father—*your* father—didn't want to be around him? But you know that's not true. You're nothing like your father."

"And how would you know that?"

"Because I know *you,* you idiot!"

"You don't know me at all," he said, letting go of her hand and leaning forward to stare out into the darkness.

"The hell I don't!"

His eyes whipped to hers. "Then let me spell it out for you—every time I'm with you, all I can think about is you. All I want to think about is you. And everything else takes a back seat. Nobody knows…" He looked away, shaking his head.

"That sometimes you want to run away?" she said quietly.

He laughed without humor. "Not sometimes. *All* the time."

"And you're somehow blaming me for that?"

"Of course not," he said on a ragged breath, then turned to her. "I'm blaming myself. Or whatever's inside me that's so much like my father, it scares the hell out of me. Yeah, I do what I have to do. But that doesn't mean I like it."

Her eyes stung. "That doesn't make you some kind of monster, Joe. Just human."

But he was shaking his head, back in rock mode. "I knew all along that Seth had to be my first priority. That I couldn't let myself be distracted. But I did anyway."

"Joe, for heaven's sake—it's not irresponsible to take some time for yourself!"

"That's like telling an alcoholic one beer every now and then's okay."

"Oh, for crying out loud…!" She pushed herself off the steps, needing to distance herself from his craziness. Once down in the yard, however, she whirled back around. "Why does everything have to be about your father?"

"Probably for much the same reason as everything's about yours!"

She lost her breath. "That was a cheap shot."

He got up and walked over to her. "I know it was. And I'm sorry. But…" His hands threaded through her hair, tenderly cradling her skull, and her insides roiled with his torment. "But don't you see? The only way for me to not be like my father is to become more like yours. And I…care far too much about you to put you through that again. I was beginning to think maybe, *maybe,* I could somehow balance all of this. That I could take Hank up on his offer and Seth and I could stay here, and you and I…" He dropped his hands, his breath rushing from his lungs. "I can't fix this, Taylor. No matter how much I want to, I can't make the pieces fit." He glanced down at the muddy ground, then back up into her eyes. "I'm accepting the job offer in Tulsa."

Well. Didn't take a ton of bricks and all that.

"Because that's what you really want?"

A pained smile twisted his lips. "Because it's the most responsible choice."

"Well, then," she said. "I wish you all the luck in the world."

She heard him whisper her name as she walked away, but what was the freaking point?

Oakley probably thought she'd totally lost her marbles when she stormed back into the house. And with good reason.

"Have you *ever* met a more hardheaded man?" she asked the dog, pacing her living room floor with her folded arms smashed against her ribs. Oakley groaned, then laid his head on his front paws, his eyes following Taylor as she paced. "Not that I'm any great shakes, goodness knows. I knew damn well what I was getting into, but did I stop myself? Noooo." She punched the air as she walked. "Just forged right ahead into a relationship I knew full well was doomed from the start." She dropped onto the edge of the sofa, shoving her hands through her hair. "What's wrong with me, Oak? Why do I keep doing this? Why?"

The dog hauled his mangy butt off the floor and came over to her to give her a nudge of commiseration. At least, that's what she was going with. He probably just wanted food.

With a huge sigh, she collapsed back into the sofa cushions, listening to her heart pound in her chest and thinking she needed to do something besides sit here and listen to her heart pound in her chest. To her surprise, that something turned out to be calling her mother. Because, dammit, right now she needed her mommy. Not to kiss it better, but just to talk to. To listen. Never mind that she'd never had that kind of relationship with her mother. Or at least, if she had, she couldn't remember. But she didn't want to dump on her friends, no matter how much they would have let her. She wanted to talk to someone with a real, bona fide, vested interest in her life.

She wanted to talk to someone about her father and her mother was the only one who could fill that bill. Whether she wanted to or not.

So when she got her mother's machine, she said, "Hi, Mom, it's Taylor. And I'm not fine, surprise, surprise." She swiped away a tear trickling down her cheek. "In fact, right now I'm pretty damn miserable, and I need you. I need to know you give a damn about me. I mean, if you don't, I guess there's nothing I can do about that. But if you do...well, I'd just kinda like to know that, okay?"

Then she clicked off the phone and carried it into the bedroom with her, where she threw herself across the bed and promptly passed out.

The phone's muffled chirping awakened her out of what felt like a drugged sleep. Eventually locating it underneath Oakley's left hip, she was still groggy when she heard her mother's, "Taylor McIntyre, what the hell makes you think I don't give a damn about you?"

Her fingers half tangled in her hair as she pushed it back from her face, Taylor stopped midyawn, instantly awake.

"Maybe because you never return my calls?"

"I never got the feeling you really wanted me to," Olivia McIntyre said, and once again, Taylor felt as if the air had been sucked from her lungs.

"Why on earth would you think that?"

"'Just calling to say hi,'" her mother mimicked. "'I'm fine, nothing new here'."

"You're a mother," she said dryly. "You're supposed to read between the lines."

"Maybe I was afraid to," her mother said quietly.

"Why?"

After a moment, her mother said, "Because screwing up is a bitch."

"I hope you don't expect me to deny that."

This time, a chuckle filled out the pause. "No, I don't." Then: "So why *did* you call?"

So she majorly dumped on her mother about Joe, and all the

complications attendant thereto, ending with, "And for some fool reason, I have the feeling a lot of this has something do with Daddy. I just don't know what. So that's why I'm calling, to talk about him. If you want to, that is."

Yet another pause. Then: "And if you had any idea how long I'd waited for this moment, you wouldn't say that." Only before Taylor could say, "What?" her mother said. "Do you love him? Joe, I mean?"

"Yeah," Taylor said on a sigh, figuring they'd deal with this now, the rest of it…later.

"And you're worried about him?"

"In spades."

"Because he reminds you of your father?"

"In some ways. But most especially because he's got it in his head that if he takes out two minutes for himself every once in a while, he's somehow in danger of morphing into a clone of *his* father. Who was a total sleazebag, from what I can tell."

Her mother sighed into the phone. "Fear's a helluva motivator. Especially fear of failing."

"Daddy was afraid of failing?"

"Of failing *again.* Of letting us down. And like your Joe, he never seemed to be able to find a balance, as if a single slip would send him back to square one." She hesitated, then said, "Except it sounds to me as though Joe has something Hyatt didn't have."

"And what's that?"

"Someone with the guts to save him before it's too late."

"Yeah, that seems to be the general consensus. Except that only works if he wants to be saved. And I'm not getting that feeling here."

"But then, it's always easier to let things ride, isn't it? Which is what I did with your father."

Olivia didn't add "and you girls," but Taylor could hear it in her voice. However, that was fodder for another time.

"So why did you?" she asked.

"I don't know. Because I was afraid he'd feel I was being

pushy? Or unappreciative of everything he was doing for us?" A beat or two passed, and then she said, "I guess I forgot loving somebody was supposed to be about sharing the load, even if the other person is hell-bent on carrying it all by himself."

"I've tried that approach. Didn't work."

"Then you have to try again." She paused. "Or walk away."

"Some help you are," Taylor said, but without rancor, and her mother said, "Hey. This ain't a science," and Taylor actually laughed.

Then they promised to stay in touch more often, the way everyone always does, only Taylor thought maybe they just might. Especially when her mother said, "Let me know how it goes with Joe. He sounds like a keeper."

"He is," she said, her eyes burning. Then she hung up, flopped back on the bed and thought, *Uh-boy.*

Chapter 18

The screen door to Joe's cabin was propped open, as was the Blazer's hatch which was half filled with luggage and boxes. Taylor rapped lightly on the door frame, taking a deep breath and then another, in a futile attempt to dispel the shakes. Joe came out of the bedroom with another box, coming to a dead stop when he saw her.

She'd never asked a man to stay before. Not since she used to beg her father to play with her instead of going into work on a Saturday. Or Sunday. And God knew she wasn't about to beg this time. But if Joe was determined to leave, then he was damn well going to leave knowing all the facts. As best Taylor could figure them out, at least.

"Hey," he said softly, that single syllable telling her there was a chance. It might be slender as a new blade of grass, but she wasn't picky.

"Is Seth here?" She held up the copy of Judy Blume's *Double Fudge* she'd bought for him. "He left this at my place."

"Oh...no. He's up at the Fraziers'. Um...just toss it in that box of books over there."

Taylor came inside, sticking one palm over her patterned sundress, one that brushed her ankles when she walked and camouflaged her big butt. And her hair was loose, too, because, not being a total fool, she knew he liked it that way. "Didn't realize you'd be leaving so soon," she said, taking in the stacked boxes still in the cabin's living room.

"Mitch wants me to start immediately, so I need to get back, find a house right away." His eyes followed hers around the room. "How we managed to accumulate so much stuff in eight weeks, I have no idea."

They exchanged brief smiles, their gazes skittering apart before she said, just to keep the conversation from falling into a deep hole, "You think it'll all fit in the Blazer?"

"If it doesn't, I can always make a second trip, I suppose."

She nodded again, her rope-soled shoes silent against the patterned rug as she walked over to an open box on the dining table and placed the book inside. "Seth can read this himself now, did you know?"

"Yeah, he told me."

She twisted to face him. "But you haven't heard him?"

"When things settle down, it's right at the top of my list."

Her stomach quaking, she backed up against the table, sweaty palms clamped to the edge on either side of her hips, all but melting at the expression in Joe's eyes. After so many years of being conditioned to let go and move on when something wasn't working, the idea of actually fighting for something—even something she believed in with all her heart—seemed almost unnatural. And definitely terrifying. But she'd come for a reason, dammit, and she was going to see it through.

"Seth doesn't really want to leave Haven, Joe."

"Taylor…"

"And I don't think you really want to, either. I think you want more than anything to take Hank up on his offer." She swallowed, but she willed her voice steady, even as Joe's gaze darkened. "And I think you want to stay here with me. But you won't do that as long as you've got it in your head that doing what *you* want is somehow against the rules."

She saw his jaw harden, his mouth thin. "Don't do this," he said, his voice raw. "You know I can't stay here. And you know why."

Even though Taylor wasn't sure her legs would support her, she pushed herself away from the table and narrowed the gap between them. "Because you can't afford to take the risk?"

"Yes."

Their gazes locked, she took another step closer. "You're not your father, Joe. Wanting a life of your own won't turn you into him."

A second passed, maybe two; then he yanked his gaze from hers, grabbing a roll of packing tape off the coffee table. He ripped off a strip, the sound echoing the mood in the room. "My life's not going to settle down, Taylor," he said through a tight jaw, then glanced at her. "Not in the foreseeable future, at least." He slammed the tape across the box of books. "Maybe not ever."

"I know that," she said gently.

He looked at her. "You deserve more."

"That's a cop-out."

His brows crashed together. "No, it's the truth. You deserve more than somebody who's already got a million other responsibilities. You deserve someone who's going to be there for you when you need him. Someone who's not going to make promises he can't keep. Someone not like *your* father."

"It could have been worse. I always knew my father loved me."

"And you've never forgiven him for abandoning you."

Her heart twisted at the bitterness in Joe's words, the pain still obviously so fresh after so many years for what his own father did to him. But she wasn't leaving this house until he understood a few things she hadn't understood herself until a little while ago.

"And it's taken me a long time to realize how hideously unfair I was being," she said, linking her arms over her middle so he wouldn't see how badly she was shaking. "He was only doing his best for his family, just like you for yours. But I was a child,

Joe. A child who couldn't connect with her own family for reasons I'll probably never understand. Of *course* I wanted my father around more—he was the only person in the house who gave a damn about me. So, yeah, I resented his working so much. Every time he had to back out of spending time with me, it felt like a betrayal. And when he died, I was angry. Horribly angry. But it was the anger of a child who'd felt as if she'd been ditched by her only true friend.

"But I'm not that child anymore. Whether or not I ever really connect with my own family again, I don't know. But I've got my work and wonderful friends and a life here I genuinely love. I don't need to cling to anyone. The only thing missing," she said, taking a deep breath, "is someone to be there for. Someone who needs me to be there for him. There's nothing more precious than knowing you're somebody's sanctuary."

Silence hummed between them for several seconds before he whispered, "But I can't be that for *you*."

Two more steps, and she was close enough to lay a hand against his rough cheek, to see tears gathered at the corners of his eyes. To see in those eyes a brutal determination not to let her change his mind.

Tough.

"You know what your problem is?" she asked.

His mouth twitched. "What?"

"For one thing, you seriously need to let go of this all-or-nothing mind-set. Not being able to fix everything doesn't make you a failure, Joe. Or in danger of becoming a bum." She tilted her head. "And for another, you've got to stop mixing me up with the desperate woman your mother was when your father walked out." She rasped her thumb over his cheek. "And mixing yourself up with the jerk that called himself your father."

Taylor stood on tiptoe to kiss his cheek, then moved away while she still could. However, when she got to the door, she turned and said, "You're already everybody else's hero. You don't have to be mine."

It took everything she had in her not to run back to her car. But when she got there, even though there was no denying the hot knot of pain lodged in her chest, she still felt as though a burden the size of Texas slid off her shoulders.

Now there was nothing left to do but wait.

And pray.

"So what do you think of this one?" Joe asked his mother, standing in the kitchen of what must have been the tenth house they'd looked at in four hours. The Realtor, thank God, was out front yakking on her cell phone. Nice lady, but a little intense.

Danielle clanged shut the oven door, smoothing her hands over her denim jumper. "Nice yard, okay kitchen, small bedrooms."

Joe frowned up at a water stain on the ceiling. Not exactly in the same league as the four-hundred-thousand dollar houses he'd be overseeing once he started work for Mitch. "Does that mean it's in contention or not?"

He hadn't meant for the words to come out as sharply as they had, but he was tired and nursing a headache, in part because after two days Taylor's words were still ringing in his head. Why couldn't she understand that what he wanted had nothing to do with it? When he could finally breathe more or less normally after she walked out of the cabin, however, it hit him just what kind of legacy his father had left him...that the bastard had robbed him not only of a father, but of any sort of real life, one where he could make his own choices.

One that included a crazy, emotional, generous redhead to share that life and his bed and his dreams and his problems, whose life and bed and dreams and problems he wanted to share, too.

Taylor wasn't the first thing he'd wanted in fifteen years, but she was the first thing he'd wanted in fifteen years that he'd spend the rest of his days regretting that he didn't get.

"Joe?" his mother said softly beside him. He looked down into concerned brown eyes. "I said I think we should keep looking."

Not what he wanted to hear.

"But not today," she said, touching his arm. "I need to get Kristen home, I can tell this is wearing her out. You want me to take Seth, too?"

"No, that's okay." Joe looked out the kitchen window, saw that the kids had found an old tennis ball or something and were playing catch. Kristen dropped the ball more than she caught it, but she was grinning and flushed and clearly having a great time. The yard wasn't much more than a plot of wilted grass bordered on three sides by a cinder block wall partially hidden by vines. Too small for a large dog, he thought absently, noticing that he could see roofs of half a dozen neighboring houses.

"I got it!" Kristen cried, holding the ball aloft and launching herself into a victory dance Seth had apparently taught her. Letting out a roar of his own, Seth pumped the air right along with her, and Joe smiled despite the heaviness in his chest. His brother and sister were good together, each one giving the other a sense of belonging they'd never really had. At least this part of things seemed to be working out. If nothing else, watching Seth adapt to who Kirsten was, not who she could have been had nature not thrown them a curve ball, was teaching Joe something he'd never seemed to be able to figure out on his own.

"He's a good kid," his mother said beside him.

"Yeah," Joe said. "He is."

"You know," Danielle said, crossing her arms, "there's no hurry about the house. We can stay in our own apartments for a while. Or you two can move in with Kristen and me, we can double up until we decide on a place—"

"No, I want to get settled." Joe turned from the window, scanning the aqua countertops, the burnt-orange floor tile. "I feel like I've been in limbo for the last several months."

"Months?" Danielle said.

"Okay, maybe for a little longer than that. But Seth needs a real home. As soon as possible."

"I agree," his mother said with a nod, then gave him a strange look. "But you want to make sure it's in the best neighborhood."

He frowned. "I thought you said you liked this neighborhood. It's stable, the schools are good..."

"Yeah, yeah, I know. But now I'm thinking...maybe something with more of a view?"

Joe sighed. "I'll keep looking."

"Because you need a better view, too, Joe," his mother went on. "One that's much more...expansive, shall we say."

He looked over at her. "We're not talking landscape, are we?"

"No. Joe..." She grabbed his hand. "I will always be more grateful than I can say for everything you've done for Kristen and me. But I never in a million years meant for you to sacrifice your own happiness for ours. If you're not going after Taylor because of us..."

He shook his head, blowing out a breath. "The timing's lousy for Seth. Right now, he needs to know I'm there for him."

Danielle's eyebrows lifted. "You don't think he knows that? Joe, *mijo,* no offense, but that little boy needs more than you. He needs a real family. And you know exactly what I'm talking about."

His mother squeezed his hand, then let go to call out the back door for Kristen to come on, just as the frosted blond Realtor tip-tapped into the kitchen with a smile that looked painted on.

"So what do you think? Isn't the backyard just adorable? Great sun, you could plant rose bushes along the west wall, maybe put in a deck at some point. And you know—" she wagged a bracelet-adorned hand toward an empty corner of the kitchen "—you don't find many eat-in kitchens in houses these days. And," she added, "my hunch is the sellers are extremely motivated, since they've already left town and all. So is this perfect or what?"

Joe and his mother exchanged glances as Danielle ushered Kristen through the kitchen. "It's not bad," Joe said diplomatically, swinging an arm around Seth's shoulders when he came in, all out of breath and sweaty. The Realtor took a tiny step backwards. "But I think we need to keep looking."

"Oh," she said, the sparkle in her eyes dimming even though her smile didn't give an inch. "Well," she said, leading them across the beige sculpted-pile carpet in the living room—brand-new last year, she'd informed them—and out the front door, "you've pretty much seen everything that matches your criteria. Four-bedroom houses in your price range are *pret*-ty hard to come by," she added with a scolding finger. "But new properties get listed every day, so you never know. How about I give you a call when something else turns up?"

"That'd be great," Joe said, and she gave a little wave and tip-tapped back to her BMW, while Joe and Seth got into the Blazer. Joe let his gaze wander down the block. It wasn't a bad neighborhood at all, neat and quiet with lots of shade trees and rose bushes. And the thought of living here gave him the willies.

"So," Joe said, starting the car. "You like any of the houses we saw today?"

Seth shrugged. "They were okay, I guess."

"Seth," Joe said, sparing him a glance as he pulled away from the curb. "Be honest. You're not going to hurt my feelings. Or make me mad."

The kid seemed to think about this for a minute, then said, "They all sucked."

They had clearly passed the reticent hurdle. "Now see…that wasn't so bad, was it?"

"No," the kid said with a little grin. "I guess not."

"Okay. Now tell me *why* they all sucked."

A good three or four seconds passed before his brother said, "Because they're not in Haven."

"Yeah," Joe said. "That was pretty much my take on it, too."

He felt Seth's eyes on the side of his face. "No kiddin'?"

"No kidding."

Out of the corner of his eye, he saw his brother's gaze slide back around. "C'n I say something?"

"I told you, you can tell me anything."

"And you swear you won't get mad?"

"I swear."

He heard the boy haul in a huge breath before he said, "I think you an' Taylor need to be with each other. Because you've been nothin' but a grouch ever since we left."

"I have not!"

"Now who's not bein' honest?"

A half smile touched Joe's lips. Except then he said, "But I thought—"

"You're not like Daddy was," Seth said quietly, his hands folded in his lap. "I'm thinking you can love her and me at the same time." He glanced over, then away. "'Cause, well, I love both of you."

Joe felt like somebody'd cracked his skull open, letting in a blindingly bright light, which in turn illuminated the one serious flaw in his approach to life over the past fifteen years:

Sacrificing himself hadn't made him a better man than his father.

Taking responsibility had never been a problem for Joe. Taking a chance was something else again. Because while taking responsibility had meant being in control, taking a chance meant letting go of that control, leaving yourself wide-open to being hurt again, of giving someone the power to break your heart. If you didn't let yourself want things, you couldn't be disappointed when you didn't get them.

Or when they were yanked away from you.

Joe'd always thought of his *father* as half a man, a wimp who didn't have the *cojones* to face up to his responsibilities. But now he realized it took a helluva lot more courage to face up to your fears. What a kick in the head to discover that taking the opposite path didn't necessarily mean you wouldn't end up in the same place…or still half a man. Jose Salazar had refused to take responsibility for others' happiness, but Joe had refused to take responsibility for his own.

Just like he'd refused to trust anyone but himself. Which might have been safe, but *whole* men learned to trust other people, too.

Well. Here was something Joe *could* fix.

But he sure as hell couldn't fix it in Tulsa.

Or all by himself.

Emotion clogging his throat, Joe reached over and cupped his brother's head. "I'm thinking you're absolutely right," he said, and Seth's whole face lit up.

"Hey," Seth said, sitting up straighter in his seat as Joe steered onto the entrance ramp to I-44, "Where're we going?"

"Where do you think?" he said, and his brother let out a "*Yes!*" loud enough to be heard clear to Kansas.

Taylor was sitting out on her porch steps, contemplating getting on with her life—or at least figuring out what to have for dinner—when, over a nearby cicada's brain-numbing whine, she heard the approaching growl of a car engine. She stood on the step, squinting through the viscous, late-day light, only to let out a quiet, "Oh my God" when Joe's Blazer lurched into view. Oakley went nuts, rushing the car and baying his head off, his frantically wagging tail practically knocking him off balance.

She combed trembling fingers through her loose hair—for what that was worth in this humidity—then dusted off the back of her full-skirted white sundress, which she was only wearing because everything else was in the wash. The car shuddered to a stop in the driveway; Seth tumbled out of it and over to her, throwing his arms around her waist and saying over and over, "We're back, we're back, we're back," until he got tired of that and added, "And we're never leaving!" At which point it was everything she could do to hold back the tears. So she hugged the boy back, hard, if for no other reason than hugging helped defuse the tear crisis. And also because hugging Seth gave her an excuse not to look at Joe right away.

Except eventually Seth got bored with the hugging, so he pulled away and he and Oakley bounded off somewhere, leaving Taylor with no choice but to face Joe.

Whose eyes were devouring her as if she were the first water he'd seen after a week on the desert.

Things were definitely looking up.

For whatever reason, he was keeping his distance, standing with one hand in his front pocket of his jeans, the other propped on the roof of his truck. "You know if Hank's offer still stands?" he asked.

Deciding to take her cue from him, Taylor stayed where she was, too. But oh, was it ever killing her. "Far as I know," she said, and the tension in his shoulders seemed to ease a bit.

"And yours?"

Somehow, she doubted her sudden lightheadedness was due to the heat. "You see a line forming?"

"Just wanted to be sure. You can never tell with women."

She crossed her arms. "You are so gonna get it for that."

He grinned. "That's what I was hoping," he said, and she rolled her eyes, which made him laugh.

"But…the job in Tulsa…?"

"Might be doing some heavy-duty commuting for a while, until Mitch can find a replacement. But I decided that wasn't what I wanted to do." He paused. "Or where I wanted to be."

Her stomach felt like a waterbed with Oakley jumping on top of it. "Gee. I'm hearing a lot of 'I wants' in there."

"Oh, honey, I'm just getting started." Then the grin dimmed a little. "I'm gonna be responsible for a lot of people for a long time. I mean, Mom and Kristen are probably gonna move back here, too."

She shrugged. "Makes sense to me."

"And you're absolutely sure—"

"I am. Absolutely."

"It's just…" He rubbed the back of his neck, peering out at her from underneath those gorgeous thick eyelashes. "I've been thinking I could use a little sanctuary from time to time."

Her heart swelled, knowing what that admission had cost him.

"I'm right here," she said, taking a step down, but he held up one hand to stop her.

"Not so fast," he said. "There are conditions."

"Conditions?"

"Yeah. Like, for one thing, you gotta promise to let me see you in that blue dress."

She laughed. "I suppose that can be arranged. But where did you have in mind?" she said, figuring on a smart-ass reply like "Anywhere I can take it off of you," or something equally man-like and predictable, so when he said, "Oh, I don't know. How about on our honeymoon?" her knees gave way and she sank back onto the porch steps.

"Ohmigod," she said.

Something like panic raced over his features. "Am I moving too fast?"

"No!" She shook her head, waving her hands in front of her. "Fast is good."

"So I take it that 'no' is a 'yes'?"

"Yes," she said, her heart racing. "You bet your butt that's a yes." She started to get up, but he put out his hand again.

"What *now?*"

"There's one more condition." His smile softened. "I'd really like to add to those responsibilities."

Took her a second. Then she flushed up to her roots. "Um, how many additional responsibilities are we talking? In round numbers?"

"Hadn't gotten that far. Thought we'd try out one or two, see how it went, then go from there."

"But your brother and sister…"

"Are my brother and sister. I want a family of my own." His gaze never left hers. "With you."

"Like I said." She grinned. "I'm here."

A smile slid across Joe's face and right on up into his eyes. "Actually," he said, opening his arms, "I'd rather have you right *here*—"

The last word came out on a *whoomph* as Oakley flew past her and mowed Joe down.

"Oakley, drop it!" Taylor cried, running to Joe and dropping onto her knees in the dirt beside him, her dress whooshing up in a cloud of cotton as she shoved the dog away, yelling, "So help me Hannah, if you've killed him, you're dead meat!" Only Joe—who was very much still alive—slung one arm around her waist and dragged her down beside him, laughing and kissing her over and over until she thought she'd explode with happiness. Even with dust in her mouth.

Then he stilled, brushing her hair out of her face and smiling into her eyes. "You got any idea how much I love you?"

Her heart singing, she looped her hands around his neck. "You got any idea how much I look forward to you showing me?"

"Hey," Seth yelled from the porch, his hands on his hips. "What the *heck* are you two doing?"

"Just waitin' on you," Joe hollered, and the kid tore down the steps and across the yard, flopping between them in a torrent of giggles. And over the boy's curly head, Joe looked over and winked at her, and the love held captive inside her for so long spilled out of her soul, and her heart, free at last.

Now she was home.

* * * * *

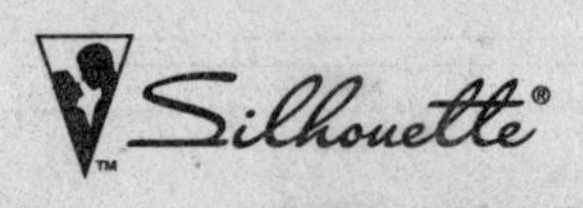

INTIMATE MOMENTS®

COMING NEXT MONTH

#1333 BENEATH THE SURFACE—Linda Turner
Turning Points
Crime reporter Logan St. John had sworn to protect Abby Saunders from her shady boss. But when Logan asked the innocent beauty on a date in order to investigate, he hadn't counted on falling for her! Soon a cover-up that could get them both killed was revealed, and Logan wondered if their newfound love would end before it even began….

#1334 RUNNING SCARED—Linda Winstead Jones
Last Chance Heroes
When a government official asked elite mercenary Quinn Calhoun to rescue Olivia Larkin from a ruthless dictator, he couldn't turn his back on the caring teacher. But an injury detained Cal and Livvie in the jungle, and passion flared between them. Could their growing love save them from the enemy, or would betrayal tear them apart?

#1335 SHATTERED VOWS—Maggie Price
Line of Duty
Lawman Brandon McCall had long since given up on his marriage to fiercely independent Tory DeWitt. Stubborn, beautiful Tory had never been willing to put her trust in Bran. But when he discovered an escaped convict's plan to exact revenge by harming Tory, he vowed to protect her at any cost—and win back her heart in the process.

#1336 DEADLY INTENT—Valerie Parv
Code of the Outback
Ryan Smith was the one man Judy Logan couldn't forget. After years away from her childhood crush, she now trusted him with the most important mission of her life—locating documents that could lead her to her family's fortune. But Ryan was keeping secrets, and the truth threatened to destroy their newfound love.

#1337 WHISPERS IN THE NIGHT—Diane Pershing
He'd been framed and sent to jail four years ago, but now Paul Fitzgerald was finally free—and getting close to Kayla Thomas was the only way to prove his innocence. But he hadn't counted on his attraction to the beautiful widow. He was determined to keep their relationship professional, until Kayla began receiving deadly threats, and he realized he would do anything to protect her.

#1338 DANGEROUS MEMORIES—Barbara Colley
Hunter Davis couldn't remember anything except an address in New Orleans and the face of a beautiful woman. So when he showed up at Leah Davis's door, she couldn't believe the husband who'd supposedly died five months ago was still alive. Could they rebuild their trust and find love again, or would Hunter's resurfacing memories cause Leah to lose him a second time?

SIMCNM1104